HE LEANED FORWARD AND
HER HEART STOPPED.

He was going to kiss her.

And she was going to die.

As confusing and frustrating and wonderful as he was, could she handle a kiss? A kiss wasn't in her plans, and men like Sawyer had a way of derailing plans, even if that wasn't their intention.

A kiss from him would cause the train to explode altogether.

Sawyer reached around her and opened her car door.

She saw spots from holding her breath.

"Okay, good night!" The words rushed out as she jumped into her car as if she were leaving the scene of a crime.

Beth buckled up and backed out, quickly putting Sawyer out of sight.

Yep, the man was a walking two-train pileup.

Something Blue

Heather McGovern

FOREVER
New York Boston

Forever
Hachette Book Group
1290 Avenue of the Americas, New York, NY 10104
read-forever.com
twitter.com/readforeverpub

First Edition: June 2022

Forever is an imprint of Grand Central Publishing. The Forever name and logo are trademarks of Hachette Book Group, Inc.

The publisher is not responsible for websites (or their content) that are not owned by the publisher.

The Hachette Speakers Bureau provides a wide range of authors for speaking events. To find out more, go to www.hachettespeakersbureau.com or call (866) 376-6591.

ISBN: 9781538737446 (mass market), 9781538737422 (ebook)

Printed in the United States of America

OPM

10 9 8 7 6 5 4 3 2 1

To My FWF, SJ, and Cupcake

Acknowledgments

This book would not be possible without the loving support of my family and the guidance of so many. Thank you to Nicole Resciniti, Emily Sylvan Kim, Jeannie Chin, and Laura Trentham. If not for them, the stories would still be in my head instead of on the page.

Something Blue

Chapter 1

Your Caesar salad darn near killed three people."

Beth pinched her eyes closed and swallowed the wince that'd been threatening since they started discussing quarterly earnings.

"Isn't that being a little overdramatic?" her sister, Aurora, whispered.

Cece, the youngest, shook her head. "Not really."

Beth hit the mute button on her phone before their accountant became privy to the peanut gallery.

"At least five members of the wedding party went to the hospital," Tom kept talking. "One of them was the governor's press secretary."

She wanted to crawl under the table and hide for the next three months. Instead, she unmuted her phone and centered it on their kitchen table. "I'm aware. I was there when it happened, remember?"

Like a slow-motion nightmare, the bad news had trickled in that night in February.

Then, it poured.

She'd pulled off the society wedding of the season last winter at the Orchard Inn, but a few hours after the sparkler send-off for the bride and groom, the first call came in.

The mother of the bride didn't feel so good. The bride wasn't doing great either. Then a groomsman got sick. Then a bridesmaid. Then another, and another. Could it be...food poisoning?

"I know you were. And I'm sorry to dig up old bones, but bad press like that is going to have negative impacts on a business. I just didn't expect it to be *this* negative. Then again, you did almost kill a *press* secretary."

"It was a salad!" Aurora blurted.

Beth patted her arm, attempting to calm and shush her. Aurora was only a few years her junior, but twice as blunt.

"It wasn't even a main course of bad chicken or fish," she muttered anyway. "Like you'd serve bad romaine on purpose?"

"Tom," Beth spoke over her sister's indignance, "I'm looking at our income and expenses year to date, and they don't seem completely dire." Just really, really desperate.

"But how many events do you have booked for next quarter?"

She pinched her lips together. That'd be zero, Tom.

"I won't insult your intelligence by telling you what this means for your bottom line." Tom had been their family's accountant for decades, and while he still called them "girls" even though they were in their twenties, he'd always respected and supported their decision to keep Orchard Inn in the Shipley family, with Beth taking the helm.

That didn't change the fact that the inn, and their wedding business, were in a pickle.

No. That wasn't fair to pickles. Pickles were delicious.

The Shipley sisters were in a great big salad of doom.

"Thanks for going over this with us, Tom. I'll look over everything else tonight and call you tomorrow if I have any questions. We won't keep you, though."

"Good luck, girls."

Aurora quirked her lips as soon as the call ended. "At least he was nice about telling us we're broke."

"We're not broke."

"Who even eats that much salad at a wedding, anyway?" Aurora asked the question like she was addressing a room of thousands. "You know the good stuff is coming out later. You eat a few bites to be polite and save up for the mains and cake."

"Can we stop obsessing over the food, please?"

"Not when the food is what got us into this mess in the first place."

And as a trained chef, Aurora was incapable of not obsessing over food, and she hadn't been Orchard Inn's chef at the time. Still working in Los Angeles, she'd been nowhere near the doomed wedding reception, but the family business was the family business to the sisters, regardless of how near or far they roamed.

"And not when we wouldn't be here if they'd only eaten a couple of bites," Aurora continued.

"I don't think E. coli works that way." Beth needed to get this thought train back on track before they spent the next hour debating and speculating. "Regardless, we can't blame guests for eating the food we served at the wedding they paid us to host."

"I know all that, and I know exactly how E. coli works, but..." Aurora let the sentence die.

"But I'm trying to be nice." Beth filled in the blank for her.

An argument of fluff and fluster, attempting to salve Beth's guilt by removing some of the pressure and blame.

Good luck with that.

Her sisters had to know by now that this disaster rested squarely on Beth's shoulders, and she wasn't sharing.

"Come on." She rose from the table in their common area, signaling the end of dwelling on their bad news. "Let's get some tea and sit on the back porch. The few guests we do have will start getting back from town soon. They may need something, and we can't wear long faces in front of them."

Besides, she was the type to dwell on things endlessly. No sense in her sisters duplicating her efforts.

"Y'all go on out there and I'll get the tea," Aurora said. "I made some little cheese biscuits I want you to try before I put them out for guests."

Beth followed Cece out of their shared family space at the back of the inn and tossed her financial file and the accountant's review into her room.

Ever since they'd invested in taking their orchard house from a private residence to the Orchard Inn, the girls had lived in a collection of four rooms at the back of the house. The house was plenty big, but it was still an adjustment. Now that Aurora had moved home, even more so.

Three grown women living in less than a thousand square feet.

Good thing they loved each other. And had several acres of peach orchard to escape into for privacy.

"You want to rock?" Beth nodded to the rocking chairs that lined the left side of the back porch.

Cece nodded, and Beth took the chair farthest from the door, saving her sister the extra steps.

It was silly and unnecessary, and Cece would flay her with one look if she knew it was intentional, but old habits died hard.

Her sister had been on her feet a lot today, working around the inn and running errands back and forth to town and the orchard's main shop. Her foot had to be killing her.

Cece dealt with exhaustion or discomfort by soldiering through it. Beth wished she'd treat herself more gently sometimes, and would realize that giving herself a break wasn't a sign of weakness.

"Here we go." Aurora showed up carrying a beautiful tray with three glasses of iced tea, a porcelain plate of little cheese biscuits the size of half dollars, and a bowl of the most perfect strawberries Beth had ever seen.

"Aurora. You didn't have to do all that." She felt guilty enough already.

Aurora set the tray down on the table next to Cece. "Yes, I did. We could use a little pick-me-up after that call."

Cece quietly took one of the biscuits and nibbled on it, her silence quickly becoming a concern.

She was always quiet—painfully so when around new people—but usually, when it was just the three of them, she came out of her shell with quick-witted comments or a thoughtful retort.

This afternoon she'd said barely two words.

Beth grabbed one of Aurora's latest offerings. If only she could bury all her worries in a biscuit.

She took a bite. Soft and buttery, fluffy with just the right bite of cheddar. It was a handful of heaven. "Oh, my word, how do you do it?"

Aurora shrugged it off and took the rocking chair on the other side of Cece. "It's just flour and water. Salt. Some cheese. And an oven."

"It's not *just* anything. You're a magician."

Cece giggled, the first sound she'd made since they'd gotten off the call. "She's a kitchen magician."

That was more like it.

Beth had another bite of her biscuit, toes curling inside her flats.

Aurora was way too humble about her talents. She had been a genius with food and flavors since they were kids, and she'd taken that natural gift and honed it at culinary school. Honed it so well she'd gone on to work in one of the best kitchens in Los Angeles.

That was, until things imploded back home at Orchard Inn and she'd come to Beth's rescue.

If she'd been working at Orchard Inn and catered the wedding in February, Aurora would've somehow prevented the salad scandal and everything would be fine. And while it wasn't fair she had to deal with the fallout, Beth was forever grateful.

She chanced a glance at her sister.

Their old catering manager had been let go, and as soon as Aurora heard, she'd insisted on returning home. She also insisted it was no big deal. She was happy to help. This was partially her business too—and on and on with why her leaving her life in LA was okay. But Aurora had to resent her for what she'd left behind.

It kept Beth up at nights.

"You're awfully quiet over there." Aurora leaned forward with a raised eyebrow. "You aren't spiraling, are you?"

"No." Only a little bit.

Orchard Inn was her brainchild. All of this was her doing.

"Mmm-hmm." Aurora wasn't buying it, but she went back to rocking in her chair.

Three years ago, when their mother announced she wanted to sell the place, get a little condo, and travel the world, Beth had come up with the idea for them all to pitch in, financially and otherwise, take out a loan, and turn their large home into *the* wedding destination in the Hill Country of Texas.

A charming country inn, complete with ideal orchard location and Texan hospitality, combined with Beth's business sense and years of experience as an event planner, Aurora's culinary talents, and Cece's eye for aesthetics and things of beauty, they were sure to be a success.

And they were. Or at least they were headed that way.

Season after season of working their butts off, and they'd made a name for themselves. Enough so that, last year, some big restaurant group courted Aurora off to California. And then came the doomed Caesar.

"We'll figure something out," Aurora tried to reassure Beth. "Try not to worry."

But if Beth didn't do something, fast, they were going to lose not just their business, but the orchard and estate that had been in their family for generations. Their employees, including the brand-new orchard manager, would be out of jobs. Worst of all, the biggest connection she shared with her sisters would be severed.

Stifling a frustrated grumble, Beth devoured what was left of the biscuit. The savory softness danced across her taste buds.

Life couldn't be that bad with snacks like this.

And it wasn't *all* bad. She had both of her sisters home now. Even if they had little else, they had each other.

When their dad took off decades ago, Beth had helped hold the family together. That was her job as the oldest. She'd started working as soon as she turned fifteen, worked all through school, and specifically gone to business school with the intention of keeping the orchard in the Shipley family name. This was her business, and, more importantly, her family.

She'd always looked out for them, and she wasn't about to stop now.

Somehow, she was going to get the inn back in the good graces of the Texas Hill Country. She'd get their finances back in the black and be profitable. The wedding schedule would once again be booked solid. Cece would not have to work as hard as she did, doing three different jobs. And she would ensure Aurora's return to California, back to the life she'd put on pause.

Beth reached for a second helping of her sister's delicious snack.

Somehow, she was going to make this work, but figuring out how was going to take more than just one cheese biscuit.

Beth snuggled under her softest blanket with a cup of honey chamomile and the accountant's report. It'd be hours before sleep caught up with her, but the tea and numbers might help.

She was neck-deep in their payables when her phone vibrated on the nightstand.

OMG. Are you still awake?! Please say you're awake! I need to talk to you! 😊

The text was from Shelby Meyers, her roommate from UT and still one of her dearest friends. They didn't talk as often now, what with life and careers, but if Shelby was texting at almost midnight, she wasn't going to stop until she got a reply.

I'm awake. What's up? Beth texted back.

I'm on your back porch! Let me in. ♡ 🙌

"What in the world?" She got up, not completely surprised by the giddy behavior. Excitement about pretty much everything was Shelby's default setting. But showing up late at night?

"Shelby?" She stepped out into the porch light to find her friend bouncing on the balls of her feet, her left hand flung out toward Beth.

"Guess what! Guess what!"

Judging by the size of the blinding rock on her fourth finger, she—

"I got engaged!"

Beth grabbed the hand that'd been thrust in her face. "Oh my gosh! Shelby! Congratulations!" She hugged her friend tight and tried to think when she'd even started dating the guy. A couple of months ago?

"Thank you! I am just beside myself. I'm so happy!"

"So, when— How? When did all this happen?"

"Tonight. He proposed tonight. We were walking around downtown after dinner—it's what we did after our first date—and he took me by the hand and told me how much he loved me, how I felt like home. Then he got down on one knee and asked me to be his wife." Shelby's eyes glimmered with joyful tears, her smile radiant.

"I am so happy for you and—" Oh jeez. Started with a G. "Garrett!"

It wasn't Beth's fault. She'd never met the guy, and she and Shelby had only talked two or three times since they started dating.

"Thank you. Can you believe it? I know it's soon and all, and people will probably think we're crazy, but we're in love. We're perfect for each other. I mean other than him and his whole family loving horses. But you'll see. I want you to meet him and get to know him. There's time for all of that."

"I know. And I think it's wonderful." Truly, she did. Marriage was on Beth's agenda too.

At some point.

That whole key element of finding someone you loved, and who loved you in return? See, that's where life got tricky.

Surely all good things in time, right? But she'd never found a good thing, and now was most definitely *not* the time.

Shelby was obviously over the moon, and if anyone deserved happiness, it was her. She'd never been anything but good to Beth and, while she put on a face for the rest of the world, she had to deal with a lot when it came to her family.

"Have y'all picked a date yet? Do you have time to get a dress?"

"Well, the date isn't written in stone yet, but funny you should ask about all that. We want to have the wedding right here at Orchard Inn!"

Beth had to blink to keep her eyes in their sockets.

"I know things have been slow around here since . . . you know."

Shelby had always said a lady didn't speak of unseemly things. Like bad salad.

"And this could really help you out. The wedding will be a big event. Garrett said his family will pay for part of it, so you'll have a nice budget to really do things up."

"That would be amazing and thank you, but don't feel obligated to—"

"You stop right there. This is not out of obligation. This is where I'd want to get married regardless, because it's beautiful and perfect and you're my best friend. And we want a big outdoor wedding that's romantic and charming, and there's no better place for that than right here."

When Shelby got nervous, she rambled.

Beth took her hands. "Okay. Just forget I said a word."

"You remember the dream box I kept under my bed, freshman year?"

She smiled at the memory. "The one with *Southern Living* magazine clippings and pictures of Channing Tatum? Yes, I remember."

"And the articles about interior design because I just knew I was going to have my own show on HGTV someday." Shelby laughed. "See? No one else knows me or could plan my wedding like you."

She wasn't wrong. Beth had heard all about the dream wedding for years. If it wasn't the oil baron who looked like Channing Tatum, it was the quarterback at Tamu, who'd surely go pro. And play for one of the Texas leagues. Naturally.

"Fair enough. I would love to give you the wedding you've always wanted."

"Eee!" Shelby started bouncing again. "And, and, and"—she flapped her hands in the air—"I think you know what else I'll ask, or you should, but would you please be my maid of honor?"

Beth's breath caught. She actually hadn't known Shelby would ask. Yes, they were best friends from college, but Shelby had close-knit cousins galore and a sister-in-law. The Meyers family was laden with potential bridesmaids and maids of honor, with a tendency to keep high-profile gigs like MoH in the family. "Of course I will. I'd be honored to do it."

She had a feeling there'd be some sour grapes among Shelby's family over this, but too bad. Beth was going to be the best maid of honor anyone had ever seen!

"So, tell me when you want to get married." Because the planning would need to start ASAP.

"Well, before it gets too hot, so...soon. Like, in two months? Tops?" Her already huge brown eyes widened expectantly. "The sooner the better, I think. Right?"

People never said no to the Meyers family. Not even when they wanted the moon.

Beth wouldn't say no because she loved her friend. She also wouldn't say no because this was a blessing in the making.

A big wedding in two months was exactly the redemption Orchard Inn needed. Shelby might be preppy and privileged, but she wasn't completely clueless. The rush-order wedding was meant to benefit Beth too.

"I think you're right. And I think you're an awesome friend."

"Aww. Don't sing my praises just yet, though. You have to deal with my mother on some of this too."

Beth's stomach turned to cold lead.

Evelyn Meyers. Old Texas money, expensive taste, impossible expectations. For everything.

Their freshman year of college, she'd berated Shelby to the point of tears because she'd wanted to pledge a different sorority than Evelyn's legacy. Shelby had won out in the end and gone her own way, but to this day, it was a point of contention between mother and daughter.

Evelyn was queen of the castle. Everybody's castle.

"Everything is going to be perfect." Beth smiled. Because she'd make sure it was. Whatever challenge came along with this wedding, she'd rise and conquer, for her family.

"This will be the best wedding Texas has ever seen," she promised her friend.

"Thank you." Shelby hugged her tight. "I know you won't let me down."

Chapter 2

Engaged. Can you believe it? Boy is barely out of law school and can't even get out of the gate before getting tied down." Sawyer shook his head and waited for a response.

Clyde, his most reliable confidant and horse, trotted along with nothing to say as they made their way around the first bend on the family property's easiest trail.

"I know, I know. He's been out of college and working for years now, but he's still young. Too young to go marry some girl this fast." In Sawyer's eyes, his brother, Garrett, was eternally underage.

Too young to go away to school. Too young to drink. Too young to move somewhere like Austin. And way too young to be someone's husband.

Clyde reached the top of the hill and came to a halt, familiar with the route of their favorite ride.

"What is he thinking?" But Garrett was going to do whatever Garrett wanted to do, same as always. Unless Sawyer truly put his foot down.

That'd only happened twice in their lives, and neither were moments he wanted to revisit.

"You talking to the horse again?" Uncle Joe came

up beside him, his steed, Malice, nuzzling into the tall grasses next to Clyde.

"Like you don't do it too."

"All the time. A horse makes a good listener. Only when they start talking back that you've got a problem."

Sawyer grinned at the long-running joke.

"Something on your mind, son?"

He shook his head but started spilling anyway. "Just Garrett and this getting-married business. Thinking he's all grown up when he's not even old enough to know better. He's known her what, a month? And now she's just supposed to be a part of the family? I've been around her exactly two times."

"He says he's in love."

"He's been in love before."

Love was a bedtime story people told themselves so they'd sleep better at night. People were people, and at the end of the day, their self-interest would always come before love.

"He says this time is different."

"That's the infatuation talking." Everything was always sunshine and a field of flowers at first. Give it time. It'd all turn to torrential rain and mudslides in the end.

"He seems pretty sure of himself."

Sawyer rubbed Clyde's neck. Garrett was always sure of himself.

He'd been sure he wanted a beat-up old Chevy as his first truck, because it was a classic. They worked for weeks getting the thing to run, only for Garrett to buy a new truck a year later. The old Chevy, still temperamental as a mule, remained in Sawyer's garage.

Garrett had been sure he didn't want to be a part of

the family business too. Then, after college, he'd used that big brain of his to change his mind and get into land-use law. He might not be a part of Silva Ranch's day-to-day operations, but Garrett regularly came to town and consulted with them on the future of their ranch.

"Garrett doesn't know what he's doing," Sawyer insisted.

They slowly made their way through a pasture, and his uncle offered no reply for at least five minutes. "Big step, getting married. Neither of us have done it," he finally said.

His statement hung there between them in the long silence, the low sounds of the horses winding around his words.

Uncle Joe was a self-proclaimed bachelor for life. Early on, it'd likely been by choice. Later, he'd been saddled with raising Sawyer and his brother.

Saddled wasn't the right word. His uncle had raised them both with a good spirit, even if with a gruff demeanor.

When their parents died, he'd taken on the responsibility, protecting and providing for them both like they were his own. And, as the oldest, Sawyer had fallen into a surrogate role of nurturer.

Garrett was their responsibility.

So how in the world was his baby brother responsible enough to get married?

And who was this girl, anyway? Shelby Meyers.

He knew the Meyers name. Everybody knew the Meyers name.

"How much do we really know about this Shelby, anyway?"

His uncle shrugged.

"I guess she seems nice enough, but she's a Meyers."

"Mmm."

Deep down, she would be just like the rest of them. Looking down their nose at everyone else in the county, or in the whole state, all because they have—or *had*—money and their ancestors settled Texas—way back in 1330 BCE, to hear them tell it.

"I'm not overly fond of that family."

"Mmm."

He wasn't fond of the rumors about their financial state either.

He'd seen an article in the local magazine featuring Shelby Meyers as one of their "30 Under 30," and she'd flat-out told the interviewer she intended to turn her family's fortune around.

Turn it around, as in turn it from bad times to good.

He didn't put a ton of stock in gossip, but where there was smoke, there was at least a flame. If even a whisper of the gossip was true, the uppity Meyers family was on much harder times than they alluded to.

Their little princess marrying someone as well-off as Garrett Silva would go a long way to ensuring the future smoothed right out for them.

He didn't like thinking that way, but in the ranching business and, unfortunately, in life, he'd learned that thinking the worst of people was often the safest mindset.

Sawyer took a steadying breath and tried to focus on the rolling hills before him, dappled with green amid dry stretches of land and grass. Over the farthest hill was a vineyard, and past that, a wildflower farm.

Beautiful country that soothed his soul.

A breeze reached the hilltop, ruffling Clyde's mane.

A ride on their property always cleared his head, the view from their favorite path a soothing reminder of all the Silvas had to be thankful for.

Today it also drove home how much was at stake.

This was his family. His blood. He'd sworn to take care of Garrett since they were little. He couldn't stand by if some high-and-mighty family was trying to take advantage of him. And in so doing, taking advantage of Silva Ranch.

"Garrett wants me to go all the way into Fredericksburg later today, to meet up with him and Shelby. Celebrate the good news and look at some bed-and-breakfast or something for the wedding."

"Mmm."

"I don't want to go."

"Mmm." His uncle kept with the one-syllable replies.

"He's going to expect me to be happy for him. I have to act happy about this."

"Folks love a wedding."

"Not folks like me."

"Mmm."

Uncle Joe was right. He had no choice but to haul himself out to Fredericksburg and make nice about this whole farce. Garrett was his brother, and if he objected outright to his engagement, they'd have a big falling-out.

That was the last thing he wanted. He only wanted what was best for his brother.

And what was best was a long engagement and time for that boy to see the light.

Come to think of it, going to spend some time with his brother meant time to talk sense into him.

Not too obviously, of course. But pointing out there was no rush. He and Shelby didn't have to move so quickly into marriage.

Sawyer could grind the gears down to a slower pace, if not halt them altogether. Give his brother time to think and see people for who they truly are.

"Thanks, Uncle Joe." Sawyer urged Clyde back onto the path down the hill.

"Anytime."

Sawyer drove to Fredericksburg, his decision made.

He'd give this wedding, and the girl, the slightest chance. But if he determined even an iota of his suspicions were true, he'd do something about it. He was not going to let someone marry Garrett just for his money. It'd break his brother's heart and God have mercy on anyone who hurt his brother.

No one else was ever taking advantage of a Silva again.

But with Garrett, his methods couldn't be heavy-handed. Give that boy anything resembling a hard line or an ultimatum, it was guaranteed to blow up in your face. Dragging the plans out, stalling the wedding long enough to ensure Garrett saw the truth—that was the way to go.

If Sawyer had only dated Melissa a few more months, he would've saved himself a barrel of heartache. But no one had warned him or been there to remind him there was no rush, to take the time to really know the woman you'd spend the rest of your life with.

Take the time to learn she loves your last name more than she loves you.

Garrett wasn't going to make that same mistake.

Orchard Inn, formally the Bluebell Orchard, sat about

a quarter mile off the main road, the drive lined on both sides with peach trees and, closer to the main house, what looked like a few plums. The house itself was a two-story, sprawling, traditional southern estate. Wraparound front porch, gazebo to the left, all in crisp white. Perfectly manicured grounds, potted plants dotting the porch, rocking chairs, and even a swing inviting you to sit a spell. Stay awhile.

He parked in the mostly empty pea-gravel lot designated for guest parking. Before he could even make it to the front porch, Garrett and Shelby bounced out the front door and onto the porch, big wide smiles on both of their faces.

"Sawyer!" Garrett grabbed his hand, pulling him into a hug. "You remember Shelby."

"Shelby. Congratulations." He put on his best manners.

"Thank you!" Shelby flung her arms around him, giving him no option but to accept her hug. "And thank you so much for meeting us out here on such short notice. We're just so excited."

"You're going to love this place," his brother added. "It's perfect for a wedding."

In other words, Please be pleasant and agreeable to everything we say and want to do.

"Is everybody here now?" A voice crossed the threshold before the person.

"We're all here. Sawyer, this is Beth," Shelby introduced the woman joining them outside. "One of my closest friends and the owner of Orchard Inn. She's going to show us around."

All air left his lungs, like he'd taken a fall off Clyde.

"Beth, this is Sawyer. Garrett's older brother."

"Nice to meet you." The woman held out her hand. Only a little shorter than him in heels, Beth had strawberry blond hair that fell to her shoulders and sharp green eyes that pierced right through him.

Words. Words would be good right now.

"You too."

Nice save.

"Now that we're all here, how about we take a look around?"

They all followed Beth into the house, and she showed them every room on the first floor with the command presence of a horse master.

"This is the dining room, suitable for small parties like a bridal brunch or groomsmen dinner. Beyond the French doors you can see the side porch. We've had guests use a string quartet, and I recommend opening the doors and allowing the musicians to play outside so the music floats in, naturally."

She went on and on about wedding details and reception ideas, a lot of which might as well be in another language.

What in the blazes was a reception *lounge* and ushers? Wasn't a wedding reception just a party that people went to afterwards? Walk in, eat and dance, throw birdseed, the end?

Apparently weddings and receptions were way more complicated than he'd ever known.

"With your tighter schedule, you'll want to start discussing a seating arrangement soon too." Beth kept bestowing wedding intel while they walked. In her white blouse and fitted, light gray pants, she was buttoned up and all business, except for a smattering of freckles across her nose and cheeks turning traitor on her strictly professional demeanor.

It was cute. Not that he'd dare call her cute to her face.

She responded to all of Shelby's questions and comments with authority. And there were a lot of questions and comments.

"What type of wedding dress do you see me in? You must go with me when it's time to shop for it. I'll need someone who will give me their honest opinion, but not brutally honest, like Mama. And I think I know who all I'm going to ask to be a bridesmaid, but there are two I'm on the fence about. What do you think about Julie?" Shelby jabbered their entire tour of the inn, Garrett somewhat forgotten beside her.

"I want to do a plated meal. Steak, of course, a fish option, and what about a vegan choice, just in case?"

"Nowadays, you definitely need a vegan, gluten-free option," Beth said.

"Did I tell you my cousins are coming in from Dallas? And Daddy said I can get all the flowers I want, and he thinks he can get the Crashers to play the reception."

Sawyer leaned closer to Garrett and kept his voice quiet. "Is she as excited about being married as she is about this wedding?"

Garrett ignored him.

At least he'd thought he was quiet. But Beth looked back at them, her green eyes flashing.

Sawyer cleared his throat. "That will be nice," he commented to whatever Shelby had said last.

"Let's go out the back of the house and circle around so you can see all of the grounds." Beth led them from the house the same way she'd led them through it. Back straight, confident in her pace, she had only the slightest sway to her hips when she walked.

Which was, of course, completely beside the point.

Sawyer told himself he noticed things like that after years of teaching horseback riding. People's stance, the way they sat. Their enticing way of walking.

"You can see more of the orchard from back here." Beth's heels clicked against the stone steps that took them to the backyard. "And we have had a few weddings out here as well, but most people prefer the front of the house. There you have photo opportunities with the porch and gazebo. The choice is completely up to you, though."

He noticed a couple of other things about Beth too.

She said the choice was completely up to them, but the look on her face said she had a very strong opinion and knew exactly what they should do.

"I think you should get married back here," Sawyer blurted.

All three of them stopped walking, drawing him up short.

He had no idea why he'd played devil's advocate. Maybe it was Beth's assuredness that made him want to engage. Her confidence calling him to match wits. He couldn't care less if they had the ceremony up front, out back, or side to side, but he couldn't resist debating even a pointless point with Beth and her freckles.

"If everyone else uses the front, why not be different? Right?"

"You make an interesting point," she said. "But it really depends on what the couple wants."

"What do you think?" He asked his brother, praying he'd take his side and make the tour a little more interesting.

"Um. Both are nice, I guess. I'd be fine either way. What do you think, Shelby?"

Shelby looked to Beth. "I think...the front?"

"You'll be happier with how it looks."

"Okay, the front." Shelby nodded, her relief plain.

"Then you can do the reception around back," Beth added.

Shelby clasped her hands together like a little kid who just found out she was getting ice cream. "Yes! This is going to be so perfect."

"What if it rains?" Sawyer asked.

They all stared at him, bordering on horrified.

"Do you really think it might rain?" Shelby pleaded.

"No, of course it won't rain." Beth cut her eyes at Sawyer.

Was she a meteorologist now too?

"And, on the way off chance it even sprinkles, we can move things inside like that." Beth snapped her fingers.

That got the group moving again, and they'd returned to the front of the house when he found he couldn't help but poke at the perfect plans again.

"Do you set up for a whole wedding inside, too, just in case? Is that how you can move locations like that?" He snapped his fingers too.

He was goading her. Why was he doing it, though? He couldn't possibly care less about how you moved a wedding inside.

Beth's green eyes flashed again.

Oh yeah, that was why.

"We have our ways," she said.

"Garrett!" Shelby exclaimed. "Oh my gosh. This would be perfect for our wedding portrait. Come see." She all but ran to the gazebo, pulling him along.

As soon as they were out of earshot, Beth turned to Sawyer. "I apologize if I'm off base here, but I get the feeling you'd rather they didn't get married at Orchard Inn." Brow scrunched, her little nose wrinkled up, and she only got cuter.

It was his turn to stare. "What?"

"Shelby and Garrett told me about his family home. Your home, Silva Ranch, and I don't blame you for wanting to have the wedding there. I'd want my sisters getting married at home too."

Huh? The last thing he wanted was to host a wedding at the ranch. Talk about a nightmare.

"And I know your family is paying for part of the event and, as such, you have a very big say in what does and doesn't happen with the wedding."

Why did it always come back around to money?

"However, since the bride and groom are certain they want to be married here at Orchard Inn, and I know we all want to make them happy, I'm sure there's a way we can compromise."

"Okay?" He didn't know where she was going with all this, but he enjoyed watching her go.

"There are events that take place before weddings. The ranch could host one."

Uh-oh. Abort, abort. He did not want a bunch of people all over his place, hobnobbing and jacking their jaws, all up in his business.

"We could also incorporate some of Silva Ranch into

the wedding day itself. Make it the best of both worlds. Tell me what you'd like to see happen."

"I want my brother to be happy." That was the God's honest truth.

"I will guarantee that he and Shelby will be beyond happy with their wedding."

"But," he quickly added, "I don't need to have any kind of party at my place. I'd like to include our ranch some-how, but it really doesn't have to be to that degree. I'll give it some thought." Being more involved meant staying at his brother's flank during all this, but surely that could be accomplished without hosting people at the ranch.

Being more involved also meant doing more with Beth.

"Great. So, we're good now?"

"We're good."

"Good news, guys." Beth immediately turned from their conversation. "Sawyer is not only on board, but he's going to help bring a bit of Silva Ranch to the event to represent both families coming together."

"How?" Shelby asked.

"We might host an event at the ranch and then bring some of the ranch to the wedding. You can leave the details to me."

"Us," Sawyer added. "Leave it to us. And we don't have to have an event at—"

"That's a great idea." Garrett gave him a huge smile. "We could do our couples shower at the ranch. Thank you." He looked as happy as he had when he'd told Sawyer about the engagement.

"You...are welcome." What else could he say? His brother's excitement didn't leave room for him to say no.

But one party was enough.

"And I was thinking, what if all of the other events like..." Sawyer looked to Beth.

"The groom's dinner?"

"Like the groom's dinner. What if we had that here? At Orchard Inn? As well."

Beth's eyes widened, the first time she'd looked caught off-kilter since they met. "Really? That would be awesome. I mean, yes, we can arrange something, I'm sure."

"Yay!" Shelby clapped again before squeezing Sawyer like a teddy bear. "See, Garrett? I told you it would be okay." She looked at Sawyer. "He was so worried about what you'd think and say about all this. I told him you'd be happy for us, but you know how he is."

Yes, Sawyer certainly did.

Chapter 3

"Tell me again why we had to come all the way out to Johnson City on a Saturday to meet Shelby's man?" Aurora twisted her hair up into a knot and pinned it as they made their way down the sidewalk.

"He's not her man. He's her fiancé."

Cece lagged half a block behind them, gazing into the window of a consignment shop. "We're also not even half an hour from home," she called out.

Beth stopped and turned to her sisters. "Huddle up."

Aurora let her head fall back with a level of drama any teenager would envy. "Not a family huddle."

"Yes, a family huddle. Come on." Beth waited until Cece joined them. "Shelby wants us to get to know Garrett better and talk wedding stuff. I think she's a little self-conscious that they're getting married so soon. By Texas standards, anyway. Plus, this gets us out of the inn for a bit. Enjoy the break. Planning this wedding is both a marathon and a sprint."

"Go, team!" Aurora stuck out her hand, palm down, and grinned.

Cece gave her hand a good-natured slap. "Some fun never hurt, and Johnson City has a new fabric shop I've been following on Instagram. Now I can go check it out in person, and if they have a nice taffeta, I'm making that dress I showed you."

"Fine, fine. I'll behave and enjoy the day. But tell me again why Garrett's brother is going to be here, if it's all just wedding talk and getting to know Garrett?"

"Because..." Beth struggled with the explanation.

She was equal parts eager and reluctant to spend time around Sawyer Silva. He wasn't without his charm, and undeniably good-looking. Big brown eyes, toothy smile, and dimples that managed to make him look more manly than cute.

But beyond all that, she sensed reasons beyond brotherly support and regular interest as his motivation.

She'd expected Shelby's mother and a mother-in-law to have the opinions and input she must contend with. Not some six-foot-three cowboy.

Then she'd remembered the Silva history from years back. Both parents had passed, decades ago.

Garrett Silva didn't have a mom and dad. He had an older brother. One who was clearly a force to be reckoned with, and she didn't need that in her life right now.

"Because why?" Aurora looked at Beth like she'd lost her mind.

"Because he wants to be, I guess. And he's involved in the wedding."

"How?"

"He's paying for part of it and wants to help. And Garrett wants him involved. And the bride and groom get what they want."

"Jeez. Don't bite my head off about it."

"Sorry. I just...I wasn't expecting a brother-in-law to

be involved. I really want this to go well. We need this to go well."

"We know," Cece assured her. "And it will. Right?" She looked at Aurora.

"Right." Aurora squeezed Beth's hand—this time the gesture was in earnest. "Quit worrying, sis. We've got this."

They walked a few more blocks and turned onto Main Street, into the heart of the festival. The midday festival crowd was light enough that it took Beth only a few minutes to spot Shelby.

In a huge, floppy white sun hat, white shorts, and pale pink top, she glowed, already looking like a bride.

The men standing near her stood out too.

Not just the groom. No, no. The other man.

"Is *that* Garrett's brother?" Cece asked.

Miles of jean-clad legs, a short-sleeved shirt that showed off thick arms and the curve of his biceps, his dark hair standing out above the crowd line.

Aurora made a noise by sucking her teeth. "No, I believe that is what folks call a tall drink of water."

"Aurora," Beth admonished.

"Please. You either didn't notice or just failed to mention he's hot."

Cece shook her head. "They're both hot. I can't imagine dating someone like that."

"Why?"

"Out of my league much?"

"They are not." Aurora shook her head. "You're out of your mind. Any guy would be lucky to have you and the sooner you get that through your head, the better off you'll be."

Beth shushed them both as they got closer to the others.

"Hey!" Shelby waved as soon as she saw them and greeted them all with a hug. "I'm so glad you-all could come."

Introductions were made to her sisters, and Sawyer greeted Beth with a smile.

Beth fidgeted, waiting for the niceties to be over.

Or maybe it was Aurora's staring at her that made her fidget. Her sister had always been bolder, and even if she thought she was being discreet, she was not.

Finally, the group began wandering down the center of Main Street.

"It's good to see you again." Sawyer matched her stride and looked her way with another smile. His eyes lightened in the afternoon sun, a chocolate brown that took her in.

"You too."

"How have you been?"

"Fine."

She wanted to roll her eyes at herself. Normally she was the master of small talk and networking, but today she kept clamming up.

Had to be the heat.

Booths lined both sides, selling every kind of food item from apple turnovers to zucchini bread, homemade crafted items, even some art. A band played on one of the side streets, the music drifting in and out.

"Busy, I bet," Sawyer said, and he bumped against her as they maneuvered around another group of people.

"Sorry about that." The palm of his hand was warm against her elbow.

She nodded, her entire conversational repertoire gone.

After another half a block of walking in silence, Aurora fell back.

"Hey, sis. Check this out." She tugged Beth aside to look at ceramics, but once they got in the booth, her sister just stared at her.

"What?"

"Sawyer keeps trying to talk to you and you're being weird."

"I know, but you keep staring at me."

"Because you're being weird."

Beth huffed a sigh.

"When a nice man wants to talk with you, you talk back. I thought we'd gone over this. Did you forget everything while I was gone?"

A more prolific dater than Beth ever thought about being, Aurora had insisted on advising her since they were teenagers.

For the most part, it was hopeless. And pointless.

Beth was good at networking and business and reaching her goals. Flirting, demurring, and having any luck with guys went beyond her expertise.

"I think he might be interested in you," her sister insisted.

"He's just being nice."

"You sound like Cece. You are not that naïve."

Beth wasn't that naïve. But Sawyer wasn't there for her. He was the groom's brother. A vitally important groom.

"I get the feeling he has a lot of…opinions about this wedding, okay? And the Silvas are bankrolling half of it."

"Oh."

"Exactly. There's too much riding on this for me to worry about whether or not some guy likes me. Especially when the guy is the groom's whole family rolled into one person."

Aurora pursed her lips, deep in thought. "I guess I see your point. Sucks, though. You deserve to have fun, too, you know?"

Sawyer, with his bright smile and warm gaze, was the kind of fun Beth didn't need right now. His insistence on being chatty and personable only muddled things even more.

No. She was there to plan a successful wedding for her best friend and have Orchard Inn rise from the ashes. She'd hang back and keep some distance from Sawyer.

"There you two are!" Shelby popped into the booth with them. "We were wondering where y'all went."

Beth picked up one of the statues closest to her. "Just looking at some of these."

Shelby glanced down at what was in her hands. "I didn't know you collected clowns."

Beth looked at the bulbous-nosed clown staring back at her. "Oh god!" She set it down quickly. "It's for a gift. But I think I'll go in another direction. Shall we?" She turned to leave the booth.

"Wait." Shelby waved her and Aurora over to the side, out of the way of other shoppers. "I'm glad I have you both here, alone. I wanted to talk to you about the couples shower. Garrett has almost convinced Sawyer to have it at the ranch."

"Convinced him?" Beth asked. "I thought he wanted to have the party there." Why else would he have been such a naysayer while touring Orchard Inn?

"Honestly? I can't ever tell what Sawyer wants or is thinking. But it does seem like the shower is a go there. However, we still need it catered." Shelby smiled at Aurora.

"Me?" Aurora all but blushed.

"Of course, you. That is if you're available. It'll be next Saturday. I wouldn't want anyone else. Please say yes."

"Yes, I'd love to. Do they have a kitchen I can use at the ranch or—"

"There's one in Sawyer's house. I'm sure he won't mind. I think. I'll let Garrett handle that."

"This is great." Beth glanced at her sister.

More exposure for Aurora, and the inn. A way to prove they could cater without trying to kill anyone. And, if the shower went well, prospective business for the future.

"And listen, thank you so much for coming out here with us today. I know it's a haul, but it's such a pretty day. And I know y'all will like Garrett once you get to know him. I don't want you to think he's some stranger I'm rushing to marry."

Beth stopped Shelby mid-fret. "We do like him."

"And no one thinks you're rushing to get married," Aurora added.

Shelby obviously didn't buy it. "Maybe you two don't think it. I know what people are saying about us getting married so soon and—"

"I don't know what they're saying, and I don't care. Neither should you."

"Shelby. There you are. Look what I found." Garrett appeared out of nowhere offering Shelby a fistful of pink gerbera daisies.

It was impeccable timing and the perfect way to stop Shelby's spiral.

"Oh, baby. They're beautiful!" Shelby popped him a kiss and held the flowers close, Garrett beaming like he'd won over the homecoming queen.

Which, to be fair, he had.

"I saw one of those dog bakery booths are here too. Thought maybe Dodger would like some treats."

"He'd love some." Shelby turned to Beth. "Dodger is his terrier, and he's adorable."

"And he loves Shelby," Garrett added. "Which is saying something, because that dog doesn't love just anybody."

They all left the booth and started down Main Street again. Eventually, Beth found herself right back next to Sawyer. This time she intently avoided glancing at her sister.

Don't be weird, she told herself, Aurora's words ringing in her ears.

"Have you ever been to this Founder's Day festival before?" she asked him, making a point to sound casual.

"Never. You?"

"Once, when we were little. But it was much smaller back then." See? She wasn't being weird. Sawyer was just a guy, related to the groom. There was no attraction here with either of them.

Nothing to see here, folks.

"Oh. I'll be back in a minute." Shelby dropped back from the group and disappeared.

As they kept walking, Beth kept her gaze off Sawyer.

They meandered down the street until they all stopped to look at an artist's eye-catching paintings.

And Sawyer touched her again.

This time it was just the tap of his fingers on her shoulder to draw her attention. "Look, it looks like your place."

Beth turned to find what he'd pointed out.

The artist had done an orchard row in vibrant acrylics, the depth so real Beth imagined she could step right in and pluck a peach from one of the trees. "Wow."

"You like it?"

"I love it. It looks like..." She let her sentence drift, anxiety kicking in over Orchard Inn and what she stood to lose.

"Home?" he finished for her.

"Yeah. Home."

Sawyer ran a hand through his tousled black hair. "Yeah," he said, and she could've sworn it sounded like he knew the trail of her thoughts. "And check these out." He led her to a series of smaller canvases, horses the focus this time. "They look alive, like you could touch them. These kind of look like home to me."

He stepped around her to reach for something, his body close enough she could've fallen back into him.

He took the artist's business card and quickly slid it into his back pocket.

Sawyer appreciated art?

She was *not* going to find that attractive.

"Garrett, come here." Shelby popped back up outside the art booth, waving him over.

They all left, with Garrett hurrying out in front. He reached for the clear cellophane bag in the palm of her hand, two perfect, bright yellow squares inside.

"Those aren't—"

"Mama Luann's lemon squares? They are indeed."

"Don't tease."

"I'm not. I saw online that she was going to have a booth here. Why do you think I insisted we come all the way out here just to meet up with everyone?"

Garrett already had one of the lemon bars in his mouth. "I didn't know it was for this."

Beth looked to Sawyer for an explanation.

"Luann's is a sweets shop in Austin. His favorite."

"We have to get some more." Garrett was about to head off in search of the booth.

"I had her put aside a baker's dozen. Already paid for."

"You're the best, you know that?" He turned and kissed Shelby, this time full on the mouth as she wrapped her arms around his neck.

A pang of envy tugged at Beth. She wasn't jealous that Shelby had found someone she'd fallen madly in love with; she was jealous she *could*.

Beth had never felt that kind of all-consuming emotion for anyone. Sure, she loved her family, but that was different.

"There's the fabric shop I was telling you about." Cece quickly turned from the group. "I'm going to check it out." The words were barely out of her mouth before she was gone.

"Yeah, I'm going back to that organic farm stand," Aurora added. "I saw some super fresh veggies that might inspire a new dish."

Her sisters couldn't have abandoned the scene any faster. Maybe they felt as awkward about the moment as she did.

They hadn't grown up seeing their parents lavish

attention and affection on each other. After their dad left, their mother didn't date for eons, so there were no examples of couples being...couple-y.

Outside of wedding days, where it was expected, and kind of required, that kind of open tenderness and consideration seemed too private and precious to witness.

Garrett and Shelby left as soon as he finished the lemon bar, and Beth realized she'd been left alone with Sawyer.

"I don't want any sweets. You?"

"Not at all."

"Good. How do you feel about street tacos? There's a truck up ahead."

She loved them, and eating something as unromantic as tacos might help with the awkward silences. "Sounds good to me."

They each ordered a taco with chorizo, shrimp, and sriracha and Sawyer was paying the truck owner before Beth could even offer.

They found an empty table, and it turned out she was hungrier than she thought and halfway through her second taco she started wishing she'd ordered a drink with her lunch.

Sawyer seemed to read her mind. "The sriracha isn't playing games, is it?"

"I'm dying over here."

"I'd kill for a beer right now."

She nodded fervently, mouth full of spicy shrimp.

"Want to finish these and hit the saloon up there?"

"Please."

They tossed their trash and headed to the saloon,

reaching the wooden front porch before she spotted Shelby coming toward her.

"Guess what! They have a vintage consignment shop."

Beth quickly moved closer to the door of the saloon.

Nothing against consignment, but Shelby was the kind of shopper who went in for the long haul. A decathlon of shopping, complete with jumping the hurdles of other shoppers, javelin-throwing of charge cards, and a shot put of coffee halfway through if you got too tired to make it to the finish line.

They'd once spent an entire day at two stores, looking at kitchenware.

It was the type of activity much more suited for Cece. Beth lacked the patience.

"You want to go?" Shelby asked.

Beth looked helplessly at Sawyer.

"Actually, we're dying of thirst after a spicy lunch." He came to her rescue. "Can we join you after?"

"Hey, baby, how about just me and you go?" Garrett offered.

"You sure?"

"Of course."

"Okay. We'll see y'all in a bit." She all but floated away with her fiancé, and Sawyer ushered Beth inside as quickly as possible.

"Thank you. That was a close call." She laughed.

"I get the feeling you've already been hit by the bullet you just dodged."

"Many times. I'm sure shopping all day is fun, if that's your thing, but Shelby can look at stuff for hours. I'm a get-in, get-what-I-need, get-out kind of girl."

"I bet."

"Hey now!"

"I'm just saying I can tell you're efficient. I can't picture you wandering about, window shopping all day."

They found two stools at the bar, and the bartender came over immediately. Sawyer looked at Beth to order.

"Your Shiner Bock on tap."

"I'll do the same," Sawyer said.

Their beers arrived and Beth took a few sips before turning to Sawyer. "I hear you're having the couples wedding shower at your place."

He finished a long draw on his beer. "Yeah, thanks to you."

"What?"

"You were the one who put the idea in their heads when we were touring your place."

She shook her head. Shelby was right—who knew what this man was thinking? "You said you wanted the ranch more involved in the festivities."

Sawyer quirked his lips and tilted his head in a way that made him too good-looking for words. "Did I, though? Did those words come out of my mouth?"

"Yes, you—" Beth thought back on their conversation outside the inn.

He'd been a bit of a naysayer about the various wedding plans, played devil's advocate on every other topic, but he hadn't ever actually said he wanted to host the wedding events or a shower at his ranch.

"Do you *not* want to host the wedding shower?"

He laughed, the sound full and round, warming her skin. "Oh, I'm hosting it now, regardless."

Oops.

"I swore I thought you—"

"It's fine." He clinked his pint glass against hers. "But I am hoping you're still running the shower show, regardless of location."

Beth blinked. Shelby had said Sawyer Silva was a tough shell to crack, and she wasn't wrong.

The man had agreed to host a wedding shower but knew nothing about how they operated.

"If you're the host, it's your show to run."

He set down his glass with a thud. "Um, that's a big no-thanks for me. I just got roped into having it at my house and paying for food and stuff. I don't want to be in charge of that chaos. I thought you liked running things?"

She did. She loved running things. All of the things. If she ran them, then life went smoothly. If she didn't, everything fell apart.

Like this shower was about to do.

"I don't know where you got the idea that I have to run things, but I'm happy to step in and help."

He gave her a knowing smirk that would be obnoxious on anyone else. "You are welcome to step in on this shower...thing. Would you mind?"

"I'd love to." Plus, with Aurora catering, the whole event would be another feather in the cap of Orchard Inn.

And they needed a lot of feathers right now.

"So, what's it like?" Sawyer turned his body more toward her, leaning an elbow on the bar. "Running an inn along with all this wedding planning and party throwing?"

The effortless charm was completely unfair.

"Like spinning a hundred plates at once. What about ranching?"

"Same. Except with horses."

Beth snorted over her beer.

"You okay?" He patted her on the back.

"I think so. Just the imagery of horses spinning around..."

Sawyer laughed, too, the full, rich sound washing over her again.

This was murky territory. Sitting here, laughing with him, being charmed by him, with cold beers and warm laughs and him insisting on looking like he looked.

Any other time, she would've soaked in the attention from a good-looking man, agreed to go out if the guy asked, and then call it off after a few dates because they'd either get mad she was a workaholic and they weren't the center of her world, or she'd realize they only wanted one thing, and it wasn't her sparkling personality.

But with Sawyer, she couldn't even go down that short path.

He was intimately tied to the Meyers-Silva nuptials, and paying for a lot of it. She never mixed business with pleasure, and certainly not when that business was the only life-support system her family had right now.

"We should probably finish these up and find the others." Beth took a long sip.

Sawyer looked at his over-half-full beer. "Okay, but I haven't chugged a beer since college. Did I say something wrong?"

"No." She was being weird again. No one had ever accused her of being weird until today. Get it together, Shipley. "I just..." What? "I thought you might be tired of me by now and ready to find your brother."

His gaze was a mix of amusement and bafflement. "We just got here. I'm far from tired of you."

She had to look away from the spark in his eyes, the curve of his lips. "Have you given any more thought to how the ranch can be a part of the wedding ceremony?"

"To be completely honest, no, I have not. Not at all. Any suggestions?"

"Incorporating your family into the ceremony is something personal. The idea will have to come from you."

"Great."

"But once you have an idea, or a few, then I may be able to help you flesh them out and decide."

His head fell back as he sighed. "Thank you. I'm out of my league when it comes to stuff like this."

"The wedding will be fine."

Sawyer straightened back up. "I'm more concerned about Garrett."

"He'll be fine too." Why wouldn't he be? The guy was clearly on cloud nine.

"I'm—I'm sure he will be. Just. You know. Big step and all. I'm his big brother. I tend to worry."

"Tell me about it." Beth sipped her beer. Sometimes it felt like all she did was worry.

"You're the oldest, too, right?"

"Thanks for noticing."

"No, I wasn't saying—"

She smirked.

Sawyer's eyes narrowed. "Ahhhh, you almost had me."

She shared a smile with him. "I am the oldest, and I worry, just like you."

"I feel like the parent sometimes, you know?"

"Actually, I do know."

She had his full focus then. "You do?"

"Beth." Shelby rushed up to the bar, miraculously

already done with her shopping. "Please look. You are never going to believe what we found."

Garrett was right behind her. She gingerly set a cardboard box down on the other side of Beth. She lifted something from the box, and unwound the bubble wrap.

It was a giant ceramic bowl, painted in yellows and greens, with a couple of hula girls on the side.

"That's pretty." Beth glanced at Sawyer to see if he had a clue what it was.

"What is it?" he asked.

"It's a scorpion bowl."

"There are no scorpions on it," he replied.

"No, that's what it's called."

"But what is it?" Beth tried.

"I don't get it." Sawyer went back to drinking his beer.

"A scorpion bowl."

"You keep saying those two words, but I have no clue what you're talking about."

Shelby tossed her hair over her shoulder with a put-upon sigh. She then cradled the bowl like it was the most precious of finds. "Scorpion bowls were used in tiki bars, starting back as far as the 1930s. You make a large rum drink and share it with your friends, using straws. This one came from the 1950s."

"Do you throw a lot of tiki parties?" Sawyer asked.

"I might now."

"Don't listen to him, baby." Garrett gave his brother a stern look. "We'll have all the tiki parties we want and he won't be invited."

"I didn't say I don't like parties." Sawyer put up his hands. "I'm just trying to understand what this is all about."

"I guess we'll just have to mix up a scorpion bowl and have you guys over. Then you'll understand." Garrett laughed with his brother.

"That's a great idea." Shelby looked to Beth.

"Yeah," Sawyer added in his vote. "We could get together, take a few of the horses for a ride, hang out."

Beth widened her eyes at her best friend, silently communicating.

"Maybe," Shelby quickly added. "But I know everyone is busy with the wedding and stuff, so we'll see. Okay." Shelby carefully wrapped her scorpion bowl back up and placed it in the box. "Garrett, do you want to grab some lunch?"

"Yeah, I'm starving. We'll catch y'all later?"

"Later," Sawyer said. "And don't forget to pick up some of that agave nectar at the booth for Lina. You told her you would."

"I know I did. I'm not going to forget."

Sawyer leveled a look at his brother.

"I'm not."

Shelby waved as they left the saloon.

"I better text him later or he'll end up forgetting." Sawyer shook his head.

Beth stared at him until his eyes met hers.

"What? He will."

Beth laughed. "You literally just reminded him."

"Doesn't matter."

"Who is Lina?"

"Our housekeeper. And she uses agave nectar in this killer lemon-limeade she makes. If he forgets, I don't get my lemon-limeade for weeks."

"Oh. Now I see why it's so important."

Sawyer laughed along with her. He nudged her arm with his. "Trust me, if you had some, you'd know. You'd be texting him too."

Her face hurt from smiling.

Beth quickly took another sip of her beer and excused herself to the ladies' room.

The entire walk across the bar, she reminded herself: Brother of the groom. Brother of the groom. So unprofessional. Just focus on the job.

But his laugh, and those eyes. The easy way he talked to her and put her at ease. He was as headstrong as her, if not more so. He'd never judge her for being obsessive about work. From what she could tell, he was the same, even when it came to lemonade.

She washed her hands and smoothed down her hair.

And not to mention those arms and shoulders.

He was the whole package. The kind of guy she'd like to date. But she couldn't. Not right now.

Maybe after the wedding?

Beth made a face at her reflection. Now that was an interesting option.

When the wedding was over, and Orchard Inn was back on track, things might be calmer. There'd be no conflict of interest between business and pleasure.

She might have time to date in general, Sawyer specifically.

This plan had promise. All she had to do was be patient. And maybe not be alone sipping drinks with him until then.

Beth left the restroom with a renewed sense of purpose and hope. A plan always made her feel good.

She returned to the bar to find Sawyer bowed up at the

bartender. "What are you trying to say, friend?" Sawyer asked the guy.

The bartender, his face the color of a tomato, sputtered and stammered. "Nothing. I was ... nothing."

"Is everything okay here?" Beth moved to get her purse. Bar fights were not her style.

"Everything is fine," Sawyer said.

But he didn't look it.

"Are you ready to go?" he asked.

"Yes, let's." She led the way out of the bar, wondering what in the world she'd missed.

She wanted to ask, but Sawyer didn't look like he was in a talking mood at the moment. Obviously something had happened, and she wanted to give him the benefit of the doubt. Still, when it came to dating and opening her heart, she didn't want it to be with someone who picked fights in a saloon.

Couldn't he see he was messing with her plan?

Chapter 4

His Friday started even earlier than usual. He never slept well when he was looking into a new horse acquisition.

There was a chestnut quarter horse stallion at another ranch, and they were looking to sell.

He didn't necessarily need another stallion, but this one was something special. Before he made a final decision, though, he wanted to make several visits. It was all part of his method.

Sawyer climbed in his truck and headed west to the ranch, the sun rising in his rearview mirror, coloring the sky yellow and blue. He tuned the radio in to his favorite classic rock station—people were always surprised that his tastes went beyond country music and all things stereotypically Texan—and thought about the day before him. Give the horse another look-over, probably his second of three or four viewings, talk paperwork and price, set up a follow-up visit.

This trip would take him most of the day and he didn't want it any other way. Being out, driving around the Texas countryside, cleared his mind.

A certain buttoned-up redhead had fogged up his brain all week.

His time together with Beth at the Founder's Day festival was barely anything. Some tacos and a beer, a little small talk, some laughs. It wasn't even a date.

She would've been working all week on the upcoming shower and he was busy running Silva Ranch.

So how come he couldn't stop thinking about her? What was she doing? What was she thinking?

How come he kept going over every word, every detail? The way her green eyes sparkled when she laughed, the way she didn't hold back and said what she meant. And that look she gave him. It'd happened more than once. A mix of surprise and, one might even say, admiration.

It was a good look, and he liked the way it made him feel.

Sawyer shook his head.

He wasn't some teenager who'd never flirted or been flirted with. What was the matter with him? He highly doubted Beth was at home, thinking about their time together, running over it in her mind.

Except what if she was? What if she'd found the kind of enjoyment that she hadn't felt in years? What if she was interested in doing it again?

"You need to stop it," he told himself, and turned up Creedence singing about the bayou.

But he didn't really want to stop it.

She'd made him smile and laugh with engaging conversation. And she was straightforward.

She wasn't what Uncle Joe called mealymouthed.

The only negative from their not-date together was

the a-hole bartender who'd started trash-talking his brother's fiancée as soon as Beth left for the restroom.

"Wasn't that Shelby Meyers who was just in here?" he'd asked the other bartender.

The guy had thought he was whispering, but he was wrong.

"I heard she's getting married to that Richie Rich kid she was with," he'd said, before singing the line from a song about gold diggers.

And that was all Sawyer could tolerate. He'd called the guy out immediately.

Sure, he'd had similar concerns about Garrett's fiancée, but that was a family matter. He wasn't going to have some random guy in Johnson City walking around talking trash.

The guy had cowered straightaway when confronted. Unfortunately, that was when Beth returned.

The non-date was over then.

He knew how the scene probably looked, but she hadn't said anything about it.

Maybe no harm, no foul. But if she brought the moment up, he'd be sure to explain.

Then again, he didn't really want to be the one to tell Beth what people were saying about her best friend.

Sawyer arrived at Northcliff Ranch later that morning. He met with the owners, Bert and Ginny Ferguson, and Peyton, their intern trainer.

The stallion, Buck, was as beautiful as ever. His deep amber color shone in the sunlight, and the wider-than-usual blaze down the center of his face and the white socks on his hind legs made him unique.

Sawyer had to have him. He wouldn't close the deal today, but Buck would be his.

"He's a beauty, isn't he?" Peyton walked the horse around the paddock.

"He is."

"I'll tell you a little secret, too, if you're interested."

"Always."

"He likes when you sweet-talk him and call him Bucky. This big guy comes across like he doesn't like anybody, but you just got to know how to handle him."

"Sweet-talk and call him Bucky. Roger that."

"Mr. Ferguson wants you to stay for lunch. He'd like to close the deal today."

"I'm sure."

"You know you want him. Why wait?"

She was awfully pushy for a college kid. "I want to be certain."

"How are you not already?"

Because he was a grown-up. And he just wasn't, but he'd get there. Life had taught him to settle for nothing less than certainty.

After lunch with the Fergusons and another visit and mount on Buck, aka Bucky, Sawyer headed for home.

He didn't make it more than fifteen minutes from the ranch before the midafternoon driving doziness hit him. He stopped at a diner on the highway for some coffee to go. A caffeine bump for the way home.

The place was a sixties-style luncheonette with counter service and booths, and the diner had a lot of patrons given the time of day. Sawyer waited at the counter after placing his order for coffee, black, and giving the lady a five to keep.

"I'll make you a fresh pot, hon."

While she brewed, he checked his phone.

No messages from Uncle Joe or Garrett, so all must be well at the ranch.

No messages from Beth, not that he expected any, but she had his number now and something could come up with that blasted couples shower that required his input.

Stranger things had happened.

No calls or voicemails from anyone, so he let his gaze wander across the booths of people. Mostly families, a few solo diners, and two couples. One couple he didn't know from Adam's housecat. The other made him do a double take.

Was that...?

No.

But it had to be. If it wasn't her, it was the spitting image.

Shelby Meyers, with her dark hair braided back and sunglasses pushed up on her head. She didn't see him, but Sawyer definitely saw her, sitting in a booth, way too close to some cowboy who was most definitely not his brother.

"What in the Sam Hill?" Sawyer muttered.

"What's that, hon?" The waitress slid his coffee across the counter.

"Oh. Nothing. Sorry, ma'am."

Not nothing, though. That was his brother's fiancée, all saddled up in a booth with some other guy.

They spoke quietly, intimately, about something.

He should say something. Go over there pretending it's casual, and bust her. But something about Shelby's expression stopped him.

What if it was nothing? He'd been wrong before about this kind of thing. If he walked over and gave any indication that he thought she was up to no good—and she wasn't—she'd go right back to Garrett.

Then he'd be the bad guy, and Garrett was the type that held a grudge forever.

But what if he was right and said nothing? How could he ever explain that to his brother?

Better to play this cool.

He'd see Shelby again, and just ask her. Not in a suspicious, prying way. He'd keep it neutral. Innocent.

Sawyer grabbed his coffee and left, determined to think the best of Garrett's new love.

Still, the feeling that this was likely the worst situation possible haunted him all day.

Saturday breakfast was an event at Silva Ranch.

Sawyer was responsible for the bacon and eggs and never-ending pots of coffee, Uncle Joe brought the Crockpot of grits and toppings, and Lina provided the baked goods, fruits, and vegetables.

No one ate lunch on Saturdays, because a breakfast like theirs lasted until dinner.

"I brought strawberries, blueberries, and some tomatoes that are perfectly ripe," Lina said, setting down her basket. "And I was feeling like cinnamon rolls this morning."

"You won't get any argument from me on any of that." Uncle Joe settled his Crockpot on the counter and plugged it in on low. "Y'all are going to have to roll me out of here today, I can already tell. You get the tire fixed on that wheelbarrow? You may need it."

"You'll be fine." Lina patted Joe on the arm. "We can walk around the ranch a bit before it gets hot. Helps the food settle."

Joe placed his hand over hers. "That's a good idea."

"Besides." Lina began pulling plates from Sawyer's cabinet, familiar with the kitchen. "We'll have help eating breakfast this time. Garrett and Shelby are coming over."

Sawyer and Joe shared a look.

"They are?" Joe asked.

"Of course they are. They're staying at the guesthouse, and they have to eat."

"We're just surprised at the good news is all." Sawyer helped her put down the place settings.

He'd hoped to see his brother, alone, before being faced with him *and* Shelby. Now, his favorite meal of the week was going to be served with a side of tension.

Garrett and Shelby showed up, Dodger leading the way into the kitchen just as Lina was serving up the eggs, over easy.

Everyone was all smiles and warm greetings, Lina doting over Shelby the way she doted on everyone. They were seated, Garrett at the other end of the table, Shelby to his left, next to Lina.

Sawyer found a Busy Bone in the pantry for Dodger, because without it, no one got to have breakfast in peace.

"What did you kids get up to yesterday?" Lina asked.

Garrett motioned to Shelby. "I just got some work done at the guesthouse. She's the one with all the excitement."

Sawyer jerked his gaze to Shelby.

This was it. Was she going to fess up to hanging out with some guy all day? Maybe it was just a cousin. Maybe he was being an idiot. But they sure hadn't appeared to be cousinly.

"Well, I spent the afternoon at the bridal shop, trying on dresses and getting measured."

Lina clapped her hands together with delight.

What?

No, she was not in a bridal shop all afternoon, trying on dresses. She'd been out near Carson, Texas, saddled up in a booth with some local cowboy.

She was lying. Which meant she was hiding something.

"Is this bridal shop in Carson, by any chance?" Sawyer shifted in his seat.

"No, it's right here in Fredericksburg. Why?"

Oh, it was, was it?

"Just wondering. I thought I saw you while I was coming back from looking at a horse."

Shelby's laugh was laced with nerves. "Only if you stopped in Magnolia Bridal."

A smile stiffened across his lips. "No. Just into a diner for some coffee."

Panic flashed in her eyes.

"How did it go at the bridal shop?" Lina interjected.

Shelby jerked her gaze from his, focusing on Lina. "What? Oh. Great. It went wonderfully. I want to go back with Beth, and my mom. Probably. There are a few I like, but I wouldn't dare make a decision like that alone."

"I didn't know women ever liked to alone." Sawyer dared her to look his way again. "Especially not for something so important."

"They don't." She took a sip of her orange juice.

Were her hands shaking?

"But since we're limited on time, I thought I'd better at least check things out."

"And you're wise to do so." Lina smiled. "I know I've said it already, but I'm just thrilled for both of you. This whole thing is just such wonderful news."

Sawyer picked up his coffee.

Sure. Wonderful news.

They continued with breakfast and Sawyer chewed on his thoughts as much as on his food.

He could keep prying, ask a lot of questions, and come across like an overbearing a-hole. Wouldn't be the first time he was accused of such.

But this was his brother's fiancée. He didn't want to push and push, and end up with Garrett, Lina, and even Uncle Joe mad at him.

He also didn't want to be wrong.

There was still a chance her coffee date was . . . innocent. Though even thinking such made him want to smack himself upside the head.

No explanation existed that made what he saw completely innocent.

After breakfast, he and Garrett cleaned up in the kitchen with Dodger tap dancing at their feet hoping for some dropped crumbs. Lina chatted with Shelby while Joe went out to the stables.

Sawyer fought the urge to bring up anything around company.

He and his brother would go out riding once breakfast settled. They did it almost every Saturday, and today should be no different.

As soon as the kitchen was clean, Sawyer asked about riding.

"I was planning to go into town with Shelby. Maybe some other time?"

But they rode every Saturday.

"We can go afterwards," Shelby was quick to say. "Go riding with your brother. Dodger can stay here with me."

She was probably being agreeable out of guilt, but Sawyer would take it.

"You sure?" Garrett asked.

For the love of Pete, she already had him whipped to the point he had to ask twice?

"I'm sure."

"She can stay here, and we'll catch up. We can take the dog for a walk and talk about the shower tomorrow," Lina offered.

"Yeah." Shelby smiled. "That sounds perfect."

"So, we're riding?" Sawyer fought to keep the annoyance out of his tone.

"Looks like."

They made it maybe half a mile on their ride before Sawyer cracked.

"I know I saw Shelby outside of Carson yesterday."

Garrett sat on his filly, Delilah, his form perfect, completely unphased. "Yeah, she said she'd be running some errands."

"She was at a diner. Not running errands."

"I guess she was hungry and stopped to eat."

"Then why didn't she say all that at breakfast?"

Garrett pulled his horse up short and Sawyer stopped too. "Why don't you just say what it is you want to say?"

"I—" He did not want to go there.

"Spit it out, Sawyer."

"I saw her having lunch with some guy."

Garrett stared at him for the longest few seconds of his life. And then laughed.

Laughed!

"Not lunch with a guy! Oh no!"

Sawyer grimaced. "Don't be a smart-ass, I'm serious. They looked...cozy."

The laughter stopped; Garrett's expression suddenly solemn. "I know you were lied to about stuff like this, but I don't like your tone. Shelby has male friends. She has a lot of friends. She has co-workers. You know how well known her family is."

"That's not what this—"

"And she can have lunch with whoever she wishes. If I didn't trust her, I wouldn't be marrying her."

"I just think you need to ask her who she was with the other day. That's all."

"I'm not going to interrogate her because you're the one who's suspicious. You're suspicious of everyone. I get why you're wary of people, but it doesn't mean Shelby has done anything wrong. That's just you."

"But I think—"

"Look, I know what you went through, but my fiancée isn't the same as yours. Just because Melissa lied and cheated on you, doesn't mean Shelby will do me the same way. I hate that that happened to you, but you can't go around suspecting the worst of everyone because you got burned."

Sawyer kept silent, his jaw cramping with how hard he bit back his words.

"You can't take that out on us."

"That's not what I'm doing."

"Isn't it?"

"I'm trying to look out for you. All that love and stuff can make you blind, and I don't want to see you get hurt. You're my brother. You're my only family."

"I know. But you've got to trust me on this. I know what I'm doing."

"I'm not—"

"We're dropping this. Right now. I want to enjoy my ride with my brother."

He'd drop it. For now. But he was not letting this go.

Chapter 5

Silva Ranch made a surprisingly ideal location for a bridal shower. Beth let a wave of pride wash over her as the Sunday sun eased lower in the sky.

No, she couldn't control the weather or the Texas heat, but if she could, she would've arranged a late afternoon just like this.

Warm, but not too hot. Sunny, but not too bright. Nice breeze, low humidity.

It was a perfect day.

Now, if she could only get a duplicate day for the wedding in a few weeks.

Shelby had chosen a Tex-Mex theme for the shower and, in a matter of days, Beth had pulled together an outdoor luncheon and made Sawyer's backyard look like the ideal if understated fiesta.

Colorful table coverings and adorable, take-home-with-you succulents decorated every table.

And, of course, Aurora's food rose beyond the occasion.

"Can you believe this?" Shelby pulled Beth aside.

"You like?"

"Like? Are you kidding? This is perfect. I can't believe you put this together so fast. And do you smell those fajitas? And there's southwestern-style caprese salad at each high-top table, with salsa verde and queso. I'd never even heard of southwestern caprese until today. Everything looks and tastes amazing."

"I'm glad you're pleased."

"You're a miracle worker."

That was her job, but it always made her happy when the miracle played out.

"My mother can't stop oohing and aahing."

"Really?" Evelyn oohing over anything was impressive. Maybe she'd ooh and aah to her friends and Orchard Inn would benefit.

"The fact my mother hasn't picked this party, and the food, apart is the greatest compliment ever. I already told your sister."

"Good." She wanted Aurora to get all the compliments. In truth, the culinary work she was doing now was at a lower level than her previous work. If everyone bragged on her and reminded her of her talent and skill, then maybe being back home wouldn't be so bad.

At least Aurora had seemed excited about some of the fruits and veggies she'd bought at the Founder's Day festival. The southwestern caprese was made with buffalo mozzarella and tomatoes from a vender she'd met there.

"You need to eat something," Shelby insisted.

"I will in a bit." But the truth was, Beth never ate until an event was over. She needed to be free to work, in case something came up.

"Okay, you'd better. I'm off to mingle. I think my aunt just got here." Shelby turned to go but stopped dead in her tracks. "No. No, no, no."

"What?"

"My mother has cornered Sawyer."

Uh-oh. Evelyn Meyers meeting Sawyer Silva was the very definition of an unstoppable force meeting an immovable object.

"We should go say hello," Beth suggested. "Also known as intervene."

"That won't help. He doesn't like me. He'll hate me after meeting my mom."

A record scratched in Beth's mind. "What? How could he not like you?"

Shelby lifted an eyebrow.

"I mean it."

"I don't know. Maybe he likes me fine. But if so, he hides it well. He's a hard one to read to begin with, and...I don't know. I don't think he's thrilled to be my future brother-in-law. My mother won't help matters."

Sawyer definitely had his reservations about the speed of the wedding, but Beth didn't get the feeling it was anything more than brotherly protectiveness. A man like him was used to calling all the shots in his world, and this was one thing he had little to no control over.

But there was no way he didn't like Shelby.

"Don't worry." Beth patted her friend's shoulder. "I'll take care of this meet and greet. You go enjoy your party."

Regardless of Sawyer's feelings about Shelby, an unsupervised run-in with Evelyn couldn't possibly go well. Running interference hadn't been in her plans today, but plans changed.

She hurried over to where Evelyn had crowded Sawyer, standing at one of the high-tops, enjoying the caprese and some of the habanero-touched pineapple punch.

"I'm sure the house is every bit as grand as Shelby described," Evelyn was saying.

"Hello there," Beth butted right in.

"Darling!" Evelyn greeted her with an air kiss for each cheek. "Don't you look gorgeous? Purple is definitely one of your colors. You should wear it always. Do you know Sawyer?"

Sawyer widened his eyes at her.

"Yes, as a matter of fact I do. Did you two just meet?"

"We did. And I was telling him how much I would love to see the rest of the place. I've heard so much about it. But he's being shy."

Evelyn and Sawyer alone for a tour of the ranch? Disaster in the making.

"Maybe later, after the shower," she suggested, hoping Evelyn would forget all about it by then. "You don't want to miss the party."

"Nonsense." Evelyn brushed off her concern like shooing away a gnat. "These people will take forever to eat and this way we'll be back in time for dessert."

Beth glanced at Sawyer, who looked ready to choke on his punch.

"Sawyer probably needs to stay close to the festivities. Just in case."

"In case of what?" Evelyn was not taking no for an answer.

"Emergency?" she tried.

"Honey, we aren't leaving for the Rockies. We're going into the house. It'll be quick."

"Might as well get this over with or we'll be here all day," Sawyer muttered to Beth, setting down his glass. "I'd love to show you around," he said, louder.

"Just the house, though," Beth quickly added. "Touring the land and stables will ruin those heels."

"Good thinking." Evelyn nodded.

"I'll tag along, if that's all right." Better to head off any issues, and better to get to the bottom of this not-liking-Shelby nonsense.

"Yes, please." Sawyer gave her another pleading look.

And so, the oddest trio of all time entered the back of the house and stood in Sawyer's great room in an awkward silence.

The terrier, Dodger, came bounding out of the kitchen to bark at Evelyn.

"Oh dear." Evelyn clutched her chest like a grizzly bear had approached them.

"Is the party moving inside?" An older, tall, slightly rounder gentleman came down the hall and picked up the dog.

"Uncle Joe," Sawyer said. "This is Beth. She planned the shower and she's planning the wedding, and this is—"

"Evelyn Meyers." Joe nodded. "Yes, we've met."

"I'm just giving the ladies a tour."

"A tour? You didn't say anything about a—"

"Impromptu." Sawyer patted his uncle on the back before herding him down the hall, speaking in a hushed tone.

She and Evelyn stood there, Evelyn's gaze wandering across the family pictures and the portraits, the vaulted ceiling and open second story.

Even when Sawyer returned, the silence remained. He obviously wasn't the tour-giving type.

"When was the house built?" Beth asked to fill the void.

"My grandparents built this house," he said without

looking at them. "Before that, the main house was what is now the guesthouse."

This was better. At least it was something.

"Would you look at this kitchen?" Evelyn's voice came from farther away.

While Beth had been watching Sawyer and Sawyer had been staring into nothingness, Shelby's mother had slipped away.

She'd gone on ahead with her tour, no need for a guide, and was nosing into other rooms. "My goodness!" she called out. "You could feed an army out of here."

"Hello, Evelyn." Aurora's voice drifted from the kitchen, followed by barking.

She was likely working on dessert before Shelby's mother barged in.

"I bet you've never cooked in a place this nice, have you, dear?"

Beth shook her head, imagining Aurora's face right now. Whatever she was thinking, Beth prayed Aurora didn't say it.

"And that's the kitchen. Obviously." Sawyer went after her; Beth followed.

How did Shelby do it? Day in and day out with this woman, year after year. Exhausting didn't come close to describing it.

"Hey, guys." Aurora plastered on a smile as they reached the kitchen. "What are y'all up to?"

"A tour. I think." Sawyer shrugged. "Has Dodger been in here with you this whole time?"

Aurora laughed. "This is where the food is, right? Figured better in here than outside begging. But he's been great. Sits right there, watches me like a hawk, and doesn't make a sound. Well, until now and when he heard y'all come in."

"I don't believe in having dogs in the house," Evelyn pronounced.

"A tour, huh?" Aurora ignored her comment. "Well, this is the kitchen." Aurora held her arms out wide. "And it's lovely and functional. Sawyer has a standing mixer I'm jealous of—"

"That's not mine," he said.

"And it's an awesome kitchen that is really busy right now." Aurora gave Beth a look as Evelyn began opening cabinets.

"Okay, how about we see what's next?" Beth tried to propel Evelyn out the other side of the kitchen.

"This *is* lovely." Evelyn eyed every inch of the room like a property inspector.

"Thank you," Sawyer managed.

"And I'm so glad Shelby will be taken care of." She brushed her fingertips along the marble countertops. "You know what I mean? She's grown up a certain way and I don't want that to stop."

Beth wanted so badly to tell Evelyn to zip it.

"It's good to know now she'll have everything she's ever wanted."

Aurora's mouth fell open.

Beth scratched at her temple to keep from groaning. The look on Sawyer's face said it all.

Her attempts to tone down Shelby's mother weren't working. They needed to wrap up this tour as quickly as possible.

"How about we check out that room?" Beth flung her finger out toward the nearest open door, to what looked like a living room or study. Simple, safe enough. Anything to get them out of the kitchen.

Evelyn beat her to the door.

"That's my office," Sawyer said from right behind Beth.

She stopped, glancing back at him with a wince as Evelyn entered. "Sorry." She mouthed the word.

"Look at this. So manly," Evelyn cooed.

Beth rushed to join Shelby's mother, wishing the hardwood floors would open up and swallow them both whole.

To be fair, though, Sawyer's office leaned heavily toward stereotypical masculine décor. It wasn't anything like Beth would pick out, but in here, it worked.

Hardwood floors covered in a deep maroon, gold, and green designer rug; leather sofa and oak coffee table; an oversized desk and comfortable chair; and at least a dozen pictures of horses.

Most were of one horse in particular.

Beth homed in on the most striking of them all. Sawyer, mounted in Western saddle, wearing dark jeans and T-shirt and a black cowboy hat complementing the horse's beautiful blue roan coloring.

"That's Clyde." Sawyer appeared at her side.

"He's beautiful. I take it he's special."

"That obvious?"

She smiled at the multitude of photos and the small portrait someone had done of Clyde. Perhaps Sawyer had a soft side, at least when it came to horses. "Only a little."

His smile lit the room.

"You have any?" he asked.

Sawyer didn't bother asking if she rode, only if she owned. Everyone in their neck of the woods rode horses.

"No, but I have a favorite horse at Mapleton Stables. I get to ride with her from time to time. Less time to do so now, but I try."

"You should come out here. I have a mare the perfect size and temperament for you, and our trails are beyond compare. Plus, we aren't as crowded as Mapleton."

"Do tell, what temperament is perfect for me?"

Sawyer tilted his square chin, his strong jawline with barely a hint of stubble because he'd shaved for today's occasion. "Well, from what I can tell, you'd do well with a social horse, curious and interested, but not aggressively so. Poppy would be a good fit for you. She's fun on a ride. Lots of personality without being easily distracted."

She liked the sound of Poppy, and the name.

"I should warn you, though, I prefer English saddle to Western."

"I won't hold that against you. I do both but like Western. We could go out on the trails one Sunday, when work isn't so crazy."

Gazing up into his brown eyes, she imagined riding with him, the wind on her face, the feel of being in the saddle again. How long had it been since she'd ridden out on some trails? The freedom and joy, the feel of it.

And riding with him.

There'd be a specific kind of security when riding with a man like Sawyer. Horses were his life, riding like breathing to him. Could there be anyone better to get away with?

Wait. Was Sawyer asking her out or was this just his way of promoting his ranch?

She may very well be getting ahead of herself here.

"Is this you and Garrett as kids?" Evelyn asked from across the room.

Beth jerked from her daydream. She'd completely forgotten about Evelyn.

"What?" Sawyer shook his head and turned away.

"This picture. Is that you and Garrett? You're just little boys."

Sawyer took the photo and placed it back on his desk. "That's us when we were five and seven."

"So cute. And look at you both now. All grown up and Garrett getting married to my Shelby. Things just work out wonderfully, don't they?"

With pinched lips, he nodded.

"We should get back to the party now." Beth approached Evelyn to guide her to the door.

She managed to get her out of the office and to the back door.

"I'm sorry about Evelyn," Beth whispered to Sawyer as soon as she was out of earshot. "I know she can be a lot."

"Really? I hadn't noticed," he deadpanned.

Relief melted her shoulders. At least he was being a good sport about this.

Sawyer wasn't so bad at all.

Sure, he had a tough outer coating and an intimidating air about him, but he seemed fair and if he could tolerate Evelyn with good spirits, then there was no way he'd find fault with sweet, sincere Shelby.

She'd have to pull her friend aside and tell her she was wrong. Sawyer was the type who'd like her just fine.

They returned to the party and she was quickly pulled away by Shelby.

"Where were y'all? You disappeared. We ran out of that caprese and some people didn't get any yet."

"What?" That couldn't be right. Aurora planned for more than enough.

"Are you sure Aurora said we were out?"

"I—I didn't ask her. But there was no more being served."

You always checked with the kitchen before assuming you were out of any dish. But then, Shelby wouldn't know that. She'd never catered or waited tables in her life.

That's why Beth was the one in charge of this event, but she'd been so caught up in Sawyer's eyes and his stories about horses and—ugh.

She knew that man was going to be a distraction.

"Let me check with Aurora. I'm sure we're not out of anything."

Shelby bit at her bottom lip. "Okay. I'm sorry I didn't think of that."

Beth turned to her. "You shouldn't have to think of it. Your job is to mingle. Mine is to worry about tomatoes and cheese. I was just...occupied. Your mother wanted a tour of the house."

Shelby's eyes flew wide. "No."

"Don't worry, I intervened the best I could."

"Which means?"

"Only a couple of overbearing moments versus dozens of them?"

Shelby groaned as they walked into the kitchen.

"It wasn't awful. I promise. I've gotten better at handling your mother over the years. Still a long way to go, but it was better than the time she came to our sorority house and told our chapter president she better bring her A game for our freshman year."

"Oh my god, I remember. I wanted to die. I thought they'd kick us out after that."

"Luckily, the chapter didn't judge us for your mother's behavior, and neither will Sawyer."

Shelby let loose with a pop of deprecating laughter.

"Stop that. How could he not like you?"

She tilted her head with a droll expression. "You've met my family, right? Not just my mom. The whole Meyers family tree. Plenty of people don't like us."

"That's your family, not you."

With a floppy lift of her shoulders, she shrugged. "I guess, but I'm telling you, he doesn't like me, personally. In his eyes, I'm not good enough for Garrett. I'm telling you."

That made no sense, but it was vexing Shelby and that wouldn't do.

Beth would have to get to the bottom of this issue and fix it.

"Okay." Beth took the punch glass out of Shelby's hands and set it on the counter. "No more sour thoughts for today. It's your bridal shower. You should be beaming with joy. Go mingle and enjoy."

"Hey." Aurora walked into the kitchen with an empty tray. "Why are y'all hiding in here?"

"We aren't hiding. Shelby thought we might be out of caprese."

Aurora sniffed at the notion. "As if I'd let that happen. I just took more out to the tables."

"I knew you'd be on it." Beth returned her attention to

Shelby. "Now, you put Sawyer Silva and your mother out of your mind. Have fun and, in a few minutes, I'll bring you some of that tres leches cake Aurora made."

Shelby took a deep breath. "You're right. I'm getting in my head too much about this. I'm marrying the man I love. I'm going to go find him and remind him."

"You do that." Beth sent her off with a shoo and downed the rest of her punch.

Now, where would Sawyer be hiding out, to avoid any more tours?

After being stopped for a few hellos and well-meaning guests asking about the inn, she found him at the edge of the yard, around a corner, talking to one of Shelby's bridesmaids.

The poor girl, Becky, looked like she'd been stopped by the highway patrol.

"How was the dress-fitting thing y'all went to?"

"What dress fitting?"

"The other day. Shelby said you-all went dress shopping." Sawyer placed his hands at his waist, managing to appear even more imposing. "How was it?"

"They went dress shopping without me?" The girl all but yelled the accusatory question.

"I don't—"

"Oh my god." Becky flew past Beth so fast she caused a draft.

"What just happened?"

"Hey." Sawyer shifted nervously. "I didn't see you there. Did you, ah, have any of the cake yet?"

"No, it's not been brought out yet." Beth narrowed her focus. "I said, what just happened?"

"You mean that?"

"Yeah, that." Her sisterly senses began to tingle. Sawyer wasn't the first guy to avoid her questions.

"Just making conversation."

"Rule number eight of wedding planning: Do not upset the bride or bridesmaids. Becky looked a little upset."

"I was just—"

"Kind of sounded like you were shaking her down about dress shopping."

"Why would I care about dresses?"

"You tell me. It's either that or you were flirting with her."

Two deep lines creased his brow. "I was *not* flirting with her."

Beth snorted with laughter.

His scowl line only deepened. "Now you're laughing at me. Great."

"I'm not." Yes, she was, but how could she not? He was kind of cute when he was indignant, and she was obviously going to have to get the full story from Becky.

"No, it's fine. Feel free." He cracked a smile.

"I bet no one ever laughs at you or picks on you, do they?"

"Only Garrett and Joe, like once a year. And now you."

She moved closer to him. "Is he your uncle on your father's side?"

"My mother's brother. He raised me and Garrett after our parents passed. Still lives here on the property."

Beth remembered hearing about the Silva tragedy when she was a child. Both parents died in a car accident. She'd forgotten about it completely over the years.

"That's right. I'd forgotten about your parents' passing. I'm sorry."

Sawyer shrugged it off. "Long time ago now. But thanks. Uncle Joe raised us, so he was our dad—and mom, I guess. Took over at the ranch until I got old enough."

"You were really young when it happened too," Beth mused aloud.

"I was seven, yeah."

Right around the time that picture in Sawyer's office had been taken.

He was a child when he'd lost his parents and had to deal with more than some adults could ever manage.

His tough outer shell made a little more sense now.

"I'm glad you had your uncle Joe."

She'd had no one when her dad left. Not even her mom. Not really. For almost a year after her dad took all of their money, savings, and livelihood, her mom had been despondent.

She slept, ate very little, drank too much wine, repeat.

Getting up, going to school, getting on with life had fallen to Beth.

She'd kept her family together, kept her sisters on track, kept the ship afloat, until their mother rebounded, and got herself together.

Sawyer's gaze met hers and, though they spoke not a word, she felt that, somehow, he knew.

She was, once again, pulled toward him, and away from the dozens of priorities that sat at her feet.

But it was so refreshing to feel like someone might understand what it was like to have those kinds of responsibilities at a young age.

"You'll have to meet him sometime," he said. "I mean, really meet him." His voice was impossibly soft; an understanding laced his words and made her heart ache.

"Maybe when I come over to ride?"

"That sounds really nice."

They stood there, unmoving, the sound of the party so far away. Beth felt as though a spell had been cast, her focus on Shelby's concerns evaporated, until there was only her and Sawyer.

Chapter 6

Y ou are going to love the new doors we put on the stalls back here. You'll want some for your place."

Sawyer followed Peyton to the other stables, the ones without Bucky.

"Are you keeping me away from my horse? Is this some kind of sales tactic?"

Peyton turned and walked backward as she grinned. "He ain't yours yet."

"He will be. You and I both know that."

"Yeah, but until you sign on the line and Bert's got that check, you have to see our stall doors and amuse me before getting quality time with my Bucky."

"Now he's your Bucky?"

"Yep. Mine until he's yours." She spun around with a laugh, her ponytail whipping through the air.

Peyton couldn't be older than twenty, twenty-one, but she had the same grit and gumption as some of the old-timers who'd been around for decades.

She was also about to try selling him on another horse, he could tell.

The Fergusons had a future star employee on their

hands. He'd have to let them know, *after* he got his horse. Or horses.

They entered the stable and, sure enough, the new stall doors were nice. Double hinged, sturdy.

Conveniently enough, the stall Peyton chose to show him contained a beautiful black filly with a big personality. She cozied up to Sawyer immediately.

"Mmm-hmm. I see," he said.

"This is Sugar." Peyton stroked the filly's head.

"I'm only looking to acquire one horse. A stallion."

"She likes you, though."

"She probably likes everyone," he argued, taking over with stroking her head. "That'd be why she's named Sugar. Because she's so sweet."

"No. She's named Sugar because she likes sweets. Check it out." Peyton began to unwrap a peppermint candy and immediately had Sugar's full focus.

"You want some candy, Shug-Shug?" Peyton placed the peppermint in the palm of her hand and held it out for Sugar.

The horse took the candy and rolled it around in her mouth, clicking and clacking it against her teeth before crunching down on it like a grinder.

Sawyer couldn't help but smile at the light in the filly's eyes. She was a beauty.

"You ought to see her with a butterscotch," Peyton said. "She is sweet too. I'll give you that. She's gentle and happy—she'd be ideal for any newbies that come to your ranch." Peyton lifted both eyebrows and waited.

"Then why don't y'all keep her?"

"Hey, I'm just trying to look out for you. Besides, we got what we need right now."

Sawyer rubbed her muzzle and she nuzzled the palm of his hand, looking for another mint. His chest squeezed as he fought the urge to make kissing noises.

A horse like this would be perfect to have now, and continue her training his way.

No, he was here for Buck, not Sugar.

"She'd make someone an excellent horse," Peyton said in a singsong voice.

Sawyer pulled his hand away. "I'll think about it."

Damn, he was a sucker for a good horse.

"Now, where is my stallion?"

Peyton silently clapped her hands together and led him out of the stables at the same end they entered. As they turned to go, movement from the other end caught his eyes.

He stopped and glanced back. "I'll be a son of a—"

Shelby Meyers. Strolling out of the stables with the same too-tall cowboy.

He was about to ask Peyton about the man Shelby was with, but as the two of them turned the corner the sunlight caught their faces, and Sawyer realized exactly who he was dealing with.

Exactly the type of person his brother's fiancée was making time with.

Clay Reynolds.

Sawyer started stomping after them.

Why was Shelby hanging around the most well-known ladies' man in town?

Clay Reynolds didn't have female friends; he had a trail of broken hearts. The two of them certainly weren't co-workers, and there was no way their social circles entwined.

Shelby's people were cocktails at brunch. Clay was beer on a tailgate.

"Where you going?" Peyton called after Sawyer.

He made it halfway down the corridor before he caught himself.

What exactly did he plan to do? Accuse Shelby of running around, right there at Northcliff Ranch? Punch Clay in the face?

This was a place of business, and one of his best connections.

He took a deep breath.

"You okay?" Peyton had caught up with him.

Sugar was whinnying for their attention, since in her world there was probably no reason for a human to come back into the stables except to bring her more candy.

"Yeah. Give me a mint." Sawyer held out his hand.

Peyton dug into her pocket. "Here."

He took the mint to Sugar, who delighted in his return. He counted to ten and rubbed her muzzle.

It didn't make sense for Shelby to be here. She wasn't a horse person. None of her family was. Everyone knew that.

There was no reason for her to be with or know Clay Reynolds.

No good reason anyway.

Sawyer knew plenty about that man and his reputation. Heat shot up Sawyer's neck. Knowing it was Clay that'd been all snug in a booth with his brother's fiancée made the whole situation worse.

Clay Reynolds loved the ladies, and they loved him. He had the reputation for easily catching the interest of any woman he wanted.

Well, his reputation wasn't going to ruin Garrett's life.

With one last rub, Sawyer turned from Sugar and marched to the stables with Buck.

He tried to get his eyes on Shelby again, while staying out of their sights. He couldn't tip Shelby off to come up with yet another poor excuse about why she was there. Or, better yet, how she wasn't even there.

Dress fittings, his ass.

But he didn't see the pair anywhere.

Peyton let him into Buck's stable and he tried to concentrate on the business at hand. The sight of those two played in his mind, though.

He had to talk to Garrett about Shelby and Clay.

This would not stand.

The next morning, Sawyer found Garrett hovering over the coffeepot in his kitchen, Dodger right by his side.

It wasn't even six in the morning yet.

"Good morning?"

"Coffeepot at my place is on the blink," Garrett mumbled and rubbed his eyes. "And you know I can't come up to the big house without this one or he's mad at me the rest of the day." He nodded toward the dog.

As soon as the machine beeped it was ready, he poured his travel mug full. "I know you always set yours to start brewing before six, so it was just easier to drive up here than to a gas station."

"I'm that predictable, huh?"

His brother smiled. "About certain things."

Sawyer filled his mug as well and leaned a hip against the counter. "I'll pick you up a new coffee maker when I'm in town today."

"That'd be great. Thanks." Garrett sipped and yawned, yawned and sipped.

"But things are okay otherwise?"

"Yep."

Sawyer worked to keep his tone neutral. "Good. You're good?"

A suspicious brow went up. "Yeah. Why do you ask?"

His brother knew he wasn't big into small talk, especially before coffee, but today he needed some information.

"No reason."

"Mmm." Garrett headed toward the back door.

Sawyer grabbed his shoes and followed his brother out. "You're heading back already?"

"Probably. You need help with something around here?"

"No. I thought we could hang out a minute. Talk."

Garrett stopped walking and turned. He put the back of his hand up to Sawyer's forehead like he was feeling for a fever.

"Would you stop? I'm fine."

"You never want to just talk." He put on his Sawyer impersonation voice: "Who has time for small talk when there's work to be done?"

"Come on. You're getting married. Things are changing. Can't I want to hang out with my brother?"

"Of course we can hang out. It's just unusual is all. I was going by to see Delilah on my way back. Do you want to go with me?"

"I'd love to."

Garrett cocked an eyebrow again, but led the way nonetheless.

They found Delilah just waking up, nuzzling Garrett

with the quiet trust of a three-year relationship. Then she lowered her head, acknowledging and inspecting Dodger like he was the oddest-looking small horse in their stables.

"What'd you get up to yesterday?" Sawyer took a drink of his coffee.

"Just working. Had a bunch of conference calls and loan agreements to review for clients. I had lunch with Joe, and Lina joined us. Hey, have you noticed the two of them hanging out more?"

"Not really. So, you didn't have lunch with Shelby?"

"Huh?" Garrett shook off the question and focused on a tangle in Delilah's mane.

"I thought you would've had lunch with Shelby."

"She couldn't. She was in Austin with her mom."

No, she was not!

She was at Northcliff Ranch, cozying up to Clay Reynolds.

"Why were they in Austin?"

"Shopping or something. I don't even know. Did you hear what I said about Joe and Lina? You seriously don't think they've been spending a lot of time together?"

"They've always hung out. Austin is a long way to go for some shopping."

"With hundreds more stores than we have here. That's my girl," he cooed to Delilah.

"Maybe, but you don't think it's weird?"

Garrett dropped his hand from Delilah's mane. "What is weird, Sawyer? You're doing it again. Say whatever it is you're trying to say."

Shelby's lying. Again.

But he couldn't say that. With anyone else, he'd grab

the bull by the horns and just tell it like it is. This was his brother, though. They'd already been through this, and Garrett would shoot down any insinuations and cut off any questions. They'd gone down this road the other day, and Sawyer had hit a dead end.

Regardless though, his fiancée was running around with the likes of Clay Reynolds, and Garrett needed to know.

"Shelby wasn't in Austin yesterday." The words flew from his mouth.

"Not this again." Garrett was already walking away.

"She wasn't. I saw her—"

His brother spun on him, finger pointed right at him. "I'm not doing this with you. You're the most untrusting, suspicious person I know. If you don't stop trying to ruin this for me—"

"I'm not trying to ruin this for you."

Dodger barked at Sawyer in response, as though scolding him.

"Really? Because you're doing a damn good job of it for someone who isn't trying."

Sawyer huffed a rough sigh. He couldn't win here, no matter what.

The last thing he wanted was to push his brother away or break his brother's heart, but that's exactly what Shelby was going to do if he didn't put a stop to this wedding.

The pain would only be worse the longer this went on.

"Shelby isn't lying to me, she isn't running around on me, she isn't anything like your ex. Okay? Get that through your head. I know you think we're rushing things, but this is what I want. You need to respect my wishes and stop with the questions and doubts. If you can't do that, then maybe you don't need to be involved in this wedding at all." Garrett turned to leave the stables, his dog hot on his heels in complete support.

Sawyer's gut hit the ground. "What?"

"You heard me."

"Garrett, wait."

But there was no stopping him. He'd made up his mind that Sawyer was paranoid and being overly suspicious. He wouldn't listen to reason and there'd be no talking him out of this wedding.

But Sawyer couldn't stand by and let him marry an unfaithful gold digger.

Obviously, he couldn't be this vocal about his opposition, though. That was a surefire way to get him iced out of his brother's life.

He couldn't keep accusing Shelby of cheating. He'd have to prove it. And that meant calling in reinforcements.

Chapter 7

S he wants another glass of tea and one of your cheese biscuits."

Aurora stopped peeling the carrot in her hands. "That woman is going to float away."

Beth shrugged helplessly. "She has to keep her throat from getting dry while listing out all she wants for the big day. I'm on my fourth page of notes."

"She's been here for almost two hours."

"Tell me about it." She filled the glass with more tea and put another biscuit on the small plate.

Evelyn had planted herself in the sitting room of Orchard Inn at one o'clock this afternoon and hadn't moved or stopped talking since.

The day had already been a long one by noon, with potential brides calling all morning, thanks in large part to the chatterbox in Beth's sitting room.

Hence the reason she kept taking notes and serving tea with a smile. She owed Evelyn the very best service.

Evelyn's penchant for gab and gossip meant she'd told anyone who'd listen—and probably even those who wouldn't—about her daughter's incomparable Hill Country spring wedding at the Orchard Inn. And if anyone brought up the unseemly salad incident, she'd dismiss it with a flick of her Tiffany-adorned wrist.

Beth could hear her now.

"Oh *that*? Well, you know, it was all because the inept caterer they had working there. He's since been fired. He's gone. Long gone. Now Aurora Shipley is handling all of the menus herself. You know she went to Auguste Escoffier's for culinary school, right? And she got a coveted position at one of the best restaurants in California. Can you just imagine what she'll come up with for my Shelby's wedding? The reception will be the party of the season—dare I say, the year."

Add to that the success of the bridal shower at Silva Ranch and Orchard Inn was officially back in business.

"Here you go." Beth delivered the treats and sat back down next to Evelyn on the sofa.

"I was just thinking, what would be best for seeing the couple off at the end of the reception? I know rice isn't a thing anymore, but I've grown tired of bubbles and sparklers. So passé."

"Has Shelby mentioned a preference?"

"No, and I doubt she cares about the finer details."

Beth begged to differ, but she could always check with Shelby separately. "Tossing petals has regained popularity, large confetti—oh, or I heard that Wildflower Farms now has butterflies they'll release. Native to the area, and they have a specialist."

Evelyn clasped her hands together. "Now, I like the sound of that. Jot that down as the top option."

Beth wrote down a few options to discuss with Shelby later.

She looked at her watch and realized how late it'd

gotten. Sawyer had an appointment in about half an hour, and she needed to get rid of Evelyn.

"Well, I think we have all we need for now. Let's see…hors d'oeuvre stations and servers before the main course, ice sculpture for the shrimp cocktail, specialty drink that Aurora will create, named either the Shelby or the Silva."

"I think Silva. Don't you?"

"I—"

"It's not every day your only daughter takes the name of one of Texas's most successful families."

Beth's forced smile felt a lot like a grimace.

After listening to Shelby's concerns about Sawyer, all talk of the Silva money made Beth nervous. While she knew Shelby's intentions were pure, and she obviously adored Garrett, she understood what it might look like to someone as skeptical as Sawyer.

"I know!" Evelyn slapped her hands together, making Beth jump. "A drink called the Silva and one called the Shelby."

Two drinks were doable.

"Do you have any input on what they contain?"

"You girls can figure it out. Something classy and completely original. Maybe bourbon in the Silva. Or tequila. Yes, a top-shelf tequila."

Beth kept jotting down notes.

"How much did you say Sawyer was going to contribute to the budget?"

"I didn't."

"You didn't?"

"No ma'am. Only that he expressed a willingness to help and be involved."

"Involved?"

"Insomuch as both families will be represented. Nothing more. I think it will be a nice touch."

"Well, if he's to be involved, then I'm sure the Silva family can afford to contribute more than a little to the budget. Did Shelby tell you they're going to the Hawaiian Islands on their honeymoon? I told her to be sure they stay at the Four Seasons. You only get one honeymoon and there's no reason to skimp on luxury, if you know what I mean."

Beth smiled politely. "Well, I think I have everything I need to get started on the reception. I'll be in touch if anything comes up."

"Are you rushing me off, dear?"

"No, no. But didn't you mention having a nail appointment this afternoon?"

"Gracious! Yes. What time is it? I'm going to be late."

It occurred to Beth that Evelyn asked and answered her own questions more often than not. She imagined Evelyn didn't need her there at all for this entire meeting. A voice recorder would've been sufficient.

"Let me run, honey."

As though Beth had been the one keeping her. "I'll walk you out."

She got Evelyn out the door, closed it, and leaned back against it with a long, slow sigh.

Finally, a reprieve.

She'd have her own glass of tea and cheese biscuit, put her feet up for five minutes, and gather her thoughts.

After a short break, she'd meet with Sawyer about the groom's dinner.

Sawyer.

He of the small dimples and deep brown eyes.

Characteristics that didn't match his more cynical nature. Sawyer with his surprisingly easy nature and casual flirtations, his soft spot for horses, in complete opposition to the tough businessman she knew him to be.

The contradiction was appealing and growing more so every time they—

No.

No, no.

Shelby's wedding, she reminded herself.

She had a business to redeem and a best friend's wedding to pull off. Sawyer and his charms would have to wait.

"How long are you going to stand there with your eyes closed?"

Beth's heart leaped out of her chest and likely hit the chandelier.

"Sawyer! My heart. I mean—not my heart. I almost had a heart attack."

"Are you okay now? Because we need to talk."

His voice was different than normal, and not in a good way either. It held an edge she didn't like.

"You're early."

"Only by a bit. Can we talk?"

Something was wrong. The clipped tone, the hard look in his eyes.

But what could possibly be wrong? Things were fine the last time they'd spoken. She'd meant to ask him about Shelby and why her best friend was of the mind that he didn't like her, but she'd gotten...distracted.

Maybe they could discuss that today, since they'd be alone and have privacy. He was even here early enough to—

Uh-oh.

He was here early. How early?

"How long have you been lurking in the hallway?"

"I'm not lurking. I'm standing. And long enough to hear about the big plans in store for me."

Beth pushed away from the door and went into the sitting room, knowing he'd follow. No reason to have their talk in the foyer, where anyone could hear.

She closed the door behind them.

"And what is it you think you heard?" she asked.

"Not *think*. Know. I heard all about Evelyn's grand plans to spend my family's money."

Beth put her hands up in appeal. "I know it probably sounded bad, but that's just Evelyn running off at the mouth. Believe me, you can't put any stock into what she says."

"No, that's her wanting to get her hooks into Silvas' resources before her daughter is even married."

"Come on, Sawyer. It's not like that." He had to know this. He was a reasonable adult, with life experience. Most of the town knew how Evelyn could be. You just took her with a grain of salt and went on with your life.

"She was the same at the bridal shower and touring my home. She all but hired an appraiser to tag stuff for retail value."

He wasn't completely wrong there.

"I know, but I promise you, I'm not going to let her run up the cost of the wedding. You have my word."

"Thank you, but it's not you I'm worried about."

Good to know, but that begged the question, "Then who are you worried about?"

"Her daughter is just like her."

Heat shot up Beth's neck as every ounce of her raged at the notion that Shelby could be anything like her mother. She wanted to yell at him to take it back or they could take it outside, because that was her best friend he was bad-mouthing.

It wouldn't be a particularly lady-like reaction, but being an oldest sister and protective friend was a heady combination.

"No, she is not," she managed to say instead. Beth knew Shelby better than anyone else, especially Sawyer Silva. She just needed to explain rationally how he'd misunderstood the situation.

"They're cut from the same cloth, and I'm not going to let my brother fall prey to some woman who doesn't love him and is only after his money."

"*Fall prey?*" Beth's hands started to shake with nerves and utter disbelief. "Are you out of your mind?" Was she being shrill? She felt extremely shrill right now. Wait. "Doesn't love him?"

What weird dimension had Sawyer slipped into?

"I'm finally in my right mind. So much makes sense now and I'm not going to let my brother be played like a fiddle."

Oh, this was bad. So, so bad. She'd seen this before: families get all stressed out and suspicious, weddings almost fall apart because Grandpa realized the groom's great-uncle once swindled him out of some cattle.

She could calm this storm.

Think, Beth, think.

"I think if we can sit down and talk, let me get you some tea—my sister makes these amazing cheese biscuits—we can sort all of this out."

He stared at her for a moment and then, "There's nothing to sort out."

The man wouldn't even sit down. Instead he stood like an oak in the center of her sitting room.

"I've got some thinking to do and...I don't know. Some work to do."

Evelyn Meyers and her big mouth. But this obviously wasn't all about Evelyn. Shelby's insecurity wasn't baseless after all. Maybe Sawyer just plain old didn't like her.

"I do wish you'd at least sit down so we can discuss this," she urged. "I'm sure it's all just a misunderstanding."

He glanced at the sofa as though tempted, but then began pacing. "No, no. I know how these things go. You bring me over here to talk and next thing you know my head is a mess and I'm doubting what I heard when I know what I heard and I know what I know."

What in the ever-loving world was happening here? Had body snatchers taken over the seemingly reasonable cowboy she'd met over a week ago? "You came over here to discuss the groom's dinner. I didn't bring you here for anything ulterior, so maybe we should just focus on that."

"I don't want to discuss any dinners. I think this whole wedding is a bad idea."

Beth's barely banked fire broke free. "It's not your wedding," she snapped. "Stop trying to ruin something that doesn't have to involve you."

"You're darn right. And the Silvas shouldn't have to pay for any of it either."

"I assume you'll let your brother know of this new development."

"He'll know about it, all right, when I tell him I think he should call off the whole thing."

Wait. What?

Sawyer stopped pacing and headed toward the door. "Garrett needs to get out now, before things get worse."

He left the sitting room and stomped through the foyer.

Beth followed him out. She'd made things worse. So much worse.

How had that happened? She was trying to be the voice of reason. But how did one reason with a man who was being completely unreasonable?

"We can talk this out," she called after him. "Come back inside."

"I'm done talking."

If he upset Garrett, then that would upset Shelby, and then an upset Shelby would mean all the Meyerses were upset and everything would snowball from there.

Sawyer Silva was not going to ruin this wedding.

Beth stopped short of chasing him all the way to his truck.

There had to be a way to fix this. He needed to calm down and reflect, if he did things like that, and she needed to come up with a plan.

As soon as he was down the drive and out of sight, she ran back inside and hauled Cece into the kitchen, where Aurora was pulling something out of the oven.

"We have a problem. A very big problem."

"What happened?" Cece's eyes were wide with concern.

"It's Sawyer Silva, and he's trying to torpedo Shelby's wedding."

"Oh, no he isn't." Aurora took off her apron. "Is he here?"

"He just left. I don't want to talk about this in the kitchen, where someone could hear."

Aurora waved them to the back door. "Let's take a walk. These cakes need a long time to cool anyway."

The inn was quiet midafternoon, and they were able to slip away without any guests stopping them for more towels or shopping recommendations.

"What happened?" Cece asked again as soon as they reached the first row of plum trees.

"Sawyer is going to try to talk Garrett out of the wedding."

"Why?"

"He thinks Shelby is using Garrett and is only after him for his money."

"Shelby has her own money," Cece pointed out.

"Not like Garrett's got," Aurora countered.

"True, but it's not like she's hard up. Her family might've had hard times lately, but who hasn't? We have."

"None of that matters." Beth stopped them. "Y'all know she isn't using Garrett. Shelby loves him."

"It's so obvious." Cece nodded.

"Some might say sickeningly so," Aurora agreed.

"And Sawyer said the weirdest thing about that too. He's convinced she doesn't love Garrett. I don't know how he could think that."

Cece chewed on her lip. "Maybe it's because he doesn't know Shelby like we do?"

"How could he not see it? They're all kissy faces and honey-baby-baby." Aurora plucked one of the leaves from a plum tree.

Cece scowled at her sister. "I thought it was sweet. But back to Sawyer, how could he have it in his head that Shelby is a gold digger?"

Beth took the leaf from Aurora and checked for spots. "I have no idea. He wasn't making any sense when he came by a little bit ago. He flew off the handle about Shelby preying on his brother, and I got the feeling there's a lot of sour grapes there for some reason."

"Hmm." Cece chewed on her lip some more and then gave them a knowing nod. "I bet Sawyer got burned by a woman who was just after his money."

"How do you know that?" Aurora asked.

"I don't know it. Not for certain. But why else would he be flying off the handle and thinking Shelby is preying on his brother? He must've gotten burned before, and he doesn't want the same thing happening to Garrett. He's overreacting, and men overreact when protectiveness and pride are involved."

Both of them stared at Cece, mouths slightly open.

Beth slowly shook her head. For someone who rarely ever dated, Cece had some surprising insight on men. "How do you do that?"

"Do what?"

"Just, know things," Aurora answered.

"I listen and pay attention. People forget I'm in the room a lot. Makes it easy to observe pretty much every kind of human interaction."

They both stared again.

"Hmm," Beth eventually puffed. "I think you may very well be right. And we cannot let him ruin this wedding for any reason, much less because of his past. This is too important to our future and the inn."

"How do we stop him?"

"I tried reasoning with him earlier, and that didn't work at all." She flashed back to snapping at him that this wasn't his wedding. "Well...kind of. I might've made matters worse."

"How?" Aurora cocked an eyebrow.

"I got a little fired up when he accused Shelby of using Garrett."

Cece crossed her arms, looking lost in thought. "Somehow, you've got to put a salve on his burn before he'll be willing to accept Shelby or this wedding without drama."

Beth shook her head. "I tried, at first, but then everything went pear-shaped."

"You're going to have to eat crow if you were mean to him," Aurora pointed out.

"I wasn't mean."

The doubting purse of her sisters' lips shut her up.

"I might've been a little brusque. But not mean."

Cece nodded again and uncrossed her arms. "You're going to have to take one for the team and apologize."

"*Apologize?* I didn't—"

Cece held up her hand. "Doesn't matter what you did, he did, you said, he said. We need this wedding and we need him to be on board, right?"

"Right."

"Then invite him to lunch or coffee, say you're sorry, eat that crow and listen to him, then convince him that Shelby isn't a woman after the Silva name and fortune. You do that and you can probably get the wedding plans back on track."

Cece was channeling her inner Beth at the moment,

and she'd be lying if she said she wasn't the teensiest bit proud—even while being told what to do.

"I could meet him for lunch. Get some barbecue."

"Exactly. That sounds perfect."

Her mind went back to Sawyer's story about only his family being bold enough to laugh at him. Her sisters were the same.

From the time they really had a moment to talk, Sawyer had seemed…relatable. Familiar. She thought she was getting to know him. Understand him.

And then this about-face on the wedding and his harsh refusal to listen.

She didn't know him at all.

"Earth to Beth?" Cece looped an arm into hers. "It's going to be okay. You can handle Sawyer. I have no doubts."

"Me either, sis," Aurora agreed. "You know I'm just teasing. Let's walk some more."

They made their way down rows of plum trees, until they reached row after row of peach trees.

When they were kids, the three of them would play hide-and-seek for hours among these trees.

Cece always kicked their tail at hiding and seeking. They'd give up before ever finding her, and she found them both way too easily.

Aurora, on the other hand, was better at tag. The same single-sighted stubbornness that took her to the top of her field made her dominate the tag game. If she wanted to tag you, by gosh, you were getting tagged.

Beth was the best when it came to the yard tricks. Cartwheels, handstands, walking handstands, Hula-Hoop, flips on the trampoline, you name it. She'd practice and practice until she could do something perfectly. Then she'd teach her sisters.

They'd grown up in the orchard as much as they'd grown up inside the house. This wedding was guaranteeing they'd have many more years here, with lifetimes of memories, even memories for generations to come.

Sawyer Silva was not going to threaten that by threatening this wedding.

Whatever his flawed logic and weird reasoning, Beth was going to convince him of the truth.

Shelby and Garrett were meant to be together and have the best wedding Texas had ever seen. And Sawyer was going to get with the program and be happy about the blessed event, whether he liked it or not.

Chapter 8

*S*top *trying to ruin something that doesn't have to in-volve you.* Sawyer gripped the steering wheel tighter. *It's not your wedding.*

He'd never said it *was* his wedding. Getting married was the furthest thing from his mind. But that had nothing to do with the issue at hand.

Beth had gone into left field from their argument, away from what mattered.

Her friend Shelby was using his brother, and she'd tried to defend her.

Shelby was seeing some other guy.

He'd heard Evelyn Meyers with his very own ears.

All that talk about the Silva name and money and resources, and how he ought to contribute plenty and Garrett ought to take Shelby to the most expensive hotels all over the world, and still Beth had the gall to try to defend that family and their intentions.

Unbelievable.

"What's eating you, son?" Uncle Joe asked.

"Nothing," came his clipped reply.

Joe snorted. "Yeah, you sound just fine. Meeting with the wedding lady go bad?"

Despite his uncle's attempt at humor and insistence on giving everyone a title to go with their name, Sawyer was far from fine.

Even with Beth firmly on the side of Shelby and Evelyn and defending this farce of a wedding, he still couldn't hear her name without part of him sparking at the sound of it.

They'd argued—there was no other word for it—and even mid-argument he couldn't be mad at her. He couldn't stop the warmth of attraction when she'd stepped up to him, brows knit and nose scrunched, telling him no, Shelby wasn't just like her momma.

Yeah. Sure.

Beth might look downright delicious defending her friend, but her defense was built on lies.

Maybe he should've told her about seeing Shelby with Clay. Maybe he should've come out with his firsthand knowledge of what it looks and feels like, being used for your name and money, and then cheated on.

To be lied to for who knows how long, and manipulated into believing someone loved you, when the only person they could love was themselves.

But Beth didn't need to know about all of that. It was in the past, and he hated the way it made him look. Not knowing who his fiancée really was, all while she worked their relationship to her benefit.

He'd been played for a fool.

But this wasn't about him.

It was about Garrett and saving his brother from a similar fate.

"So is your silence a 'Yes, the meeting with Beth the wedding lady went to crap'?"

Sawyer shook his head and chuckled despite himself. "It's just Beth, Uncle Joe. Not Beth the wedding lady."

"I think that's got a nice ring to it."

"Kind of long, though. I like Milton the mailman better. Or even Lina the house lady."

His uncle cleared his throat. "She's just Lina. So, I guess I can go with plain ole Beth."

Beth wasn't plain ole anything.

With green eyes that flashed whenever she was interested or aggravated, and hair that matched the fire within, Beth was a force.

Sure, she was full of manners and graces, a professional with a mind like a trap, but he saw the careful, deliberate side of her crack when she'd gotten mad at him. That might make some people mad. Turn them sour on someone who looked ready to gouge their eyes out for saying something about their best friend.

Not him.

He understood that kind of reaction. That level of protectiveness.

It was exactly how he felt about Garrett.

Beth made sense to him—most of the time. He liked her. Plain and simple. And she'd almost convinced him to sit down and let her talk him into believing in Shelby and Evelyn, and supporting this wedding.

But he couldn't let his affinity for her get in the way of doing what was best for his family.

"You going to answer the question, son?" Joe interrupted his thoughts. "Y'all were meeting about the groom's dinner. Did you get it sorted?"

"Not exactly."

"You better hurry up. How many more days until go time?"

Not enough days, that was for sure.

"There are some issues I need to fix first."

"Issues. That doesn't sound good."

It wasn't, and Sawyer was usually great at resolving issues. But this one had already blown up on him two or three times.

"Anything I can do?" Joe asked.

There may as well have been a lightbulb flipping on over Sawyer's head.

Uncle Joe's help was exactly what he needed. If he could get his uncle on Team Stop This Wedding, then Garrett would finally listen.

Joe was their mentor, their father figure. They loved him, would do anything for him, and vice versa. If Joe had concerns, then Garrett would take heed.

"You going to drive right by Farm & Feed or slow down?" Joe asked.

Sawyer hit the brakes and cut a quick right, barely making the turn.

"Don't kill us before we get supplies."

The Farm & Feed was only slightly less crowded on a weekday but remained one of Fredericksburg's hottest social scenes on any given afternoon.

Sawyer and Joe had to stop twice to talk to folks before they even made it into the air-conditioned barn area.

"You want to divide and conquer on this list?" Joe flicked the notepad paper in his hand.

Normally, that was their MO. Today, Sawyer needed to bend his ear and gain an ally.

"We don't need much. I think we can stick together."

"Hey there!" His uncle waved at one of their neighbors and went over to chat.

Sawyer said hello and waited patiently for his uncle to finish gossiping about the couple that'd bought the land next to them.

At this rate, he'd never have time to talk about Garrett.

Finally, Joe finished chewing the fat and they headed to the aisle with the galvanized tubs.

"About the groom's dinner meeting," Sawyer began, with no segue or soft opening. "I told Beth I'd like to wait on scheduling that just yet, since I have some concerns about this whole wedding to begin with."

His uncle stopped in the middle of the aisle. "Has this got anything to do with that same nonsense you pulled at the breakfast table the other morning?"

"It's not nonsense. I'm telling you, Shelby is hiding something. She isn't trustworthy. I heard her mother telling Beth about all her big plans for spending Garrett's money."

"Spending money is all that woman ever talks about. That don't mean nothing. I know Evelyn Meyers can be a lot to handle, but you can't judge Garrett's girl based on the dam."

"She's not a horse, Uncle Joe. She's an opportunist and she's using Garrett the same way Melissa used me."

They both fell silent. The softness in his uncle's gaze was more than he could bear.

Joe was the person he'd confided in when he'd first learned the truth about his fiancée. He'd gone over to Melissa's house to surprise her with a trip to San Antonio, in celebration of their engagement.

So stupid in love, he hadn't stopped to wonder what some flashy Mercedes was doing in her driveway.

He'd been struck silent, finding her with another man.

Even later, she'd tried to make excuses for her actions and said a bunch of crap about how she'd felt rushed and she'd gotten scared, wanted to slow down, and how this was, in essence, all his fault.

He should've told her where she could go with all the bull she was shoveling, but he knew nothing good would come from saying another word to her. His love for her had ended at that exact moment.

So he'd walked away.

To this day, he was angry at her, but sometimes the best thing a man can do is walk away.

A few nights later, at Bronco's Bar & Grill, he learned from one of Melissa's tipsy friends that she'd actually "traded up on fiancés." See, Chad with the Mercedes was a stockbroker from Dallas. Chad managed hedge funds and was moving her up in the world.

She'd never loved Sawyer or felt anything for him, except excitement at the opportunities being Mrs. Silva might have brought her.

That was the extent of Melissa's true feelings for him.

The next day, after sobering up, Sawyer had gone out to one of the barns and punched a feed bag until his knuckles were raw.

That was where Uncle Joe had found him, and where he'd spilled out the whole sordid tale.

"Shelby ain't Melissa, son," Uncle Joe said to him now.

"I know she isn't, but she's cut from the same cloth."

"How so?"

Sawyer looked at his uncle.

"No, seriously. Following that logic, how do you get she's the same as your ex?"

He spit out the truth. "I've seen her hanging around a guy I know is no good. For no good reason."

"Did you ask her why?"

"No. She doesn't even know she's busted."

"So, it could be completely innocent?"

"No way."

"I suggest you ask her and find out the truth about what you think you saw before you go digging yourself a big ole pit to fall in."

"I asked her at breakfast, and you heard her. She made up a lie."

Shelby wasn't going to be honest about what she was up to, which is why he'd called a friend of a friend who did a little investigative work on the side. Nothing over the top, just someone who could do a little digging, a little following up on his would-be sister-in-law.

Something he should've done for himself, back in the day.

Joe shook his head. "Don't go making judgment calls on people until you talk to them and get to the bottom of things. You know this, and we deal with it in business all the time. I've taught you as much for years."

Oh, he'd get to the bottom of things. That much was certain.

But this wasn't business. This wasn't horses and land, training and riding and breeding.

This was personal.

This was his brother and the woman he was planning to marry. She was going to be family.

Family was more important than business.

*   *   *

After the Farm & Feed, they had an appointment with Mitchell, their financial advisor. There was an account Uncle Joe had and he said he wanted to check on it and make a few changes. He was vague on details, so Sawyer didn't pry.

Instead, he waited in the clean, sleek lobby while his uncle conducted his business.

"Sawyer?"

"Garrett." He stood to greet his brother. "I didn't know you were meeting Joe here."

"I'm not. I just wrapped up a separate appointment with Mitchell and ran into him. Funny seeing you guys here too."

What was Garrett doing at Mitchell's office? Mitchell handled only their long-term finances, savings and investments. Garrett didn't need to make any changes to his savings. Unless...

A knot twisted Sawyer's stomach.

Surely he wasn't adding Shelby to any accounts already. They weren't married yet.

He'd raised his brother to be smarter than that.

But how to ask.

"What are you doing here?"

Not smooth, but it'd have to do.

"Nothing much, just talking about options. Stuff about the future. You know."

He did know. That was what worried him.

"But not making any changes right now. Right?"

Garrett rolled his eyes. "Sawyer," he grumbled as he turned to go.

Sawyer followed him out. "I'm just asking."

"You're being nosy. They're my accounts. I can do what I want."

"And some of them are our accounts."

Once he reached his car, Garrett spun on him. "You really think I'd be doing anything to our joint, family accounts without telling you?"

"I didn't say that."

"It's what you meant."

"I didn't mean anything. I was asking a question. I know you're all in love—I've been there, and it can make you do things—"

"I'm not you," Garrett snapped.

They both fell silent.

"Look. I know you mean well, but after breakfast and then whatever happened at the bridal shower—"

"Nothing happened at the bridal shower."

"Obviously something happened, because some brides-maid came running over to Shelby upset about them going dress shopping without her, and Shelby is convinced you hate her."

Great.

This wasn't going his way at all. He wasn't going to convince his brother to call it off, but what if he could at least convince him to slow it down? Buy himself time to get proof of Clay and Shelby.

"I just think you're moving too fast. What's the rush?"

"It's not too fast."

"Why now? Why does the whole thing have to be what Shelby wants?"

"Let's just stop talking about this, okay? You've made it clear how you feel about her, the marriage, and now where we're getting married."

"I don't care about where you get married." He just wanted them to stop moving forward.

Garrett stuck his finger in Sawyer's face. "Do not bring this up again. You understand? Not Shelby, not the wedding, none of it, or so help me God, you won't be a part of any of it."

Sawyer's gut clenched and Garrett got in his car before Sawyer could say anything else.

He drove off, leaving Sawyer in the parking lot like a dog someone had abandoned.

An older lady studied him from the other side of her car.

"Ma'am." He nodded her way before going back inside.

With a grumble he slumped onto the couch. This was going south fast. The harder he tried, the more he pushed his brother toward Shelby.

His tactics were all wrong. He was creating the Romeo and Juliet syndrome, and everyone knew how that ended.

He sat up a little straighter and tried to clear his head.

Everything he'd tried ended up with him being the bad guy. Flying off at the mouth had put him on the outs with Beth and now Garrett.

He wasn't the bad guy, but they couldn't see that.

Sawyer had to make himself the good guy. Turn things around so he was back on the inside, and then he could get to the bottom of what was going on.

Shelby was hiding her relationship with this guy, and he'd have to have his proof before he could ever bring this up with Garrett again. He wasn't going to confront her about it, only to have her lie again and cause even more issues between him and Garrett.

No, he'd sit tight and wait until he had facts in hand before bringing anything up again.

Beyond that, though, he'd be Mr. Nice Guy. He wasn't going to let Evelyn Meyers break the bank with her big reception plans, but otherwise, he'd play along with this wedding game.

That was the only way to ensure his brother didn't lose.

Chapter 9

Beth finally got around to pouring herself the glass of tea she'd wanted over twenty-four hours ago and plodded down the separate hall to her bedroom. Luckily, her room sat on the other side of the living room from her sisters'. She needed privacy for this conversation. No one wanted to eat crow in public.

She sat on her bed and quickly ran through her opener—half in her head, half mouthing the words.

"Hey, Sawyer. It's Beth Shipley. I would like to apologize for the other day. The whole conversation got out of hand, blah, blah, blah. I'm sorry. Let me take you to lunch. How about Frank's BBQ? I will hear you out and even answer any questions you may have about Shelby. Without being defensive. You will see she is the best kind of person. I'm sure we can get everything back on track."

Or something like that.

Maybe she'd get lucky and go to voicemail.

She hit his contact in her phone, because, yes, he was now a contact in her phone, and waited as it rang.

"Hello."

Dang it. No voicemail.

"Sawyer. Hey. It's Beth. Shipley."

"I know. Your name popped up when you called."

She was in his contacts too.

"Right. Okay. Well. I'm calling because…"

I want to apologize.

Just spit it out. Take one for the team even though he'd been snippy and defensive, too, not to mention completely baseless in his accusations against one of the nicest people on the planet.

Beth took another deep breath. "I'm sorry."

A pause drew out into too-long silence.

"Because. See, the other day, when you were here, things got—"

"I know. I'm sorry too."

Beth drew back the phone and looked at it. He was sorry too? In her experience, the men of Texas rarely, if ever, apologized.

"Things got way out of hand. The way Shelby's mom was talking rubbed me the wrong way and I have my own, justifiable, reservations about my brother getting married so fast, but I didn't need to go barking at you about it. I was out of line."

Beth sat back against her pillows, stunned.

"Don't get me wrong. I still think they're rushing into this, but I realize I went about things the wrong way."

"I'm…that's good to hear. And I realize I was defensive and a bit…snippy. But I know what a good person Shelby is, and she really isn't anything like her mother."

Silence from the other end of the phone, but at least there was no argument otherwise.

"I know you were concerned with some of what you

overheard," she kept going since he wasn't pushing back. "Why don't we get together and talk about it? You can tell me what you'd like to see and you can continue to be as involved as you'd like to be. If you still wish to be involved?"

"I do."

Her shoulders slumped with the sigh of relief. "Great. Then let me take you to lunch tomorrow. Maybe to Frank's? And we can sort everything out. I'm sure."

"I can't go to lunch."

Dang it.

"But I can meet you for dinner."

Oh.

"Okay," she answered, probably too quickly.

Dinner with Sawyer. On what planet was this a good idea? She was supposed to be corralling the enemy. Buttering him up so he didn't ruin this whole thing. Not gazing into his big brown eyes over candlelight.

Actually, Frank's didn't have candles. Just BBQ and beer. That would be safe enough. Nothing romantic about either of those things.

"I'll meet you there at seven tomorrow?" he asked.

"Sounds good."

"See you then," he said, and waited for her to hang up first.

Beth set her phone on the bed and began picking at a loose string on her quilt.

The call had gone okay. Right? Kind of felt like she'd blacked out for a moment after he apologized.

But he had definitely apologized, so that was a good sign. He knew he was out of line with all that warning-Garrett talk and trying-to-ruin-the-wedding nonsense.

Not that Garrett would listen.

Any fool could see how much he loved Shelby, and how she loved him.

It still bothered her why Sawyer would ever think the worst of her best friend, but she could use this dinner to poke around and get to the bottom of why.

Frank's BBQ looked out across the vast fields of Firewheel Farms, one of the Hill Country's famous wildflower farms. At sunset, the views would be so clear you could see for miles.

There were two different stories about how the Firewheel flower got its name.

The flowers were vibrant yellow around the edges, red centered, and daisy shaped.

Legend had it that, in the time of the Aztecs, bright yellow flowers grew everywhere. Children played in fields of wildflower blooms. Young ladies collected the flowers and decorated themselves with necklaces of these yellow flowers.

Then Cortés arrived and conquered the nation. The blood of the Aztec people stained the flowers with red.

Beth shivered at remembering the tale. It was a dark legend.

Some believed the Firewheel was named for the Texas horizon at sunset. The sky would color a deep burnt orange, the sun setting low beyond the peak. It looked like fire in the sky.

Sawyer had beaten her to the restaurant and waited for her inside the door near the hostess station.

She smiled, thinking he'd probably heard the exact same stories growing up, as all locals did.

"Good to see you." He smiled back.

Remembering he was the enemy was going to prove quite the challenge.

And, as it turned out, for dinner service, Frank's did have candles.

Yay!

They were the short, fake tea-light variety, but they still created an ambience that Beth didn't need right now.

"Inside or outside?" the hostess asked.

Sawyer looked at Beth for a vote.

Was one more inclined to business than the other? She defaulted to what she always wanted if the heat allowed.

"Outside. If that's okay?"

"Outside sounds good," Sawyer agreed.

"Right this way." She led them to a table at the edge of the back deck.

No candles on out here yet, as the sun hadn't set just yet. Which meant they'd be here for sunset.

She couldn't win for trying tonight.

Beth sat before she could catch on that Sawyer had pulled out her chair for her.

This was not a date, she told herself. Don't get side-tracked. She was here to set him straight and they weren't leaving until he was on board with the wedding, and Shelby, and the whole shebang.

"You look nice," Sawyer said after he sat down, mentioning it so casually that she almost didn't catch it.

For over an hour she'd deliberated between jeans or a dress. It was BBQ. Jeans, obviously. But it was higher-end BBQ and business, and sometimes Frank's had someone playing music later and she'd be with Sawyer.

In the end she'd opted for a casual dress. Nothing fancy. Not trying too hard. Just a sheath dress in deep green. Aurora may have once mentioned that emerald green was her best color.

"Thank you. You...you do too," she finally managed to reply.

At any other time, her conversational skills were unparalleled. A huge part of her career included talking to people.

But around Sawyer, tonight, particularly when he wore a white dress shirt, folded up at the sleeves, his sun-kissed forearms just out there, for anyone to see? Her cool confidence faltered.

"I appreciate you agreeing to meet with me, and I hope we can come to some kind of a compromise and understanding, as far as Garrett's wedding goes."

There. That sounded like her usual self.

Sawyer opened his mouth to reply, and the waiter showed up to take their drink orders.

They both opted for a beer.

"That's my hope as well," Sawyer said, once the waiter disappeared. "I was thinking about it yesterday, about how we could include Silva Ranch and contribute without giving the Meyers family free rein over spending. If you know what I mean."

"Of course."

"I'd like to keep my financial contribution to the wedding itself. That's the most important part anyway."

"It is." And, typically, less expensive than getting into reception costs.

Sawyer wasn't completely clueless about weddings.

He knew he was minimizing his exposure to Evelyn and the over-the-top expectations he'd overheard the other day, but Beth couldn't blame him.

"I'll talk to Garrett about what we could do in the ceremony that'd be special to the Silva family. That way he can run it by Shelby for approval, and everyone is happy."

He wanted Shelby's approval. Such progress.

"Wonderful," Beth said.

This all sounded surprisingly reasonable compared to their talk in the sitting room.

Should she be suspicious and ask why the sudden change of heart?

The waiter showed back up with their beers and Sawyer raised his glass to hers. "This way we've officially set the parameters and we'll avoid any confusion going forward."

"Sounds good to me." She tapped her glass to his and took a sip.

Frank's brewed their own beers, two IPAs, a lager, a stout, and a Hefeweizen style. She was a sucker for a Hefe.

"Man, that's a good beer." Sawyer all but smacked his lips.

The fruit-forward scent filled her senses as the flavor danced on her tongue. Hint of clove, cold and crisp. Perfection. "One of the best."

Sawyer smiled again and she looked away.

Why did he insist on being so agreeable tonight? So likable in general, even if he was a bit of a hardhead?

"Would you look at that sky?"

Gladly.

Beth focused on the sky so she wouldn't have to think about the man sitting across from her.

"I love sunsets. My sister Cece is a sunrise person, but not me."

"Me either. Sunsets are better. Especially out here. You ever hike out here in the country?"

Of course he loved sunsets and hiking. Because everything was conspiring against her will to keep this purely business. "Not in a while, but I used to go with my sister pretty often."

"I hiked a lot this winter. Needed to get out of the house, stretch my legs doing something besides riding."

"How often do you ride?" she asked.

"Every day, unless work is crazy."

"Really?"

"I have to. It's the business. But I also want to. No better feeling in the world."

Beth nodded.

"Well..." He stopped there and took a sip of his beer.

Beth did the same to keep from blushing. There was *something* better than riding horses, but she did not need to think about that in conjunction with Sawyer.

Or how it would be if it involved Sawyer.

"So," she said a little too loudly. "How old were you when you learned to ride?"

"I don't even know. A baby, it seems like. Uncle Joe says I was about three years old when I first sat on a horse, and around six or seven when I really learned to ride on my own. On this little pony named Gulliver."

"I think it's nice that you and your uncle are really close."

"Yeah. For having no kids of his own, he was great at raising us. And he's still my mentor."

Beth envied him that.

"Listen. About your friend Shelby."

Beth opened her mouth to defend her immediately, but Sawyer put up a hand for her to wait. "I was wrong to go off about her the way I did the other day. I was all fired up, and, yeah, I was raised better than that. I was way out of line to say all that."

She appreciated his ability to admit as much, especially face-to-face.

"And I'm sorry I raised my voice at you like that. I'm not...that's not okay where I come from."

"Thank you. Apology accepted." She took a sip of her beer. "And I'm sorry I made matters worse. I normally defuse situations and high emotions. Comes with the territory. I did not handle our meeting well, though. I just...I can get riled up when it comes to my friends and family."

Sawyer laughed as he nodded. "I'm the same. No harm, no foul. That's why I flew off the handle about Shelby and her mom. It involves my younger brother. I worry about him, and I only want the best for him. I know, in my mind, he's a grown man and can take care of himself. But in my heart, I forget all the time and I jump in, trying to take over. I don't know that it will ever change either. If that makes any sense."

Beth envisioned Aurora having to work at Orchard Inn after reaching the pinnacle of success in LA. It physically pained her to see her sister taking a step backward when she'd gotten so far. Or Cece and how hard she worked to compensate, just to be like everyone else. When, in reality, Cece was extraordinary and better than pretty much every person Beth knew.

"Makes perfect sense to me."

Sawyer lifted his gaze to hers with silent understanding.

That kept happening. No matter how inconvenient, she couldn't deny they were kindred personalities.

The waiter showed up to take their order, bless the interruption, and Beth drank more of her beer.

They both ordered the house specials and ate dinner as the sun set. They talked about growing up in Fredericksburg and about the wedding. Finally, they got to the subject of Shelby.

"I know you want them to be engaged for a year or whatever," Beth said. "But that's not what they want. They're great together, and so in love. I've known Shelby since we were eighteen. She's good people, but it's clear you have doubts about her. Why?"

Sawyer pushed some food around his plate and then started turning his pint glass on its coaster. But he didn't answer.

She wasn't letting him off that easy. Beth sat in silence and waited.

"I think it's just doubts in general," he said. "I'm sure she's not a bad person, but he's my only brother and…look, I'll deal with my doubts. I'm not going to go running off at the mouth again, I promise. There's just some stuff I need to deal with, but that's on me."

Beth studied him, the strong lines of his face, the way he quirked his lips in deep thought, the depth of his dark eyes.

"Fair enough," she said. "But I can vouch for my

friend. You'll see. She's going to make Garrett a wonderful wife."

Sawyer nodded solemnly but wouldn't meet her gaze.

They finished their meal and the beers, talking about other places they loved to go in town. The conversation was enjoyable, but something kept niggling at the back of Beth's brain.

She brushed it off as they walked to their cars. Sawyer stopped with her when she reached her driver's-side door.

"Thank you for agreeing to meet with me tonight," she said. "I'm happy with the progress. Your brother's wedding is going to be amazing. I promise."

Sawyer stared at the sky before swallowing hard. "Look, I know I can be a pain in the ass to deal with. Pardon my French."

Beth fought back a smile.

"I've known this about myself for a long time now. But…" This time he met her gaze, and the power of his sincerity made the ground tilt. "I don't want you to think this has anything to do with you. My reactions and, you know, overreaction, has nothing to do with you or your skill and dedication to what you do. Or my thoughts on who you are as a person."

Beth blinked up at him.

"I just wanted to say no matter what happens, I appreciate all you've done for Garrett, and the wedding. And me."

Her pride swelled a bit while her stomach knotted.

No matter what happens?

What was going to happen?

"I'm glad we met," he said.

A moment passed before she could respond. "Me too."

The space between them held so much weight, some of which she wondered if she even fully grasped.

There was obviously something there, with them. Some potential, some spark, some something.

She might even be a little fond of him, but she also kind of wanted to punch him in the arm.

That wasn't a normal, healthy reaction.

Was it?

"I hope that…" He studied the sky again. "Maybe someday, when this is all over, we can hang out. I'll understand if you don't want to—"

"Why wouldn't I want to hang out?" Beth scrunched her nose and studied him.

"I don't know." His voice drifted. "But we'll see. This wedding stuff first, though."

She stared, trying to piece the puzzle of Sawyer Silva together.

"Sound good?" he asked.

Beth shook off her confusion. "Yeah, sounds good."

"Good night, then."

He leaned forward and her heart stopped.

He was going to kiss her.

And she was going to die.

As confusing and frustrating and wonderful as he was, could she handle a kiss? A kiss wasn't in her plans, and men like Sawyer had a way of derailing plans, even if that wasn't their intention.

A kiss from him would cause the train to explode altogether.

Sawyer reached around her and opened her car door.

She saw spots from holding her breath.

"Okay, good night!" The words rushed out as she jumped into her car as if she were leaving the scene of a crime.

Beth buckled up and backed out, quickly putting Sawyer out of sight.

Yep, the man was a walking two-train pileup.

Chapter 10

"I think an autumn wedding would be more romantic, don't you?"

Deanna Nikolas, oldest child of the Nikolas family, of Nikolas Olive Oil, was one of three appointments Beth had booked as a result of Shelby's bridal shower.

Nothing moved a business forward, or backward, like word of mouth. And, in this case, the mixture of positive word of mouth and the close connections in a town like Fredericksburg meant Orchard Inn's business was looking up.

"I agree. Autumn is probably my favorite time of year," Beth agreed. "Shall I go ahead and meet with my sister Aurora on the special menu items you mentioned?"

Say yes to the inn, she repeated silently. Yes to the inn.

"Yes, absolutely." Deanna flashed a bright white smile, her mother beaming with pride beside her.

"Are you sure your sister can manage? We will have family coming over from Greece. They will expect authentic Greek food."

"It will be no problem. Aurora loves to step outside of the usual Texas wedding fare."

"And you're certain your other sister—Cece, is it? She

can create the look we want for the reception area? If we can't have the wedding in Crete, it had better look like a wedding in Crete."

"I'm certain. She'll check with you every step of the way with her design ideas and progress, and I'll make sure she knows how important the proper feel is for the happy couple and their families."

"This is going to be so perfect." Deanna clasped her mother's hands.

Their big day would be perfect, Beth thought, because she treated every wedding like it was her own.

She'd come to realize that pleasing people and making them happy with the result of their ideas was ninety-five percent of her job. She dealt in dreams and making them come true.

And, if she could pull together Shelby's wedding, Deanna's, and the other two prospective nuptials in her appointment book, then her dream would come true too.

Orchard Inn would be the top pick of Texan brides, maybe even brides from all over. She'd solidify her family's security and future, and finally find some peace with the path they'd chosen.

She walked Deanna and her mother out of the inn on floating feet.

"Your land and the views here are just stunning," Deanna said as they reached the porch. "That's what made me tell Mom about this place, even though she'd heard differently and crossed it off her list for their anniversary party."

Beth's feet hit the ground, hard.

"What do you mean, she heard differently?"

Color rushed to Deanna's cheeks. "I'm sorry, I didn't

mean—it was just some gossip from town. I don't pay any attention to that stuff."

"But what was the gossip from town?"

Deanna glanced down at her feet before speaking. "Something about Sawyer Silva pooh-poohing a wedding here. One of my mom's friends overheard him. I told her either she was mistaken or he didn't know what he was talking about."

A knot twisted in Beth's stomach. She tried not to clench her teeth as she asked, "What exactly did Sawyer Silva say?"

The idea that he would say anything even remotely negative about Orchard Inn, after all they'd talked about, their mutual understanding, made her temples ache.

"I didn't hear him say it," Deanna explained, unnecessarily. "But Mom's friend Nancy overheard him outside of Wellford Advisors yesterday or the day before. He was telling his brother not to get married here."

"What?"

Deanna flinched.

Beth reeled in her temper. "Sorry. I'm just surprised to hear he'd say something like that."

"I didn't pay any attention," Deanna tried to reassure her. "Nancy said between that wedding in the winter and Sawyer Silva warning his brother against it, she was out. But she's all about town gossip, and what would Sawyer know about weddings and anniversaries anyway?"

He knew enough to know better than to go bad-mouthing her inn and business in a town like Fredericksburg.

"Are you okay, dear?" Mrs. Nikolas asked.

"I'm fine."

She had a clear head, for once.

There she'd been, thinking Sawyer was a kindred spirit, someone who knew what it meant to run a family business with the people you loved most.

She thought they understood one another.

She'd thought he was going to kiss her. And she would've let him.

Beth ground her back teeth together. Good thing he didn't try a move like that, after trash-talking her inn.

Of all the overconfident low-moral nerve!

She'd go over to his ranch and give him a piece of her mind.

"I'm fine," she repeated. "I can't wait to work with you both on the special day."

"Good." Mrs. Nikolas patted her hand as much as shook it. "Then we'll be in touch, dear. Thank you again!"

She watched them leave, but her mind was on Sawyer.

Whatever his problem was with her and Orchard Inn, she would find out.

Right now.

She made it to the Silva Ranch in record time.

Knocking on Sawyer's front door, she planned what she would say. She wanted to know what possessed him to speak negatively about the inn, especially knowing they'd reached a treaty.

More than anything, she wanted to know why he'd lied.

Lied wasn't the right word.

He'd feigned support of her business, and her. He'd acted like he believed in her, even when he didn't believe in his brother getting married. He'd said he liked her and wanted to spend time with her when this was over.

His claims of liking her made his actions a thousand times worse, and he had to answer for that.

Beth knocked again.

No answer.

His truck was there, lights were on inside. He was clearly home and simply not answering the door.

She moved to knock again, but their housekeeper appeared at the door, smoothing back her hair.

They'd met briefly, before the bridal shower. Beth wasn't sure the woman would even remember who she was.

"Beth? Is everything all right?"

But then, maybe she would.

Taking in Lina's flushed cheeks and hurried breathing, she almost asked her the same thing.

"Everything is fine. I'm looking for Sawyer."

Uncle Joe appeared in the foyer behind Lina, color in his cheeks to match hers.

Lina glanced back, communicating something silently, but Joe just stood there. She gave up and re-focused on Beth. "He's in the stables. The pregnant mare started pacing and fussing like it was time, and he likes to be there for the labor whenever pos-sible."

Sawyer was delivering a baby horse?

She wasn't going to let that dim her anger at him, and yet...

"You're welcome to wait here until he gets back." Lina smoothed down her apron. "I was just in the kitchen making samosas for dinner, if you'd like some."

Beth focused on Lina rather than thinking about Sawyer helping a new foal come into the world.

She didn't realize a person could get that rumpled making samosas.

"No, that's okay." She was clearly interrupting everyone.

"Don't be silly." Joe stepped forward, urging her inside. "Come on in here."

"Have something to eat," Lina added.

"And drink. It's a scorcher out there today."

They both ushered her into the kitchen to wait, the savory scent of garlic and cumin filling the room.

"What brings you out here?" Lina asked, scooping out a tablespoon of the potato mixture to place into the dough.

"I wanted to talk to Sawyer about some stuff. Wedding stuff."

"Here, try one." Joe shoved a plate with a samosa into her hands.

"I thought they were for dinner."

Lina shook her head, but there was a smile on her lips. "If any make it to dinner. This man can't stop snacking on them as soon as they're ready."

Unable to resist the smell, Beth took a bite. A little spice, a little salt, a little sweet. The textures and flavors came together perfectly, making her salivate for more.

No wonder Uncle Joe kept eating them before it was time for dinner.

"I wish Garrett were here for your visit," Lina kept talking. "But he's off with Shelby, I believe. You should see that boy. He practically floats around the ranch every day. Head in the clouds. How are things going with the wedding planning?" Lina folded the edges of the dough to make a little pocket for the potatoes blended with spices.

"Good?" Beth tried to keep the insecurity from her voice as she finished her samosa.

Joe took a couple more and settled on a stool at the kitchen's bar. "Doesn't sound that good."

"Well, things are okay, but..." She was just going to spit it out. "It seems Sawyer still has some reservations about Orchard Inn as the location."

"What do you mean *still*?" Lina looked completely confused.

Joe groaned. "That boy has always got reservations. What happened now?"

"I'm not one to put much stock in gossip, but it seems he's going around town saying he doesn't want Garrett getting married at the inn. Maybe he really would rather have it here."

Lina's pop of laughter almost made Beth drop her plate.

"Oh, honey, he would never bad-mouth you."

"And he would never have a wedding here at the ranch," Uncle Joe said.

"He wouldn't?"

"No," Lina answered for him. "Besides the fact that he has no clue how to throw any kind of party, he'd never muddy the works of running the ranch with things like weddings. Not to mention how hurtful it'd be since his own—" Lina pinched her lips together and quickly went back to stuffing dough with filling.

"Since his own what?"

Lina shook her head. "I've said too much."

Beth looked to Joe.

"Guess there's no sense in hiding what most folks already know." Joe patted the stool next to him, and Beth joined him at the counter.

"See, back...what was it, Lina, just over a year ago?" Lina nodded.

"Sawyer was engaged."

Beth's eyebrows shot up. That was the relationship Cece had so insightfully predicted, but more than a girl-friend. Sawyer had a fiancée.

"And he floated around here just like Garrett is doing. Maybe even more so. He was going to have the whole shebang here at the ranch because that's what the girl wanted. Sawyer would just as likely sneak off down to the courthouse if he had his way. He's not one for show, as you probably already know. But nope. The girl wanted the big wedding and all that, but then...things didn't work out."

"It was bad," Lina added.

"And the wedding was off."

Uncle Joe picked up another samosa. "As happy as Sawyer was when engaged, he was equally as unhappy when things went sideways."

"More so," Lina added. "He had so much anger and hurt." She shook her head.

Beth was a little surprised that they'd share this in-formation so openly with her. Then again, it shouldn't be too surprising. Folks loved to talk, and they knew she and Sawyer were friends, so—

Wait. Were they friends?

She would've qualified them as such after their dinner at Frank's. Friends with the potential for more.

But now?

Beth didn't know what they were.

Anger and frustration at him still simmered beneath the surface, very close to a rolling boil, but now she also had compassion for what he'd been through.

Uncle Joe patted her hand, surprising her. "I love that boy to the ends of the earth, but he can be more difficult than an ornery mule if he gets in his head about something. He probably doesn't have a problem with your inn or you planning the wedding, or anything that's got to do with this wedding in particular. His problem is with weddings, period."

So much made sense now. His hesitancy with committing to something if he wasn't the one in charge, his hang-ups about the timing of his brother getting married, his suspicions about Shelby.

His dag-blasted insistence in believing the worst of people.

She now understood why he resisted at every turn, but he needed to move past it. If his brother was his priority, like they'd talked about at Firewheel, then Garrett needed to be the priority. Not Sawyer's fear.

But how did you tell a man like Sawyer to get over himself?

She couldn't stomp up to him, as originally planned, and chew him out. He'd only become more obstinate and refuse to cooperate with anything.

No, more flies with honey. That was the way.

She'd ask him about trash-talking the inn—that was a must—but she couldn't match fire with fire or all she'd be left with were ashes.

"You know"—Beth pushed herself off the stool—"I can call Sawyer or come back later. It's not an emergency."

"Are you sure?" Lina left her spot by the counter.

"I'm sure."

"Well, I'll tell him you stopped by."

Uncle Joe insisted on walking her out, and Lina insisted on giving her food to take with her. Beth eventually left the house with a renewed sense of purpose, and a Tupperware of samosas.

She followed the path from the house with every intention of calling Sawyer first thing the next day and arranging a time to meet for coffee. She'd ask him what he'd said about Orchard Inn, and if he'd really said what he was accused of, she'd set him straight with a come-to-Jesus he'd never forget, and he could forget hanging out after the wedding.

If he hadn't talked trash about the inn, then that was another story.

Regardless, though, the wedding would move forward. That was what really mattered.

A low voice coming from the nearest stable pulled her from her thoughts.

She followed the sound, recognizing his voice, but not the tone. She stepped into the stable and saw him standing just outside the last stall, in the far corner.

"You're doing great. That's it. It's okay. No, don't get up. Easy does it," he cooed.

The last stall was twice the size of the others, and deep bedding hay was strewn out into the corridor.

"That's it, Bella. Nice and easy."

Beth approached quietly. Sawyer was oblivious to anything around him. In his jeans and a white undershirt, he had eyes only for Bella and her baby, which must be on its way.

Beth made it to the edge of the stall and saw the sable mare on her side, her back legs moving up and down slowly, side to side, as two black hooves edged into sight.

The moment was here.

"Oh my goodness," she whispered.

Sawyer's gaze jerked to her, his eyes rounding. "What, ah— Hey."

Surprise, she thought.

"Hey." She kept her voice low.

"What..." he began, but then shook his head. "Did we have a meeting or...?"

"No, no." She moved closer. "I wanted to talk to you, but Lina told me you were busy. I was leaving but I heard you in here and..."

Now she didn't want to leave. She wanted to stay here. With him.

Say it.

"Do you want to stay?" he asked. "Watch the birth?"

"Can I? If that's okay, I'd love to."

His eyes widened even more. "Yeah, of course. I didn't think—never mind." He waved her over, closer to him. "You can see a little better over here. Have you ever seen a foal being born?"

"No." She'd been around horses her whole life but had never witnessed a birth.

"You're in for a treat, then. At least, I think it is. Mileage varies depending on people's point of view."

He meant some people didn't have the stomach for things like births.

Beth had a stomach of cast iron.

"I like to let the mother and Mother Nature take the

lead," he explained. "I'm here in case I'm needed, but mostly, thankfully, the momma's got it under control."

Beth moved closer to him, her arm brushing against his.

Bella made a few low noises, but not ones of distress.

"It's taken her foal a little while to breach, but this is her first, and I think we're on the other side of things now.

"No, no, baby," he cooed to Bella again, his mouth so close it ruffled Beth's hair. "Don't get up. It's okay, girl. There you go."

Bella lifted her head, her huge dark eyes on Sawyer before she tried to see what was going on.

"Just keep pushing. You can do it."

Sawyer's hand touched the small of Beth's back as he leaned down as if to whisper in confidence. "She's trying to see what's going on, like, what in the world is happening down there."

Beth nodded.

"But instincts kick in and she'll know just what to do. It's the most amazing thing. I'm glad you'll get to see this."

The awe and admiration in his voice made Beth's heart clench.

Bella let out a neigh and laid her head back down, another movement of her hind legs, and more of the foal emerged, dark legs visible through the placenta.

"Baby is going to have her coloring, I bet," Sawyer said. "Good. She's got a great color."

A few moments later, a mouth and muzzle appeared. Then the long bridge of a nose.

"You're doing great, momma," Sawyer encouraged. "You're almost there."

Bella's body moved up and down with her efforts and breathing.

"That's it, girl. Rest a sec. You're almost done."

His encouragement and positive coaching touched Beth. How could this be the same naysayer from her sitting room? The cynic who'd toured her home the day they met?

Putting the two sides of Sawyer together was a puzzle.

"There's the head." He nudged Beth.

The foal's head emerged, followed quickly by the body. Another push and the hindquarters were out.

"You did it!" Sawyer exclaimed. "You did it! Look at that!"

The baby's head was fully out of the sack. The foal took its first deep breath, and something squeezed Beth's chest. Her eyes pricked with a burn before her vision went all liquid with joy.

She tried to blink back the tears and the knot in her throat, but it was no good.

Sawyer would just have to know she was a big weepy mess sometimes, and get over it.

A baby horse lay on the hay, and it was one of the most beautiful things she'd ever seen.

She risked looking at Sawyer, prepared to have him patronize her for that kind of reaction.

Instead, she lifted her gaze to his, and found his eyes were damp, too, with a smile on his face so wide it made her heart ache.

Chapter 11

That was incredible." Beth gazed up at him, her eyes sparkling with unshed tears and wonder.

"Wasn't it? It never fails to amaze me and put things in perspective." His face hurt from smiling.

The foal was already trying to move about, with Bella maneuvering around to lick at her baby. She licked at the foal's face, its haunches.

The sack pulled away as Bella slowly made her way to stand.

"Easy, girl. Nice and steady. You've had a big day."

Bella stood and hooved the ground, moving hay around. She then began cleaning the foal again, in earnest.

As she cleaned, the foal's color became clear. Dark points with a chestnut coat. A bay, just like its mom.

"We need to name the foal," he said, as it rose on wobbly legs.

"It's all knobby knees and legs, isn't it?"

"Definitely. Easy, there. There you go. Take your time."

Bella kept cleaning her newborn, nuzzling and licking and attempting to help it stand.

"A name." Beth smiled. "I don't even know where to start."

"I prefer something not too cutesy. Bella means beautiful, so something more in line with the mother. And it appears..." Sawyer bent down and waited for the appropriate view. "It appears we have a female, so something that matches Mama Bella here."

Sawyer took in the moment. The tawny coat of the foal, just like her mother's, the warm glow of the waning day. This was his second sunset with Beth, the sky the same golden orange, a warm, rich tone.

"What about Amber?" he asked her.

"Amber. I love it."

The foal took shaky steps and lilted to one side but managed to keep her balance. Sawyer couldn't stop the smile of pride that broke across his face.

He loved these moments. Easily his favorite part of being a horse rancher was watching one come into the world, the mother's tender care, the first unsure steps that would one day turn into a confident stride.

He glanced at Beth and caught a new glistening of tears.

"You okay?" He moved closer to her.

"I'm great. It's just...this was really beautiful and I...okay, I confess, I can be a big softie about stuff like this."

His heart clenched as it swelled. "I know. Me too."

It continued to surprise him, how well she fit with him. They fit and it felt right. Except for attempting to work on the wedding. But then, wasn't that mostly his doing?

Birthing foals? Totally his wheelhouse. He was in his element, and happily so. His brother getting married

to a girl he barely knew, from a family he didn't like?
Unhappily out of his element.

"I could stand here all day and watch them." Beth
rested her arms on the stall door.

"Same here." Especially with her there.

They remained in place for an endless moment. He
had no idea how long, watching as Amber went from
barely being able to stand to clumsily walking around and
even nursing.

Mother and daughter were doing well. He could ask
for nothing better, but he wouldn't leave them without
eyes on them for another hour or two.

"I thought you left an hour ago." Uncle Joe's voice
boomed down the stable.

Beth straightened, color touching her cheeks. "Oh. I
was, but..."

"She got to see the foal, Amber, being born."

Joe reached them, all smiles and sneaky twinkle in
his eyes. "Well, that's nice, huh? Ever seen anything like
that, Beth?"

"No, I haven't."

Sawyer didn't much like it when his uncle twinkled.
"What's up, Uncle? Everything okay?"

"Yeah. Just thought I'd relieve you. Let you grab some
grub. I know you don't like to leave them alone until
some time has gone by, but it's past dinner."

As if on cue, Sawyer's stomach growled like a bear
coming out of hibernation.

"I should get going anyway," Beth said.

"You hungry? You can stay and have dinner if you're
hungry." Said another way, he didn't want her to leave.
Not just yet.

"I don't want to impose. Plus, I've got the samosas already and—"

"Those can be your contribution to dinner. If I know my uncle at all, there are none left up at the house, so you'd be doing me a favor by sharing yours."

Beth paused, considering his offer.

Behind her, his uncle was still grinning and twinkling. They were going to need to have a talk about that.

"Okay," she answered. "If you're sure you don't mind."

"Quite the opposite. Uncle Joe, Bella and Amber are all yours." Sawyer escorted Beth back to the house, ignoring his uncle though he tried to get Sawyer's attention.

He knew exactly what his uncle was going to do anyway. Something silly like giving him two thumbs up or making a good-natured but goofy face. Joe was anything but subtle.

Encouraging, sure. But not subtle.

"I'd like to wash up a bit," Beth said as they reached the house.

He pointed her to the hall bathroom and went into his office's bathroom to do the same. As he washed his hands, he reminded himself this was just a friendly dinner. A gesture in return for meeting him at Frank's BBQ and extending the olive branch.

That should've been his move, but she beat him to it.

Figures. Beth was a woman who kept him on his toes, as she was always on hers. He found he rather liked that about her. His mind liked to be busy, and busily thinking of her was big improvement over worrying about the most mundane of tasks at the ranch.

At least he'd been the one to tell her he liked her. Basically. Now wasn't the time to get into dating or anything beyond just hanging out. If his worst suspicions about her friend proved true and he brought those to light, he doubted she'd want to be around him at all. But he was tired of keeping his interest in her at bay, tired of pretending he didn't notice they made quite the pair.

So, before the bottom fell out, and just in case it didn't, he'd had to let her know.

"Sawyer?" she called his name from the hall.

"In here. Sorry. Just washing up too." He met her at his office door. "I was thinking I'd grill some steaks, maybe toss on some potatoes. I've got salad, you've got Lina's samosas."

"That sounds delicious. I'm starving."

"Me too. C'mon." They went into the kitchen, where he grabbed the steaks he had marinating, a salad Lina had already prepped, a couple of potatoes, and aluminum foil.

Lina must've gone for the night, but the kitchen still smelled like spices.

Beth carried the potatoes and foil and he led her to the back patio, location of the bridal shower, and some of the best fajitas he'd ever had, come to think of it.

"I meant to tell you already, but your sister Aurora is one mean cook. Those fajitas from the shower were incredible."

Beth beamed with a bright pride like she'd cooked them herself. "I'll tell her you said so."

"I already did. I think I had two at the party, but once everyone left, I ate about three more in the kitchen, standing by the sink. She was still here cleaning up and laughing at me."

"She didn't tell me that."

"They don't always tell us everything, huh?"

"No, they do not."

"We don't either, though. Goes both ways."

"I guess, just because we saw ourselves as responsible for them when we were kids doesn't mean we are now. Or that they see us that way now."

He saw what she was getting at, with him feeling responsible for Garrett, but that was different. Marriage was a big deal.

But then, careers were too.

He finished wrapping the potatoes and moved to light the grill.

"I know Aurora is a grown woman," Beth continued, "and the very definition of independent, but I worry she's unhappy because she had to leave LA."

"She seems really happy to me."

"But she could be doing so much more out there. Did you know she was the top of her class at culinary school?"

"I did not know that."

"And she was the youngest chef to ever be hired by that restaurant group in LA. I know the hours were crazy and she was stressed most weekends, but after a couple of years there, she could've written her ticket. Gone anywhere, worked at any restaurant, maybe even earned a Michelin star level."

"Hmph," Sawyer responded. "Will you hand me the potatoes?"

"*Hmph*? That's it? What do you mean, *hmph*?"

He turned to her, chuckling. "No, I mean, that is impressive. And I'm sure Aurora could do pretty much anything she set her mind to, but I also got the impression she's doing exactly what she wants, exactly where she wants. She didn't seem stressed while in my kitchen. And she was telling me about how the town needed a farm-to-table restaurant, and how she'd met with some vendors. She didn't come across like a person who was unhappy with where she was, career wise."

Beth stared at him, a potato in each hand.

"Can I—" He waved her over. "Think I can have those now?"

"Oh. Sorry." She handed them over. "I just…so she seemed happy?"

"Very." He nodded. "And she was saying something about the freedom of doing the food for the shower. Because she got to do basically whatever she wanted, how she wanted."

She continued to stare as he worked the grill. "I never thought about her liking it here more than being in Los Angeles. I thought that was her dream."

"Dreams change," he said. "And you never know. Maybe she likes being home."

"Yeah, and our home is especially awesome so…"

He laughed and closed the grill's lid. "Those will take longer than the steaks. I'm assuming and hoping you don't like your steak charred beyond recognition."

"No, medium rare at most, thanks."

Be still his beating heart. "You want something to drink? Soda, beer, wine?"

"A glass of wine would be nice, if you have some."

"We always have red wine on hand. Doctor told Joe that red wine was good for his heart, so Joe took that to mean he needed to have a glass of upper-shelf red almost every night."

They went inside and downstairs to the small cellar in the basement.

"My gosh, this is so cool." Beth went to the corner where they kept the wine and ran her fingers across the bottles.

"Well it's cool down here. Best place to keep them. Ever had a wine from Valley Falls Vineyard?"

"I've heard of them, but no."

"I think they only grow grapes for two or three of their wines, but the winery puts out six or seven varietals altogether. Lina swears by this Tempranillo. Want to try?" He turned, wine in hand, to find Beth staring at him in the dim cellar light. "What?"

A smile curled the corners of her lips. "I just didn't expect to ever hear you talking about wine varietals with such surety."

"Is that a nice way of saying you didn't think some ole cowboy like me knew a Tempranillo from a Merlot?"

Her laughter filled the basement. "I didn't say that. But you can be full of surprises sometimes."

"I'll have you know that I am a Renaissance man," he teased her.

Her laugh grew louder and his chest filled.

"Fine, maybe not exactly," he admitted, "but I know something about some things."

Beth's eyes and smile were so bright she lit up the dark corners of the room. "You are too much, Sawyer Silva. I bet people around here would be shocked to know how good-natured you can be."

"Are you insinuating folks in town think I'm bull-headed?"

"I'm not insinuating. I'm straight-up saying it."

It was Sawyer's turn to laugh as they left the basement, Beth ahead of him. "Oh, so now you're funny?" he baited.

"I'm always funny," she said, glancing back at him, eyes flashing green.

They returned to the back patio and he checked on the potatoes while she poured the wine. She brought him his glass and they stood near the grill in a comfortable silence.

"Are you warm enough?" he asked, as the temperature was quickly dropping.

"I'm great." She smiled and sipped her wine.

But a moment later, "There is…one thing I'd like to talk to you about."

"Good thing or bad thing?"

"I'm not sure, actually. At first, I was convinced it was very bad."

His stomach plummeted through the patio's stone. She knew. She'd found out about his checking up on Shelby.

"Now, though, I'm not sure what to think."

Or not. "Okay, go ahead and we'll see."

"I met with a potential bride earlier today. Her mother had heard from another lady in town that you were bad-mouthing Orchard Inn to your brother, in a parking lot downtown for all the world to hear. Is that true?"

She didn't take a breath between sentences.

"No, that's not true."

"You weren't outside of a bank or financial office building saying your brother shouldn't get married at our inn, like the inn is trash?"

"I did not say the inn was trash. Who told you this, again?"

"That doesn't matter. I thought we'd moved beyond all of this."

"We have."

"Then you didn't say he shouldn't get married at the inn?"

"No, I...it wasn't like *that*."

"Then what was it like?" Beth crossed her arms and waited.

Sawyer was no longer worried about a chill in the air. He was sweating bullets.

"I have absolutely no issue with Orchard Inn. I think it's the perfect place for a wedding and any other event. I was upset with Garrett because—"

If he said they'd had a confrontation about Garrett putting Shelby on his accounts, that would only make Beth more upset and likely cause another argument. He refused to do that again. His issue had nothing to do with Beth.

"I was upset because he was making some financial decisions and being covert about it. I didn't want him spending even more money on the wedding when I'm already committed to help, and he needed to slow down and not jump things. There was no reason to rush to get married."

Beth stared him down. Unsurprisingly, she was not easily convinced.

"I can see how that'd be misinterpreted, given my tone and my..."

"Intensity?"

"Yeah. Fair enough. Intensity."

She gave him a slight nod and sipped her wine. At least she'd uncrossed her arms, yet she remained silent.

"I'm sorry that kind of message got back to you. Especially after what we've been through and sorted out. I don't want you to ever think that I doubt your inn, your job as a planner, or you. Any...issues I have are family issues. They're my issues with my brother. Not yours. Please don't ever think differently."

She nodded again, more firmly. "You promise you are not out and about trash-talking the inn? And you aren't going to?"

He held up one hand as if he were being sworn in. "I swear I'm not, nor will I ever be, trash-talking the inn or you, or anything to do with Orchard Inn."

Beth took a steadying breath and gave him a final nod. "Fine. I'll take you at your word."

And that was all he could ask for.

He knew better than to air family business in public. *Any* family business.

He'd been rash with his brother, acting hastily instead of letting his temper cool. Over the years, he'd gotten better at taking a walk or at least counting to ten before confronting an issue with anyone, but with Garrett, that had gone out the window.

"I'm going to put the steaks on now," he said, swearing to himself he'd do better.

It took mere minutes to have the steaks ready, and they sat at the outdoor table, with refilled wineglasses, mixed greens with a balsamic vinaigrette, steaks, and baked potatoes with butter, salt, and pepper.

The ideal meal, with the best dinner companion he could ask for.

"You still warm enough?" he asked.

"I'm good." She raised her wineglass. "Fruit of the vine helps."

They began eating and once Beth bit into her steak, she moaned around her fork.

Sawyer shifted in his seat. "Good?"

"So good. Oh my word."

"It's all about the quality of the meat. And Texas has the best."

"You'll get no argument from me."

They continued eating and, while he loved that they didn't need to fill up the evening with pointless small talk, he did want to finish their talk about her sister.

"We were talking about Aurora and her cooking earlier. Do you think you'll ask her if she's happier being back in Texas? Or see if she wants to go back to LA once business turns around at the inn?"

She chewed in thought for a long moment. "Maybe? I don't know. If it comes up? It's a catch-22 because she may think I want her to go, or she may feel obligated to stay. The timing has to be right."

"And it's hard to say the right thing. I'm sure I come across like a bull in a china shop with my brother sometimes, but I only want to spare him some of the mistakes I've made."

"Exactly! I don't want Aurora to give up her dream of owning a restaurant one day so she can cook at the inn forever. That wouldn't be fair to her."

"Yep. And I want Garrett to learn from what I've done, how I've messed up, and save himself the pain of finding out the hard way."

"Like with your ex?"

Sawyer's gaze flew to hers, but in her eyes he found no judgment, no prying intent. Just a need to understand.

"Yeah. Like with my ex." He took a sip of his wine. "So you heard about that?"

"Not really. A little."

He smiled, already knowing the truth. "Lina and Joe told you earlier, didn't they?"

"Yeah."

"I'm not going to ask how that topic came up. Not sure I want to know."

"We were talking about your... hesitancy regarding the wedding. I didn't understand why. So they told me. I imagine it was awful."

"It was, but it's been over a year now. Time to move on."

"Sure, maybe. But that's not always how the mind works. Sometimes it takes a little more time."

"Maybe. We'd been engaged for a couple of months and, boom, it all went to hell and we were through."

"What happened?"

"What usually happens. What we had was built on a lie so it didn't last."

Beth's gaze softened. "I'm sorry you went through that, but to be fair, that's not what usually happens."

"In my experience it does." He recognized how bitter he sounded, but there was no reason to hide how he felt from her.

"What was the lie?"

"That she loved me. I found out she was seeing someone else while she was with me. Probably even before we got engaged. I thought I knew her. I thought she was the one. I'd always been a good judge of character, but I was so far off base with her."

She nodded. "Love can make us blind."

"Exactly."

"But not always. Some love is good, and real, and it makes us see."

Not his experience, but he guessed it was possible. "I suppose."

"Do you think all women are like your ex?"

"No. Not at all."

"Do you think you'll be able to trust again?"

"Yeah. With the right woman, I think so."

Beth smiled softly at that and sipped her wine. "It's not just about it being the right woman, though. Your trust comes from you. You must be willing, and ready. Otherwise, it won't matter how right the woman is."

"Guess I'll just have to go out on a limb and trust her?" He shared her smile.

"I guess you will."

He didn't break eye contact as a slow and steady warmth spread across his skin. It had nothing to do with the wine.

Beth leaned forward and set down her glass. His muscles tightened as he wondered about what she'd say or do next.

"You should let me handle cleanup, since you cooked," she said.

Disappointment relaxed his muscles. "You don't have to do that."

"At least let me help."

They rose and she gathered up their plates. She took them inside and he followed with the empty salad bowl and grilling tools. They went back outside for the rest, and Beth stopped him with a hand on his arm.

"Thank you for dinner," she said, standing so close to him.

"You're welcome. I enjoyed this."

"I did too." Her eyes sparkled as she smiled again. She seemed impossibly close. Close enough to kiss.

"You sound surprised by that."

Beth dipped her chin and laughed. "Not surprised, exactly. Just...okay, maybe a little surprised." She met his gaze again, and in her eyes he saw his attraction, his desire to know more, mirrored.

He slipped the salad dressing bottle from her hands. "I can finish cleaning up."

"Uh-huh."

"You should come back and see Amber in a couple of days. Once she's up and moving around at full capacity."

"I'd..." She wet her lips. "I would like that."

He touched her empty hands with his fingertips.

"And I'd like to kiss you. Right now."

She barely managed a nod before his lips met hers.

Her lips were warm, soft, and giving. He kissed her until she leaned into him, molding her frame to his. His hands found her waist, the side of her face, then the curve of her neck.

She smelled like the evening air and felt like heaven, and when the smallest sound left her lips, he had to pull away a moment to contain himself.

Beth's gaze sparked in the moonlight. "Wow," she whispered.

His sentiment exactly, so he kissed her again, this time his fingers in her hair, cradling the base of her neck. She kissed like she lived. With intention, and purpose, passionate, leaving no room for doubt about what she thought or how she felt.

It was everything he'd wanted since the moment he met her. He could've kissed her all night, but her phone began to ring inside her purse.

They ignored it at first, and the call went to voicemail.

Then it immediately rang again.

"I better get that."

Chapter 12

With a disgruntled huff, Beth grabbed her purse and dug around until she found her phone. The number was local, but she didn't recognize it.

"Hello."

"Is this Beth Shipley?"

Some telemarketer better not have interrupted their kiss, or she was going to—

"This is the administrations desk at St. Anthony's Hospital. You're listed as emergency contact for Cece Shipley."

Oh god, what had happened?

"Yes, this is Beth Shipley. Cece is my sister."

"Okay, hon. Well, your sister is here in our emergency room."

"Oh god."

"Now, don't worry. She's okay, but she requested we call you so you can come get her."

"What happened?"

"I'm sorry, I can't go into all that. HIPAA and all that, you know. But can you come down here now?"

"Yes. Yes, absolutely. I'm on my way." Beth hung up on the nice lady. "My sister is in the ER. Something has happened to her but they can't say what."

Sawyer rushed closer, his hand on her shoulder. "What can I do?"

Beth looked around, frantic for her purse, which was still right in front of her.

"Let me take you to the hospital. You shouldn't drive if you're upset."

He led her to his truck and they made it to the hospital in record time. She called Aurora to let her know what was going on as Sawyer pulled right up to the ER door. "Go on in and I'll park. I'll wait in the lobby if they let you on back."

She found she didn't really want him waiting in the lobby, which made no sense. He wasn't family, but she wanted him close. She wanted him with her.

Regardless, she jumped out and hurried inside. Once through security with its one security guard, she reached the front desk to find someone ahead of her.

They took what felt like an eternity to check in. Finally, it was her turn. "I'm here to see Cece Shipley. Y'all called me. I'm her sister Beth."

"That's right. If you'll just sign in."

"Is she okay?" Beth asked, as she wrote her name with shaky hands.

"Well," the lady whispered. "I couldn't say so before because our manager was making rounds, but I think she just broke an arm or something. Nothing too major, honey. Don't worry. She should be fine."

Sawyer showed up behind her. "Is she okay?"

"Just a broken arm, they think. Can he come back with me?"

"Sure. But he has to sign in."

She turned to Sawyer.

"Are you sure? Your sister may just want you there."

"And I want you there."

His eyes widened.

"If that's okay. Even if it's just standing in the hall."

"Yeah, no, I get it. I'm happy to go." He quickly scrawled his name on the list and they went back.

Cece was in one of the last alcoves on the hall, the farthest from the nurses' station. Maybe that was a good sign.

She lay inside, eyes closed, reclined back with her leg elevated and wrapped. Her bad leg.

"Cece." Beth couldn't keep the worry and sympathy from her voice, even though Cece detested both.

Her sister's eyes fluttered open. "Hey, Beth. Hey, Sawyer," she said as well, without missing a beat. "You can come on in."

Beth rushed to her side. "They said you broke your arm."

"Not exactly." Cece wiggled her whole leg at the hip.

"Don't try to move it."

"It's fine up here. It's my ankle. They don't know if I broke it or—"

Beth's hands flew to her mouth.

"Or maybe I only fractured it."

"A fracture is a break."

"Relax, I could've just sprained it. They don't know yet."

"Relax?" How was she supposed to relax when her sister was in a sling? How was Cece so calm about this?

"Yes, relax. I'll be fine."

"What happened?"

"Well, I don't know exactly." Cece lifted her shoulders

and eyebrows in unison. "I was hiking, making my way down a hill, and I guess the decline was kind of steep, but not really. Next thing I know, I roll my foot. I lost my balance, gravity took over, and then, *splat!*"

Beth winced.

"I did roll a little bit at the end." Her sister chuckled. "Wound up on my back like a turtle, just lying there." She flailed her hands in the air.

"Cece! This is not funny!"

"You weren't there. I bet it was a little funny. And I'll be okay! I'll be in a boot for a few weeks so it will heal right, but I can still help with the wedding and stuff."

"Don't worry about the wedding right now. That doesn't matter."

"Um, yes it does."

Beth stared at her sister silently as Aurora joined them in the room.

"Are you okay?" she asked.

Cece insisted she was fine as Beth seethed.

Her sister had resilience like no one else she'd ever known, and the strongest spirit, but sometimes it was flabbergasting. And aggravating.

"Stop looking at me like that," Cece finally said to her.

"Are they giving you crutches to go with the boot?" Sawyer asked.

"Yeah. I should be able to get around pretty good. I have lots of experience."

"Me too." He nodded.

Everyone stared at him.

"I fell so much as a kid, off bikes, hiking on rocky terrain, being where I wasn't supposed to on the ranch, you name it. I've dislocated my shoulder, broken my arm, sprained both ankles, fractured a foot one time too—oh, and there was the time I got a stick jabbed into my leg. I thought Uncle Joe was going to pass out when that happened."

Cece laughed, shaking the bed.

Beth looked back and forth between them, wondering if they should both be committed. "All of this when you were a kid?"

"The stick in the leg was last year."

Cece laughed even harder, making Sawyer laugh in return.

"You're both nuts," Beth decided.

"Nah, just a way to cope." Sawyer shared a knowing look with Cece.

"I am kinda doped up on meds right now, but a stick in your leg is pretty funny."

"You want funny, have Uncle Joe tell you the story. You'd swear I was impaled through the chest when I got home. Blood everywhere, to hear him tell it."

Aurora sniffed with laughter as Cece cackled.

"Okay, okay. I think that's enough of the war stories for now. When can we take you home?" Beth asked.

"The doctor should be back in a moment with the X-rays and a boot."

A moment was more like over an hour, but sure enough, Cece had broken her ankle. They placed her in a boot and discharged her with crutches and a wheelchair ride to the front door.

"I don't need that," she told the nurse.

"I'm sure that's true, but hospital policy says you have to be taken to your car in one."

"Seriously?" she asked, with more than a little attitude.

"Seriously." The nurse had an expression on her face that left no room for argument.

"Don't worry," Sawyer interjected. "You can cut wheelies in it on the way out."

Beth and the nurse both opened their mouths to object.

"I'm joking. Cece knows I'm joking."

Beth wasn't so sure.

Sawyer gave her a quick hug and held out his hand to the chair like he was asking Cece to dance.

That got a smile at least, and she complied.

"I'll pull the car around. Be right back."

"I like him," Cece said, as soon as he was out of earshot.

Beth glanced at the nurse as she rolled Cece out.

"Were y'all on a date when they called or what?" Aurora asked.

The nurse did her best to look disinterested, but it was still a very poor portrayal.

"No, not a date. Just...work stuff. For Garrett's wedding." The last thing she needed was people in town spreading the word that Beth Shipley was trying to move in on the elder Silva while planning the younger Silva's nuptials. She'd undoubtedly be seen as a social climber and gold digger trying to get her hooks into Sawyer.

"You should ask him on a date." Cece chuckled.

"You should sleep off those pain meds."

"If you and Sawyer can handle it, I'll head on home to help get her in the house."

"Y'all are making way too big a deal of this," Cece insisted.

Aurora ignored her and walked away as Sawyer pulled up in his truck.

"Let's get you home." Beth locked the wheelchair in place.

Sawyer hopped out and came around, helping Cece up. "Beth, why don't you put those crutches in the back and you can get on in and sit in the middle. Then I'll help Cece in."

She would be squeezed up against Sawyer. "Sure."

Sawyer got Cece in the truck like he had a side job in hospital transport, and got them home via the smoothest ride ever. Cece was already nodding off as they pulled into Orchard Inn's long driveway, her head on Beth's shoulder.

"I think she's asleep," Beth whispered.

"I can carry her in."

"I'm not asleep," Cece whispered back, "but you can still carry me if you want."

Sawyer laughed, his body warm against Beth's. Her thoughts immediately turned to their kiss, her body pressed against his, even warmer than now, his kiss growing hotter with each passing second. Bone-melting. She might've even made a noise of need. She'd be embarrassed if she could bother to care.

But she didn't. Sawyer's kisses wiped away any other thought or concern about pretty much everything.

It was almost midnight when they pulled in, but Aurora was on the porch waiting, front door standing wide open.

"You need any help?" she asked Cece as she opened the passenger door.

"Hang on, I'll help you out," Sawyer insisted.

Cece pointed to the back. "Aurora, just get me the crutches. If you aren't going to carry me, as promised, then I guess I'll have to do it myself," she teased Sawyer.

"I'll carry you."

"Eh." Cece waved him off and took the crutches from Aurora. "I got it. Carry Beth. I think she's the one struggling the most."

Her sister scooted her way out of the truck and eased down to stand up. Aurora helped her up the stairs and into the front of the house.

"Are you struggling?" Sawyer nudged her with his elbow.

"No, she's just giving me a hard time because I'm mother-henning her."

"Gotcha." He reached for her hand and squeezed it.

They hurried inside to join her sisters in their great room.

Beth helped Cece get settled on one of their couches in their living area, while Aurora hurried to get some tea and snacks.

"I'm fine. Really," Cece insisted, but no one really listened. They fussed over her until she was comfortable on the sofa, both legs up, a glass of tea in one hand and half of a turkey sandwich in the other.

"By the way, I called Mom." Aurora settled in the chair closest to Cece.

Beth bit back a groan as she sat next to Sawyer on the other sofa.

"I bet that went well," Cece muttered.

"She's in Florida until next week but said she could drive back tomorrow."

"No." Cece shook her head. "This isn't life-threatening, and she loves visiting the Gulf Coast. She can swing by next week."

Their mother was on the opposite end of the hen spectrum from Beth. She'd treated the girls as completely independent adults since about the age they were able to drive.

To be fair, raising three girls alone had to be a lot for any mother to handle. Better to teach them to take care of themselves than to crumble under the stress of trying to do it all.

How her mother had managed to let go and trust that they'd be okay was beyond Beth.

"So, what happened out there?" Aurora asked, pulling Beth back.

"I don't know, exactly. I was hiking the trail by Miller Creek and I rolled my foot on a rock or something. Next thing I knew, I was flat on my back with pain shooting up my leg."

"How did you get out of there and get to your car?"

"Luckily, I was near the end of the loop trail so I wasn't far from being done. Some other hikers came along and got on either side of me to help me back."

"Cece." Beth's stomach churned. Her sister might still be out there if those hikers hadn't come along.

As if reading her mind and knowing the wayward path of her thoughts, Sawyer spoke up. "I know that loop. I hike it a lot. Luckily, you were on a very busy trail. Someone is always bound to come along."

"Still." Beth shook her head. She didn't want to think about a worse scenario.

"I'm fine, sis." Cece held up her sandwich as if that were some kind of proof. "All in one piece. Doc says I'll be back up and at 'em in a few weeks."

Cece handed her empty plate to Aurora. "I'm about full as a tick now and ready to get to my room and clean up."

Beth got to her feet. "You need to take another pain pill before bed, so you can sleep."

"Roger that, will do. And will you help me get my jammies on too?" She batted her eyes up at Beth in jest.

"Yes, and make sure you brush your teeth and all that. Cut me some slack—I think getting that call tonight took a year off my life."

Beth held out a hand to help Cece rise.

"I know, I know. I'm sorry they scared you when they called, but I'm not sorry I was out living life and just had an accident."

"I'm not asking you to be sorry."

Sawyer had the good manners to look away from the sisterly discourse.

"Good. Because I'm not."

"Okay." Aurora handed Cece her crutches. "Why don't we head on back to our rooms and y'all can clean up out here."

Cece grabbed her crutches and thudded her way down their hall to her room and Aurora followed.

Beth let her head fall back as she sighed.

"When you go back there, tell her don't make me come in there and tell her my stick-in-the-leg story again," Sawyer added. "Because I'll do it."

His jest brought a smile to her face and helped her relax. At least a little.

"I'll give them a few minutes and then go back to help. I'll be sure to give her your warning."

He took her hand in his. "I know tonight scared you. Are you okay now?"

"I think so. I just worry, you know?"

"I know exactly."

"And she's so stubborn. She acts like I'm nagging or just big pain in her neck the whole time."

"But she had them call *you*," Sawyer said.

"What?"

"Cece had the hospital call you to come be with her. Not Aurora. Not your mom. She might act put-upon, but you're the one she needs right now. It's pretty obvious."

Beth studied him, again at a loss for words.

"Go check on them. I'll wait out here. Maybe help myself to one of those turkey sandwiches?"

"Oh, yes. Please. Where are my manners?"

"Your mind is on Cece, where it should be. I can take care of myself. You go. I'll be right here if you need me."

Beth rose up on her toes and gave him a quick, gentle kiss.

She didn't overthink it, didn't weigh out the result. She just did it. And it felt great. "I'll be back in a bit."

But a bit turned into at least half an hour. It was almost 2:00 a.m. when she returned to the living room, and Sawyer was stretched out on the couch, fast asleep.

Beth's heart warmed at the sight, and she couldn't resist the urge to tuck him in.

She left his boots on, for fear of waking him up, but covered him with a blanket and left an extra pillow by his head, just in case.

With another soft kiss, she wished him good night.

Chapter 13

The smell of coffee lifted his head off the pillow. He vaguely remembered where he was, and then why.

At the moment, all of that came secondary to the rich aroma of coffee.

He wanted to float up and have his nose lead him to the source, as though he were some cartoon character.

Instead, he had to sit up, rub his eyes, find the bathroom, and then find the coffee.

Luckily, the coffee came to him, in the form of Beth, in the cutest cream-colored cotton pajamas with bright llamas all over them, carrying a carafe on a tray with cream and sugar, followed by Aurora holding two mugs in each hand.

"Good morning." Beth's voice was like a song.

She had no business looking that good first thing in the morning.

"Morning."

"Coffee?" Aurora asked.

"Always."

"Same here." Aurora set down the tray, and everyone poured their own.

Cece hopped in with her crutches and he got up to move an ottoman in front of the chair she'd chosen.

Beth settled beside him on the couch, smelling wonderful, the morning coziness only making her more beautiful.

He had to work hard not to grin into his coffee mug like a dope.

She fit so perfectly beside him. Did she feel it too? He wanted to believe that Beth felt this thing growing between them, the way he did. But something deep inside still reared its ugly disbelief.

He'd thought he found this before, only to learn he was wrong.

Still, Beth was different. He didn't want to compare her to his past.

He squashed down the doubting voice, determined to savor this moment.

Then knocking on the back door startled all of them.

"Who in the world?" Aurora was the first to stand up, and shuffled her bedroom feet to the door. "Shelby?" She opened it, and Shelby rushed in, eyes wide, as though she'd been awake for hours.

"Oh my god. Cece, are you okay?" She bypassed everyone and reached Cece's side.

"I'm fine. Y'all are overreacting. You know that, right?"

"That's one of my fears, except I fall off a horse in the woods and lie there all night because no one knows where I am and I can't call anyone for help because there's no signal and I hear coyotes and—"

"We get the picture, Shelby." Beth got to her feet and walked over to her friend.

"Sorry." Shelby shook it off. "I just freaked when I

heard. Beth texted and said you were doing okay, but I wanted to come over."

"We're glad you did. We were all worried, but Cece's doing great." Beth shared a look with her sister that silently spoke volumes.

"Yep. I'm great. What's in the basket?"

"Oh!" Shelby pulled the towel off the top of the basket and lifted out an entire pie. "I brought homemade pecan pie."

Cece smiled and hugged her. "I know it's early, but I'm not above having pie for breakfast."

"Me either." Aurora raised her hand.

"I didn't know what you might need and I was nervous waiting to check on y'all this morning, so I was up early and baked."

"I'll get the utensils and plates."

"Pie is always perfect. Stay and have some." Cece waved her toward the empty chair on her other side.

Shelby stood and, possibly for the first time, realized Sawyer was there. "Oh. Hello. I, um, I wasn't expecting to see you."

Thankfully, Beth jumped in to save them from the awkwardness. "He took me to the hospital last night and it got so late after, he fell asleep on the couch."

He managed a smile and ran a hand through his no-doubt-unruly hair.

"Well." Shelby paused, still awkward. "There's plenty of pie for everyone."

Aurora returned and cut five perfect slices of pie. She got an extra coffee mug for Shelby, and all of them sat around the coffee table eating and chatting.

Eventually the chat turned to everyone's injuries from

childhood to present, each person trying to outdo the one before.

"Remember when I fell off my bike when I was ten?" Aurora laughed. "Skinned up both knees, both elbows, both hands, and my chin."

"You just skidded down the road with your whole body." Cece shook her head. "The boys we were with said you looked like roadkill."

"So sympathetic." Shelby giggled.

"Mom thought you were near death because you came back home bleeding everywhere," Beth added. "We were all in so much trouble and I wasn't even with y'all!"

"Eh, nothing was broken."

Shelby grimaced and rubbed her arm and shoulder.

"I think Sawyer has us all beat," Cece pointed out. "I was pretty doped up last night but I remember a long list. One included a stick in his leg."

"A what in your leg?" Shelby looked scandalized.

"He can tell you all about it."

Shelby looked to him, and he hesitated before he spoke. "I...I was running. Just messing around in the woods like kids do. But Garrett had said he was faster than me or something that goaded me enough not to let it go. So we took off running, not paying a lick of attention to where we were going. Just going as fast as we could. Next thing I know, *Bam!* Pain shoots up my leg, I fall over, and there's this dang stick, about yea long"—he held his hands out around two feet apart—"sticking straight up out of my leg."

All four of them sucked air between their teeth or made a noise of disgust.

"Best I can figure, I'd run into a fallen limb or something, with a smaller branch sticking out just so."

Beth leaned into him and then away. "Gah! You're making my leg hurt."

"I guess I must've yelled or something because Garrett came running back. He freaked out, and when I pulled the stick out—"

All four of them made the exact same noise Garrett had made that day, and Sawyer laughed at the memory.

"When I pulled it out, he made that noise just like y'all, then started freaking out, but I told him to help me get home. We finally made it, with me hobbling and him helping me balance. Uncle Joe is pretty good when it comes to injuries, all those years on a ranch and all, and he knows enough to look for splinters."

"Oh geez, don't say it," Aurora interjected.

"So he sees one, gets the tweezers—"

"Oh nooooo." Beth squeezed his arm.

"And pulls out this splint of wood about three inches long." He held up his fingers for effect.

"Uuuugh! Gross!" Cece grinned with delight. "Was there pus?"

"Cece!" Beth fussed.

"No, because it hadn't been in there long at all." He decided to throw her a bone and mess with Beth at the same time. "But another day or two and I'm sure it would've had plenty of pus."

Cece laughed and clapped at the look on Beth's face.

"That word." Beth shook her head and waved her hands in front of her face. "So gross."

The rest of them all laughed.

"Y'all are gross." Beth finally laughed too.

"I'm done. I promise." He put his arm around her and squeezed.

He didn't have to look around to know three sets of eyes were watching his every move. But he didn't care. He wanted them all to know of his interest in Beth, and he couldn't hide it even if he wanted to.

"The pie is delicious," he told Shelby, being completely earnest.

She smiled as though it were the ultimate compliment.

"Yes." Beth nodded and patted his leg. "Let's talk about pies or food or anything else besides . . . you know."

"Pus?" Aurora snickered.

"I have a funny story that doesn't involve injuries," Shelby announced, and proceeded to share a time, in college, when both she and Beth locked themselves out of their apartment and thought the best solution was an attempted breaking and entering.

Sawyer sat with his pie and listened to them laugh their way through the memory, at times in such hysterics he couldn't understand a word they were saying. Around him, the sisters and Shelby all laughed, reliving more memories, talking about the times they'd been there for one another, including Shelby.

Rescuing Aurora from a particularly bad date, the time they all went to prank Cece's crush and almost got caught by a sheriff's deputy, and the time Shelby confronted Beth's first boss, who was being a gross jerk. Shelby told the man if he didn't stop leering at her friend and trying to get her to go out with him, she'd get him fired so fast his head would spin.

Evidently he didn't listen, because she got him fired and had to deal with his wrath afterwards. Luckily, her position in life helped her deal, and he never bothered either one of them again.

The story was impressive, considering he'd never known a Meyers to do a single unselfish thing, ever.

In all of their stories, he could recognize their actions as something he would do, especially Beth's and Shelby's. He and Shelby weren't exactly polar opposites. He'd admit she did have some endearing qualities, and he could see why she and Beth were such loyal friends.

Beth also wasn't wrong when she'd labeled him over-protective last night.

Took one to know one, but true nonetheless.

He might have to rethink *some* of his assumptions about Shelby.

Not all. And he'd have the inside line on the full truth soon enough, but until that time, he may have to give her some benefit of the doubt.

A new take on things for him, for sure, but he could try.

"Do you want any more pie?" Shelby asked him, a timid timbre to her voice.

No doubt a result of his hard-line approach toward her.

She knew he didn't like her, and he hated seeing that in her eyes.

"That was the best pecan pie I've ever had—don't you dare tell Lina—but I'm stuffed. Thank you for bringing it over."

The warm smile on Beth's lips confirmed he was doing the right thing.

He could do this. He could at least soften his opinion on Shelby until he knew she was what he suspicioned.

That was all Uncle Joe had really told him to do too. Give her a chance.

Cece lifted her legs off the ottoman. "I'm going to crutch around outside for a little bit if anyone wants to come."

A marked improvement from last night.

"I'd love to," Beth said.

"Me too." Shelby got to her feet. "It's so nice out this morning."

Sawyer stood as well. "I should head home. Busy day and Uncle Joe will be on a holy roll once he's done with his coffee and breakfast."

"Thank you again, for last night and everything." Cece hopped over and gave him a one-armed hug that made his breath catch.

"You're welcome."

Beth smiled at him again. "I'll walk you out."

She followed him out and they reached his truck before she spoke. "I want to thank you too. You were a huge help and I'm so glad you were here."

"I'm glad too. I liked meeting your sisters. And Shelby."

"Really?" She beamed.

"Yes, really."

She took a step closer to him, reaching out to take his hand in hers. "That makes me very happy."

He smiled. "Good." He tugged her closer and kissed her.

The kiss was warm vanilla and cinnamon. Nutty and sweet, made sweeter still by her lips, by her arms wound around his neck. He wanted to hold on and let go sometime after lunch.

But he pulled away, to spare them both the audience that was sure to emerge soon.

He did give her one more quick kiss, and then

remembered. "You know your purse is still in my truck and your car is still at my house, right?"

"Shoot!"

"It's okay. Joe and I will be out and about a lot today. If you want, I could drop it by later?"

"You'd do that?"

"If you don't mind me driving your car."

"Of course not. That would be a huge help, actually. We have a crazy day today and I doubt I'll have time to come get it until tomorrow. But I won't need it today either, so if it's any imposition—"

"I said I'll drop it by. I'll leave the keys on the tire if y'all are busy."

"Thank you."

"I'll call you later," he said.

"I sure hope so."

He kissed her gently, one last time, before climbing into his truck and watching until she reached the top of the porch stairs to wave.

Sawyer's drive home was a blur. It wasn't until he pulled in that he realized he had no memory of the drive.

Had he stopped at all stop signs? Obeyed traffic lights? Used turn signals?

He had no clue.

All he'd thought about the whole way home was Beth.

Trying to shake off the daydreams and failing, he turned the corner into the kitchen to skittering feet.

With a scowl, he found Lina at the kitchen's island, and Uncle Joe sitting at the counter.

"Did one of you almost fall?"

"What?" Lina asked, her voice a notch or two louder than necessary.

"I thought I heard one of you shuffling around like you fell."

"Umm," Lina drew out the word.

"Me!" Joe exclaimed. "It…it was me. Darn near fell off this stool. But I caught myself."

Sawyer studied them both. "You okay?"

"Yeah. Great. Why?"

"You're winded."

"Boy." Joe shifted on the stool. "Don't make me get up offa here and show you winded."

"Fine, fine."

"Are you hungry for some breakfast?" Lina changed the subject.

"No, I'm okay, thanks. I'm going to change and head to the stables."

"Yeah," Joe piped up. "Where have you been anyway? Let's hear about that."

"What's gotten into you?" he asked his uncle.

"Nothing. You've been gone all night, apparently, so what's up with you is a better question."

Sawyer waved him off and shared a look with Lina. "I'll be back down in a bit and I can finish off that coffee, but I'm not hungry. I'm going to leave him here for you to deal with."

Lina's laugh was a tad high-pitched.

Sawyer walked away and headed upstairs, shaking his head at both of them.

Chapter 14

She'd managed to change clothes two fewer times than when she'd met him for dinner at Frank's. It would've been exceptional progress if not for the fact that they would be riding horses and she had only three riding outfits.

In the end, she'd settled for her gray riding pants and white top. Only slightly less comfy than the other outfits, but twice as cute. At this point, there was no denying she wanted to look good around Sawyer.

The flash of heat in Sawyer's eyes when she arrived at Silva Ranch meant she'd made the right decision.

"You ready to go?" His smile curled with appreciation. "You look ready."

"I'm ready."

For the most part, anyway.

Shelby's wedding was her priority, but one afternoon of fun wouldn't destroy her whole schedule. Right?

Even with a rushed-deadline wedding like Shelby's, she was on target. Mostly. She'd work extra hours this week to make up the time, finding a printer that would overnight invites. Aurora had a menu almost done for the reception, and Cece had come up with the most beautiful settings and decorations for the ceremony and reception. Everything was right on track, except for a wedding cake.

She'd get it taken care of, though.

"It's been a few months since I was at Mapleton Stables." Beth tried to focus on the here and now.

"Don't worry. We can go easy at first. There's a trail that leads to the edge of our property. I was thinking we could check it out."

She nodded, paying more attention to him in his element than the words coming out of his mouth.

Sawyer always had a kind of self-possessed magnetism. Something that probably came naturally, due to confidence and experience. But when he was out on the ranch, talking horses and riding, working with them, taking care of them, he exuded intention, self-assuredness, and strength.

Combined with his riding gear—true Western style of dark cowboy boots and jeans, plaid shirt, and his black hat—it was a heady mix.

Beth was far too practical to be a swooning, tee-heeing type of gal, but with Sawyer she could imagine the possibility.

"Uncle Joe wants me to go check out the new neighbors, too, as if I'll be able to see anything but a wide swath of their property."

"Sounds very spy-like. I'm in."

His laugh rippled across her skin. "I should've figured as much. Up for any kind of mission, huh?"

She followed as he started toward the nearest stable. "Absolutely. Are we going to need binoculars? Maybe crawl through some scrub brush to get a better look? I could've brought my camera."

"Remind me never to let you and Uncle Joe hang out too much, 'kay? That'd be major trouble."

Sawyer led her to the nearest stable and introduced her to Poppy.

"She's the one I told you about at the shower."

"I remember. Curious and interested, wasn't it?"

"Something like that. And this fella over here." He crossed to the other side of the corridor. "Is my guy, Clyde."

Clyde lifted his head, welcoming Sawyer's touch.

"Isn't he a handsome fella?" Beth cooed.

"He certainly thinks so."

With Sawyer's cowboy hat set low, his smile beaming beneath, Beth saw that Clyde wasn't the only handsome fella. How was she supposed to concentrate on riding with all of *that* on a horse next to her?

They brought their horses out of the stable and into the yard. Without asking, Sawyer provided a mounting block in case she wanted one. Beth always wanted one, whether she needed it or not. Aurora didn't tease her for being Safety First Shipley for nothing.

They mounted and Sawyer took the lead to a trailhead beyond the stables marked THE BABBLING BROOK.

"This one is gradual slopes, well marked and smooth. Good for a casual ride."

He and Clyde went first and, true to his word, they walked at a nice, steady pace while Sawyer pointed out things on the trail like he was a seasoned tour guide.

"Up here on your right we'll pass a little open field where some wildflowers bloom. We can stop and take a look."

Sure enough, little yellow blooms dotted an open field, as picturesque as a postcard.

The sun shone bright and a breeze moved across the field, creating a golden wave of color. The horses lifted their faces to the breeze, and Beth did the same, closing her eyes, the sun warming her cheeks.

It was one of those perfect spring days. Still early enough in the season not to be sweltering this early in the day, but warm enough that the breeze was blissful.

"This is my brother's favorite trail." Sawyer spoke and she opened her eyes. "I should let him know the flowers are out. He's so busy nowadays he might miss it if he doesn't ride down here soon."

"Sometimes it's hard to get away."

"Yeah, but you've got to get out, even when you're busy. Especially when you're busy. Fresh air and being outside is good for the soul."

Cynical Sawyer a lover of nature and believer in its healthful properties.

With each new thing she learned about him, she only liked him more.

They rode on for another couple of miles as the forest thickened around them. The trail became more shaded and narrow, the air cooler. Poppy's hooves softly thudded along the packed dirt, and a calmness spread through Beth's limbs.

Ahead of her, back straight, shoulders broad, Sawyer rode Clyde with a casual certainty that came only with years and years of day-after-day riding and a horse known to the rider like a best friend.

The man could be blindfolded, his hands zip-tied, and he could probably sit atop Clyde and maneuver any trail with confidence.

She was a decent rider, but nowhere near his level. She

might even be a teensy bit jealous if she weren't enjoying the view so much.

Then she thought about Shelby. If her friend could see him riding right now, poor Shelby would envy Sawyer's skill and comfort level no end. Most people thought Shelby Meyers had it all, but that was one thing most all of Fredericksburg, and Sawyer in particular, had over on her.

As they reached the end of the Silva property, they came upon an open field, cut shorter, and a copse of trees around a shallow brook that did, indeed, babble.

"Place screams for a picnic, huh?" Sawyer asked.

"I was just thinking the same thing."

He dismounted and came over to help Beth do the same, his hands warm and firm on her waist as her feet touched the ground. He held her there as she steadied herself.

When she turned around to face him, he tipped his hat back, his brown eyes taking her in as he placed his hands on her waist again. "Your cheeks are flushed from the wind and the sun."

Beth nodded, words escaping her with him this close.

He leaned in closer. "I like it."

She could play coy, be patient, and wait until he kissed her the way she wanted. But coy and patient weren't her thing.

Beth closed the distance between them and kissed him.

She could tell it caught him off guard at first, but he must've liked it. His grip on her waist tightened and he pulled her closer, the softest growl deep in his chest.

She clung to his shirt and opened to him, and he deepened their kiss, answering her call for more. They kissed until her heart flew free from her chest, her legs seeming to melt. And dang it if she wasn't swooning after all.

Sawyer broke away, his breath hot against her cheek. "You make me forget myself."

"What do you mean?"

"I'm trying to be a gentleman. In control. A proper host. But I've got to say, I don't feel proper at all right now."

Beth dipped her face into his neck. "That's okay. I don't either."

Laughter rumbled in his chest, and he wrapped his arms around her.

She curled her arms in against him and figured she could stay there forever. In his arms, held safe and steady against him. Someone as strong-willed and headstrong as her, even more so. Someone who could be a rock, if that's what he wanted. And if she let him.

The realization that Sawyer was exactly the kind of man she'd always imagined, but didn't believe existed, struck her.

Beth stiffened, straightening up, trying not to panic.

When she looked up, she found Sawyer smiling down, the same as before. Handsome, surprisingly charming and complex, considerate and capable.

The reassurance calmed her. She remembered to breathe.

Then Sawyer's hat fell onto her face.

"Clyde!" Sawyer laughed and turned, still holding her. He lurched forward but held on. "Clyde! Fine. Jeez, fella."

Beth lifted his hat away to find him chuckling as he was bumped and nudged by his horse.

Sawyer chuckled as he spoke. "Think he wants something?"

Beth began to giggle at the sight. "I'd say so."

"You thirsty, boy?"

Clyde neighed and raised his head.

"Okay, okay. Let's bring the horses over here for a drink. Someone is feeling bossy."

They broke away, still laughing at Clyde's antics. They took the horses down to the water and they drank of the cool brook.

"Seems Clyde is the worst wingman ever," Sawyer teased. "Thanks for nothing, buddy."

Beth smiled and patted his horse. "Ah, it's okay. The guy's got needs."

Sawyer took Clyde's reins as he finished drinking and led him to a grassy area by the creek. "Next time we come out here we'll have to have a picnic," he said. "Stay longer. Stay all day if you want."

Another date, spending all day with Sawyer, sounded ideal.

"I could probably get away in a few days." She didn't really have that kind of time, but she found she was willing to make the time, if it meant spending the day with Sawyer. "Once I know Aurora has all she needs and Cece is getting around better, I could probably break away."

"How is Cece doing?" Sawyer passed her a bottled water from his saddlebag.

Beth took the water and measured her response. "She's getting around pretty good, now that she's accepted the fact she needs the crutches, but she's in pain. She refused to take the pain meds after a day, so she's just powering through it. But she's okay. For the most part."

Sawyer raised an eyebrow, clearly picking up on her careful tone. "You sure?"

"Yeah. Sorry. I just...I worry."

"I know, but she's going to be fine. And changes at this stage add to the production costs, are time-consuming and, most important, might increase the likelihood of other errors appearing when she's up and at 'em again, she ought to come out here and hike sometime. We've got a lot of great trails that are good for hiking as much as riding."

"I wish she'd stop going off alone to hike at all." The truth was out of her mouth before she could stop it.

Sawyer studied her. "If you're worried for her to go alone, go with her."

"I can't. She goes off for hours and I don't have that kind of time."

"We'll be out here for hours today."

"Which causes me some deal of anxiety, but I'll work late tonight to make up for it and it's why I rarely do this."

Sawyer's face tensed. "Rarely? That can't be good."

"Cece doesn't want me with her anyway. Going on her hikes is her thing. Her getaway and mental health break."

He reached for Beth, rubbing her arm. "You know the other day was just a freak accident, right? You said she hikes all the time and she said that's her first accident."

"In a while, yes. But it's not her first."

He made a thoughtful noise before repeating, "She's going to be okay."

"I know, but I'd never forgive myself if something happened to her."

"You say that like it'd be your fault."

"Because I'm supposed to keep her safe."

"Why is that all on you?"

"Because it always has been," she snapped, and immediately turned away.

She couldn't explain where the emotion came from, the vehemence. The built-up frustration and pressure.

"Hey. Hey, c'mere." Sawyer turned her toward him, plucking the water bottle from her hand to pull her closer. "What's going on? Talk to me."

"Nothing. It's stupid." She looked away, cursing the burning in her eyes and lump in her throat, swallowing it all down.

"No, it's not. I don't know what it is, but I promise you, if you're feeling it, it isn't stupid." He rubbed her arms again before taking a finger to tilt her face back to his. "Tell me what's wrong."

She swallowed again and took a steadying breath. "I don't know," she admitted. "I worry. I *am* worried. I can't help it. It's how I'm made. She could've gotten seriously hurt, Sawyer. She still could get badly hurt and there's nothing I can do. She could've hit her head, still be in the hospital, or worse, and all I could do was get the call and deal with the aftermath. I'm responsible for her safety, her health, her happiness, but I can't do anything to stop stuff like that fall."

Sawyer stopped rubbing and held her arms. "But why are you responsible? Cece is a grown woman."

"Same reason you feel responsible for Garrett," she bit off.

"Whoa, whoa. I'm not responsible for Garrett's safety or health—that's on him. I want him to be happy and I'll do anything to help, but it's not all on me. You're telling me you feel solely responsible for your sister's safety and I'm trying to understand why."

Beth let her head fall back. "Because that's the way it's always been." She shook her head, trying to shake off the past, but the past wouldn't budge.

"See, our dad left when we were kids. He couldn't just leave, though. He got into some trouble with the wrong kind of people."

"I remember my uncle talking about that. People in town were worried about your mom and all of you."

"Exactly. And when he left, he took a bunch of money from the orchard. Luckily, his bookies never bothered us. Unluckily, my dad was the one who ran stuff at the orchard. My mom did her best, but she struggled. It was all she could do to keep the place from going under. She couldn't do it all, so she told me it was my responsibility to help with my sisters."

Sawyer nodded.

"I didn't mind helping. I love them, but I didn't understand the level of responsibility. One day, Cece got into a yellow-jacket nest that was in an old tree stump. She got stung five or six times. I told her not to go over there, but she had to learn the hard way. My mother really let me have it that night. I was supposed to be watching her. She said she couldn't do it all and keep a roof over our heads and keep an eye on us. I had to help, like I promised I would. Especially with Cece."

"Why especially with Cece?"

Beth took a deep breath. "Because Cece was premature and there were...complications. The cord was around her neck and cut off some oxygen for a bit. The doctor said she was fine, and with all my parents had going on, they didn't notice anything for a while. She was healthy and happy, but when she started crawling and toddling around, we noticed something was up with her foot and the way she walked."

Sawyer made a noise of sympathy.

"Later, another doctor said it was a very mild case of cerebral palsy. My dad wanted to sue the hospital, but my mom refused to hear that it was even true. She treated it like a curse or a bad word. She took Cece to therapy. We couldn't afford much, but she insisted Cece had to be normal." Beth used air quotes. "She had to do all these exercises the therapist said would build strength and balance. Mom insisted Cece practice every day. She didn't have time to help with that so—"

"You had to become Cece's therapist."

"Yeah."

"How old were you?"

"I don't know, eight or nine? When we started. And it went all the way up to when she was old enough to tell me to leave her alone and shut her bedroom door in my face."

"So the other night, when you tried to help her…"

"It's always best if Aurora can be involved in helping, if needed, and not just me taking care of Cece. Or if you're involved helping out, turns out. She's a lot more receptive to anyone's help but mine. And I get it! I do. But sometimes I can't stop myself. It's an old habit and she resents it."

Sawyer pulled her closer, wrapping an arm around her.

"You didn't do anything wrong by trying to help. And neither did Cece." He stroked her hair, comforting her. "It wasn't fair to either of you, what you went through as kids. Setting up that kind of relationship between sisters? Sounds like a recipe for disaster." He shook his head. "I had to keep an eye on Garrett growing up, but nothing like that. You weren't able to just be kids and sisters."

"Sometimes we could. We made do and just played, when we had time. Aurora was always a kind of buffer, though. I hate to think what it would've been like if it'd only been me and Cece. How would we have switched in and out of those roles? Turned it off and on?"

"Aurora probably made a good buffer and distraction."

Despite the heaviness of the conversation, Beth smiled. "She was very good at being a distraction. At one point, when Cece was still doing some physical therapy, I was supposed to be making her practice some strength exercises that included—I don't know—calf raises and walking stairs. In the middle of exercising, when Cece was getting really fed up with me and practicing and all of it, here comes Aurora. She starts walking the stairs with us, but she'd taken some of my mother's fanciest high-heeled boots. The tall kind. On Aurora, they looked like go-go boots or something. Anyway, she had on old shorts and dirty old playclothes, but these shiny boots she could barely balance in. She's lucky she didn't break her neck, but we laughed and tried to keep quiet, which only made us laugh harder."

Sawyer chuckled with her at the memory.

"And it worked. It made the whole thing fun, and kept us from being upset with each other. Cece being mad at me for making her practice and me resenting that I had to be the one to force her."

"I'm glad she was there to be a cutup."

"Me too. And I'm sure she knew that rested on her shoulders—to put us back into a playful, family mode." To this day, Aurora deflected or circumvented situations by cracking jokes or being the smart aleck who didn't care, even when she cared a lot.

"Was it tough for you and Cece when Aurora moved to LA?"

"Honestly? Yeah. Not only did we miss our sister, but it was like we were off balance with just two of us. We're okay most of the time now, as adults, but when something like her falling happens, we're definitely better with all three of us here."

Beth sighed, managing to smile. She felt...lighter? Like pounds of pressure had eased off her shoulders.

She'd never told anyone about any of the stuff with her and Cece. Not even Shelby. Because Shelby was friends with all the sisters, it had sort of felt like a betrayal to do so.

Sawyer kissed her temple. "You guys are very lucky to have come through your childhood and that dynamic, to still be sisters and friends. It could've gone the other way."

"I know."

He brushed her hair back, stroking the length of it. "I'm glad you talked to me about this. I could tell something was weighing on you, and it's okay to unload. Especially with me. I get it. And I'm here."

Beth closed her eyes, leaned into his touch, and let go of her guilt.

With Sawyer, opening up about all of the stuff from the past didn't feel like betraying her sisters. It felt like...healing.

She could share with him and he'd listen, help her bear that weight, and anything they talked about would end there. He'd never go tell someone else her business or bring it up to hurt her or use against her. He wouldn't judge her for any of it.

Beth had always kept her own counsel. Held it in and dealt with her problems alone.

That was what family leaders did.

But sharing with Sawyer felt…good. Maybe even great.

And normally, she'd feel the weight of guilt for playing hooky all day. Enjoying some personal time in the middle of planning a wedding would've caused her so much anxiety she'd stay up all night to make up the work. Her head would ache from the responsibility.

But right now? There was no guilt. No anxiety. No ache.

She leaned into Sawyer's arms, let him support her, and kissed him. Not the heated, needy kiss from before, but something gentler. Warmer and content.

Theirs was a generous, giving kiss.

The kind of kiss that came when your soul understood the other, and your heart was at ease.

Chapter 15

Beth smiled as she finished texting and set her phone down.

Across from her, Cece worked on her laptop, her leg elevated in a chair beside her. She glanced up. "Another text from Sawyer?"

"How can you tell?"

"You make oogly eyes when you text with him. Totally gives it away."

"I don't make oogly eyes."

Cece eased the top of her laptop down just enough to do a dramatic interpretation of mooning over something imaginary, complete with eyelash batting and face fanning.

Beth laughed at the ridiculous display. "Okay, I may be a little oogly-eyed, but I know I don't do all that."

"Maybe not that bad, but close."

She tossed a wadded-up piece of paper at Cece.

"Seriously, though, I think it's nice. It's good to see you happy."

Beth was definitely happy. It'd been a week since their horseback riding date. They'd texted and chatted every day since, and a few days ago he'd asked her out on a one hundred percent legitimate lunch date to the new southern bistro in town.

Turned out both of them had a guilty love of pimento cheese, so when the waitress brought out little pimento cheese sandwiches as an appetizer, they'd not only demolished the entire plate, but ordered a second.

They'd taken a long walk downtown after, to walk off the 'ninner cheese, as her sisters liked to call it, and ended up swinging in the little park. He'd kissed her goodbye at her car and she'd been worthless all afternoon, her mind constantly drifting from Shelby's seating chart to Sawyer's lips.

"You're oogly-eyed again, sis." Cece threw the paper back at her.

To top off a great week, she and Cece had been fine all week. Under the circumstances, she was particularly grateful.

Over the years, they were rarely if ever openly mad at each other. Any open expression of anger was always between Beth and Aurora.

In contrast, whenever Beth and Cece were out of sorts, they got quiet with each other. Cece hated confrontation and Beth hated who she became when in a confrontation. So they walked around not talking, knowing everything wasn't okay but never addressing it, until Beth cracked a few days later. By then, time had passed and they usually moved forward without event.

Her rare arguments with Aurora, on the other hand, always included confrontation, yelling, Aurora slamming a door or two and banging around the kitchen.

But this week, she and Cece had gotten along just fine. A stark contrast to any other time Cece was hurt or in need. Plus, she was getting around quickly on her crutches, no more pain meds, and they'd reached a compromise that, at least for the first few weeks once back to hiking, she'd hike with a partner.

Maybe it was the talk with Sawyer that made the difference. She was more aware of her actions and her reactions to Cece, but also gave herself the grace to want to help her little sister and not feel guilty about it.

"Do you two want any more coffee or a snack before we get started?" Aurora popped her head in to ask. "I have some leftover pastry from the guest breakfast this morning."

Cece sat up a little straighter. "What kind of pastry?"

"A strawberry cream cheese strudel."

"Yes!" Beth and Cece answered together.

Aurora brought them a piece of strudel and a carafe of coffee for their meeting. "We'll need to walk later because we also have a cake testing with Shelby and Garrett today."

"We don't have to eat the cake, though," Beth pointed out. "It's the bride and groom's job to taste and decide."

"Yeah, but it's Shelby. You know we're going to eat the cake."

This was true.

They all got going on the details of Shelby's wedding. The sugar rush from the strudel helped, and they powered through finalizing the seating chart, confirming the band and their set lists, finishing orders with all of the food vendors for the menu, and ordering the last of the flowers for the reception.

By the time Shelby and Garrett showed up for their cake tastings, Beth had checked off everything on her list that she'd wanted to accomplish that day. There was no better feeling in the world than a completed to-do list.

Beth was showing Shelby into the dining room when her phone buzzed with a text message.

It was from Sawyer, letting her know he'd gotten reservations that evening for the patio at Sunset Street Bistro. She imagined the romantic meal with him, the stroll downtown before and after, him kissing her near the town square.

Correction. There was a better feeling in the world than a finished to-do list.

"What are you smiling about?" Shelby nudged her as they sat down at one of the larger tables in the dining room.

Beth glanced up to find that Garrett was still in the hallway, distracted by talking with Aurora. "I'm having an early dinner with Sawyer tonight," she confessed.

Shelby's eyes widened as she smiled. "Oh, really?"

"Yes, really. But I don't know if Garrett knows we're hanging out a bit so—"

"Oh, he knows. You and I are going to need to talk later because evidently a lot has happened this week."

Her relationship with Sawyer had grown much deeper since she'd helped him with Amber's birth over a week ago.

The old Beth would be in a panic about moving so fast, but all she felt right now was happiness.

"How is Cece doing? I texted her the other day but only got a one-line reply about how she was fine."

"Much better. The physical therapist said the boot may be able to come off earlier than expected, but I don't know if it will be before the wedding."

"She'll make it work for her, I'm sure. She's such a trooper."

Garrett soon joined them, while Aurora and Cece took seats on the other side of the table.

"We're here in case you need a fourth and fifth opinion." Aurora grinned.

"We'll take all the votes we can get," Garrett said.

"This is a new bakery to us," Beth added, "so I went with the cakes you mentioned, plus three of their most popular options. You can do all one flavor, or what's popular now is to have a different flavor on every layer. We have traditional, lemon, strawberry, chocolate, and the ones you mentioned: white with raspberry crème filling and tiramisu."

"Ooh, tiramisu." Aurora leaned forward.

"Okay, everyone has their own fork so let's pass these around, starting with traditional." Beth handed the cake to Shelby first, then Garrett tried, around to Aurora and Cece, and she tried each sample last.

Traditional tasted like, well, it tasted like wedding cake. Delicious wedding cake, but nothing earth shaking. Next up was the lemon, and it was already steps above the usual. Everyone mmmed and yummed over the cakes, and when the strawberry finally got around to Beth, Garrett turned to her.

"Sawyer tells me the two of y'all are dating now."

Beth choked on her strawberry cake.

"Whoa, you okay?" Garrett patted her on the back.

In her mind, yes, the two of them were dating. There was really nothing else you could call it. She just hadn't heard anyone say it out loud yet.

Hearing it from Garrett like that, such a statement of fact, caught her off guard.

And Sawyer was talking to his brother about her?

Garrett handed her a glass of water.

"Thank you."

"I didn't mean to blurt it out like that and make you choke. I'm just happy to hear he's dating and especially dating you."

Warmth crept up her face. Everyone at the table was looking at her.

"Thank you?" she tried.

Aurora rolled her eyes and passed the chocolate cake to Cece.

"I think it's great too." Shelby smiled, pulling the white with raspberry crème closer. "We should all hang out sometime. Before the wedding."

Shelby had to be relieved that Sawyer had called off the figurative dogs when it came to his anti-wedding stance. Since their dinner at his house, and Cece's fall, he'd made a big turnaround. Beth had finally gotten through to him, and he'd spent a little time around Shelby now.

He'd gotten to see for himself what a sweet soul she was.

"Yeah, we could all meet for lunch and check out that new bike rental place in town. You can rent them by the hour, ride on the trail by the river, and then drop them back off. It'd be great."

Dinners and horseback riding with Sawyer, lunches and biking with him and friends. All these personal plans, all this fun. Who even was she anymore?

Beth hadn't gone anywhere or done much of anything outside of Orchard Inn in years. This place and the wedding business was her life, but with Shelby's wedding almost in the books, maybe it was time for her life to get a little bigger.

She could do both, right? Work–life balance and all that stuff people talked about. She'd never had any kind of balance before, but then again, she'd never wanted it. When her mom wanted out of the day-to-day of the struggling business, Beth had gladly taken the reins. She'd been satisfied with burying herself in Orchard Inn.

Maybe now was the time to dig out a little and see what else the world had to offer.

"Dinner and bikes sound wonderful. Maybe next weekend?"

Garrett smiled. "Sawyer and I will arrange it all. You and Shelby have done all this; the very least we can do is plan a great date night."

"Speaking of…" Shelby passed the final cake sample around. "These are all delicious, but…"

"None of them are quite right," Aurora blurted. "Sorry. I know it's not my wedding, but—"

"No, you're right." Shelby shook her head. "They're wonderful cakes, but not what I had in mind. They aren't…us. I don't know why, though."

"Because you want something uniquely yours." Aurora pulled the raspberry crème sample back over to her. "Something that says Hill Country, and Shelby and Garrett, and late spring wedding. This raspberry one is close, but it's no winner, winner chicken dinner."

Beth studied her sister as she tasted the raspberry again, then the traditional, then the strawberry.

Aurora had the best nose and palate of anyone she knew, and she could come up with flavor profiles that Beth would never dream of. She also knew how to bake, but, most importantly, she knew Shelby. She knew what this wedding meant.

"You should make the wedding cake," Beth said.

Aurora's jaw dropped. "What?"

"Yes!" Shelby exclaimed.

"But I'm not a pastry chef or cake expert."

"Your tres leches cake at the shower was the best dessert I've ever had."

"Yeah, but that was one little dessert. Wedding cakes are a whole other thing. The weight and structure. They have to look a certain way and hold up."

"I don't care about the structure if it's your cake." Shelby turned to Garrett, who shrugged.

"I'm good with whatever you want, baby. As long as it tastes good."

"You say that now, but you're going to want a wedding cake that looks like a wedding cake. It's going to be in pictures. It's a huge focal point of the reception and, most importantly, I've never done one."

"I'm sure you could figure out the structure part," Cece spoke up. "You know so many people in the industry who could coach you and be a source of info."

"But this is a totally different thing. I don't—" She stopped midsentence. "Although..."

"See?" Cece pointed at her. "You already have an idea. I can tell."

"I don't know that you want to be my wedding-cake guinea pig, though. What if it's a disaster?" Aurora's eyes were wide, shining with fear and insecurity, but there was a desire to try, to rise up to a challenge, etched in the line of her brow.

Reassure her, Beth urged Shelby silently. Aurora

needed to conquer this, and it didn't need to be the big sister doing the encouraging this time.

Beth knew she'd found her baker, but Aurora had to step up to the challenge on her own, not be forced.

"Nothing you make would ever be a disaster," Shelby said. "Please make our wedding cake. I would love to be your guinea pig."

Aurora shook her head, but she was smiling and laughing. "I hope you don't live to regret this."

"So, is that a yes? Say yes to the stress!" Shelby clapped. "Of making your first wedding cake."

"Fine! Yes! But my sisters cannot be mad at me when I'm a wreck leading up to the wedding."

"We won't," they both promised.

This new development delighted Shelby and Garrett no end, and they left the inn with huge smiles.

"Thank you so much for taking this on." Beth gave Aurora a one-armed hug.

"And anything you need from us, all you have to do is ask. We may just end up with a new line of business!" Cece grinned.

"Let's not get ahead of ourselves here. We'll see how this goes first, and yeah, you better believe I'm going to need help."

Beth checked the time on her phone and excused herself to get ready. She had plenty of time but wanted to look her best for dinner.

Moments later, her sisters were in her room, Aurora on her bed, Cece sitting in her chair, both offering their opinions on any and all things.

"Look at you, picking out a cute outfit on the first try." Aurora picked a piece of lint off her top.

"Your flattery is too much."

"Where are y'all going?" Cece asked.

"Sunset Street Bistro."

"That place is so nice."

"And romantic."

Aurora flopped back on Beth's bed, messing up her throw pillows. "So, are you two getting super serious or what?"

"I don't know."

Cece scoffed. "You like him and it's obvious he likes you."

"Oh my gosh, are we going to have a Silva in the family?" Aurora sat up suddenly, grabbing a pillow to hold in her lap. "You'll be like Fredericksburg royalty."

"Stop it."

"Aurora does have a point. You'll be the talk of the town, for sure."

Beth did not want to be the talk of the town, unless it was in relation to her stellar wedding business and how fabulous Orchard Inn was.

She hadn't thought too much about that aspect of dating Sawyer. Gossip was a part of life in a town like theirs, and the two of them dating would definitely be juicy news for a while. Eventually it would all die down, though, and, all things considered, it didn't really matter.

She was happy, so let them talk.

The only thing that'd kept him sane today was the promise of an evening with Beth.

An order of feed had been lost somewhere, clear on the other side of Texas, one of his trainers had called in sick for the week, and the new neighbors started putting up fencing without so much as a mention of it to anyone at Silva Ranch.

Uncle Joe had hit the roof about all three issues, but particularly the fence. Sawyer had to talk him off the ledge of that one, all while dealing with his own concerns about the week.

But a dinner and time with Beth waited on the horizon. They could sit back, de-stress, talk about their day. Have a laugh. Take a walk. Make out in the moonlight.

He loved work, but he'd come to love his time with her too.

Since when had he ever thought about the joys of making out with someone under the moonlight? Good lord, he was turning into a sap, and he didn't even care.

He pulled up at Beth's and she was already halfway down the front steps.

She hopped into the truck. "If you don't want to spend an hour being interviewed, we better go."

"Is a news crew here or something?" He purposefully made a show of looking around, already knowing who Beth meant.

"No, but my sisters are."

"I take it they know we've been seeing more of each other."

"Yes. I got shaken down for details while trying to get ready. Spanish Inquisitors would have nothing on my sisters."

"And what did you tell them?"

She quirked her lips. "That it's nothing special and we're just hooking up."

Sawyer's laughter popped out as he drove through the orchard, away from the inn.

"Actually, I told them to butt out. Which never works."

"I bet. That's only going to feed their need for more intel." He stopped at the end of the driveway before pulling onto the road. He turned and waited for her gaze to meet his. "Just for the record, though, it's not nothing."

Her soft smile made his heart kick. "Not for me either. It's definitely something."

He couldn't shake his Cheshire Cat grin for the next five miles.

They arrived at the bistro a few minutes later, for a 6:00 p.m. seating. The evening weather was cool enough to sit outside on the restaurant's patio. Sawyer had purposely gotten one of their earlier reservations in order to have a longer date.

Beth picked the wine and they sat beneath a canopy of trees and lights, sipping a Pinot Gris and snacking on a plate of meats, cheeses, and a bread service.

Somewhere inside the restaurant, a guitarist played music, and it floated outside, adding to the magic of the twinkle lights strung high and greenery decorating the outdoor space.

"This is so nice."

The place was romantic was what it was.

He knew it when he'd made the decision to bring her here, when he'd made the reservation, and when he'd put on dress pants.

Not jeans. Not sweats. Dress. Pants.

No denying it, he only ever wore real pants to special occasions and tonight, to impress Beth. This was a special occasion too.

Because he was falling for her.

Even with all his big ideas about getting the inside

track on the wedding, closer to her, inching in so he could keep an eye on Shelby and even disrupt the event altogether, all he'd really done was get closer to Beth.

The wedding was still moving forward, he hadn't seen hide nor hair of Clay Reynolds in over a week, Shelby and Garrett were supposedly happier than ever, and Sawyer had done nothing to stop the progress since he'd hired the PI.

He was loath ever to admit he was wrong, but it'd happened before. In life. He might have to come to terms with misjudging things completely.

Regardless, time was running out. And if he was wrong, he found . . . he'd be glad of it. He'd happily be wrong.

Which was a first, but true nonetheless.

The waiter appeared and they both ordered pasta dishes with seafood.

Once he left the table, Beth leaned forward, her green eyes sparkling as she looked at Sawyer. "How was your day today?"

He chuckled. "My day? It was interesting, for sure. Uncle Joe was on a holy tear about the neighbors."

"Uh-oh, what happened?"

"They had the nerve to start putting up a new fence, down the property line in the back. Now mind, there's always been a fence on the property line. For decades we've had a fence, but it's our fence. A Silva fence. Nothing big, just standard for a ranch."

"Then what's the issue?"

"The new folks have put up a taller fence, with wiring. And it's not a Silva fence."

"So that's bad?"

"To an old-timer like my uncle? It's the worst.

Neighbors talk before they go throwing up fences. Now I have to hear about it for who even knows how long, go over there to the neighbors and see if there's some kind of situation, and basically suss out what's going on and handle it."

"Have you met them before?"

"Briefly. Only because we went over and introduced ourselves, took them some food, naturally. Haven't heard from them since."

"That's odd."

In Texas, you made nice with your neighbors. You went out to meet new neighbors, you took food, maybe a houseplant, you always sent a thank-you note when someone gifted you, and if you were standoffish, folks got suspicious.

"Real odd. They're a younger family. New, new money, from what I could tell. They seem nice enough, but now that they threw up that fence, they might as well be a bunch of cannibals as far as Joe is concerned. He won't rest until I find out what's going on."

Their food arrived and Beth tsked before starting on her pasta. "I bet your uncle was a hoot to grow up with."

Sawyer laughed as he ate, thinking about one particular incident with Garrett. "You have no idea. One time, when Garrett was in high school, he lied to Joe and said he was staying over at a friend's house. One of the guys from the football team. Well, lo and behold, Joe gets a call in the middle of the night, and Garrett had been in a car accident out on the highway, headed to Carson."

Beth covered her mouth.

"He was fine, and the girl he was with, at two in the morning, was fine too."

Her eyes went wide.

"Exactly." Sawyer took a sip of his wine to wet his whistle. "Turns out, little Garrett had told a bald-faced lie, went to his girl's house—with her parents out of town—and they were out, driving around, leaving some bonfire or something and whoo-boy!" Sawyer slapped his thigh, thinking back.

"I hadn't ever seen Joe that mad. He was beet red and vibrating with anger. He was so mad I had to drive out to the site of the accident. He was too mad to even get behind the wheel. Both of them were fine. The girl's parents had to come back into town to get their daughter and we hauled Garrett home, but Joe made him ride in the back of my truck, all the way back to Fredericksburg."

Beth shook her head and they continued to eat.

"Y'know…" Sawyer thought about it. "To this day, I don't know exactly what all happened. All I know is Joe and Garrett stayed outside for a while, and he wasn't allowed to go anywhere the rest of the school year. He stayed home and worked on the ranch and went to school, and that was it."

"Wow."

"Later on, he told me he hadn't been drinking, but he'd taken his eyes off the road and that's all it took. He also said he'd never been in that much trouble, but he's never gone into details. I asked Uncle Joe about it later, but he never told me anything. He said it was Garrett's problem and his business, and he was making it square." Sawyer shrugged. "And that was that. But I'll never forget Joe's face that night. I thought he'd pop a vein."

They kept eating and near the end of the meal, Beth laughed, almost to herself. "Poor Uncle Joe. Y'all probably put him through the wringer growing up."

"Poor Joe? Poor us! He lowered the hammer on us regularly."

Sawyer reached for her hand. "Seriously, though. We put Joe through a lot. He was a bachelor and then a single dad."

He'd given up dating and going out all the time, because they needed him. He'd put his wants and needs second and put them first.

Sawyer had often wondered, if it weren't for raising them, would Joe have met someone? Maybe even gotten married?

Sawyer shook his head. "I can't imagine. But he did a great job. He had to be strict with two headstrong boys, and...I really don't know what would've happened to us without him."

Her gaze softened as she squeezed his hand. "He's a special man, for sure."

"Honestly, I don't know what Garrett or I would do without him now."

"I don't know if you know this, but you light up when you talk about your family."

"Yeah? So do you."

She nodded. "I'm sure I do. Family is important."

"Speak of the devil." Sawyer waved to his brother as he and Shelby approached.

"I didn't know you were coming here. Nice choice." Garrett grinned and bumped his shoulder.

"Yeah, yeah."

"We don't want to impose." Shelby tucked a strand

of hair back and reached for Garrett's hand. "When Beth said y'all were going to dinner, I didn't realize it was here."

"You're not imposing," Sawyer caught himself saying.

He was happy to see his brother, and he was warming to Shelby. Things had been a little tense between him and Garrett since the financial advisor's office, so having him come over and be so openly friendly and happy was nice.

Maybe all was forgiven when it came to that incident.

"What are you guys doing after this?" Garrett asked.

Beth shrugged. "I don't know. Sawyer?"

"Nothing etched in stone. Thought we'd walk around, enjoy the evening."

"We were going to do the same. Maybe walk down to McGrady's Mini-Golf. You want to join us?"

His brother was inviting him to hang out. A far cry from their last encounter.

"You interested?" he asked Beth.

"As long as we can get some ice cream at their shop."

"We better be," Shelby exclaimed. "I love their cookies-and-cream hand-dipped."

"Sounds good to me." Sawyer nodded to their waiter. "I just need to settle up and we can head that way."

Garrett and Shelby waited for them in front of the restaurant, and all four walked the half a dozen blocks to McGrady's.

They played mini-golf, and it turned out Shelby was as competitive as Sawyer and Beth. Garrett was the only laid-back soul among them.

At one point, Shelby got a hole in one and she screamed like they were watching the Longhorns or Raiders play.

"I just like actually being good at something!" she exclaimed, jumping up and down and clapping.

"I'm sure you're good at stuff." Sawyer laughed and shook his head.

"You'd be surprised." Shelby carried her club and ball to the next hole. "I'm so terrible at so many things."

He found that hard to believe, but he glanced at Beth and she nodded discreetly.

Once out of earshot, she leaned into him. "It's true. Shelby is glamorous and great at social events, but sports and, like, physical activities? That was never her strong suit."

But she kicked all of their tails in mini-golf.

"I think winner should buy the ice cream," Sawyer teased.

"Hey! I think winner should be gifted with the triple crown."

The triple crown was the McGrady's Ice Cream Parlor special: three different scoops of ice cream with a choice of two toppings and whipped cream.

"Fine. I'll buy," Sawyer announced, "and you can get the triple crown."

Chapter 16

Hours later, they pulled into Orchard Inn and Beth led him along the paved path to their private entrance. She let them in the back door and they quietly moved into the living room. It was late and her sisters were long since asleep on their side of the living quarters.

They kept their voices low just the same.

"What are you going to do when you guys outgrow living in the basement?" Sawyer whispered.

"I don't know, exactly." Beth sat on the sofa. "I've thought about building a bungalow on the property, but then again, Aurora isn't likely to be here much longer and there's plenty of room for just me and Cece."

He joined her on the sofa. "True. And who knows, you meet people, move forward in life, get married. You'll all want your own place. A new home."

Beth's heart beat faster.

A new home.

The thought was at once exhilarating, promising, and frightening.

This was her home, her anchor. But she wanted more in her life, eventually. Marriage, kids, a dog. All of it.

But these were all things that seemed very far away.

Off in the future, not until she had things in order. Not until she met the right man for her.

The notion had been inconceivable.

Sawyer's gaze met hers, and her breath caught.

Until now.

"I really enjoyed tonight."

Beth tucked a piece of hair behind her ear. "I did too." Maybe the most fun she'd had in a long, long time. Definitely the most fun she'd ever had on a date.

He angled himself to face her more fully. "Where do you want to go next?"

Beth smiled at the idea of going out with him again and again. "I don't know. Anywhere? But it may have to wait until after the wedding. We're about to hit terminal velocity on the big day."

Sawyer shook his head, even as he gave her a soft smile. "I'm not waiting a week to see you again. I'm sure we can work something out. Coffee break in town. Heck, I'll help move flowers and string up lights if you want, as long as I can see you."

His warm smile set against such a hard jawline never failed to undo her. And he made no secret of his feelings about her.

It was refreshing on its own, but her feelings for him made it intoxicating.

"I don't think you'll have to move flowers. I could probably manage coffee dates. Even lunch," she said.

Sawyer leaned forward and kissed her. "I'll take it."

"But if you really want to help put up lights, then I'm adding you to the work list."

He chuckled, his chest rumbling against her. "I'll help you with whatever you need."

Sawyer's lips met hers again and his words reverberated through their kiss.

Beth knew, with everything within her, that his words were true. Sawyer would be there to help her, anytime she needed him. He wouldn't lie and walk out. He'd stand by her, even when times got tough.

She hadn't expected it, especially not the day he came to visit Orchard Inn with his brother and Shelby, but she'd gotten close to him. She'd let him in.

Sawyer deepened the kiss and she pulled him closer. Never before had she felt so safe, and so certain. He fit her, like a piece of the puzzle she didn't know she was missing.

"Do you want to stay the night?" she asked before she could overthink it.

Sawyer eased away, his dark gaze flickering with fire. "Are you sure?"

"Yes." She'd never been more certain of anything.

"I would love to."

He rose to his feet and held out his hand for her to take. With her heart flying high, Beth led Sawyer to her bedroom.

Sawyer pulled her close and kissed her as she closed her bedroom door.

She awoke, hours later, warm and sated in Sawyer's arms. When she stirred, he brushed her hair back from her face and kissed her temple.

"Hey," he whispered against her skin.

"Hey." She stretched, and then cuddled into him again. She never wanted to move from her bed.

"You okay? Can I get you anything?" he asked.

Beth shook her head. All she needed was this.

Sawyer kissed her forehead, her temple, then her lips. She sighed, unashamedly content. "I'm so happy right now," she admitted.

His soft laugh was warm against her. "Me too."

On the nightstand, Sawyer's phone buzzed with a text.

"You have got to be kidding me," he grumbled, and ignored it.

Then his phone buzzed three more times.

"That could be an emergency and not Joe complaining about the neighbors." With a grunt, he rolled over and checked the message.

Whatever it read had him sitting up in the bed.

"Everything okay?"

"No. I mean yes, but..." Whatever he was going to say drifted into nothingness as he kept reading.

"What's wro—"

"I'm sorry. I have to go." He jumped out of bed.

"What?"

Sawyer seemed to catch himself as he dressed, and he stopped to talk. "I'm so sorry I have to go. I hate rushing off like this, but I have to. That's...that was Uncle Joe."

"Is everything all right?"

"No. But it's not...it's not life or death. Something is...um, one of the horses...something is up with one of the horses. And I need to go take care of it. I'm so sorry."

Something didn't feel quite right in her gut.

"No. It's okay," she said, even though it wasn't. "You go."

Sawyer finished dressing, and she couldn't stop the

niggling feeling that there was more going on here than an issue with a horse.

This wasn't like him, even with an urgent issue. His eyes seemed shuttered, his body language withdrawn.

Normally, he was all about making sure she was okay. He considered her first. Now, his mind was thousands of miles away.

"I'll call you tomorrow," he said, grabbing his wallet and keys and dropping a kiss on the top of her head.

"Okay. Be careful," she managed.

Sawyer had left sometime around midnight, but Beth didn't get to sleep for hours.

She lay in bed for a while, but her mind kept chewing on his words, reviewing them over and over, trying to pick up some morsel of meaning.

If she didn't get up and do something, she'd start to spiral.

As quietly as she could, she slipped on her robe and slippers and went to the kitchen to make tea.

Once done, she sat in bed with her honey chamomile and sipped it while scrolling through social media.

That always took her mind off her life and responsibilities.

But her feeds were full of the locations and vendors she followed for work. Everything was wedding and events, flowers, food, and décor. It only made her think about the upcoming wedding, which made her think about Sawyer, which made her think about how weird he'd been when he left.

"Stop." She groaned at herself and tossed her phone down.

His reason for rushing off probably really was one of

the horses. She was being doubtful for no reason. Getting all up in her head over nothing.

Perhaps her paranoia was because she'd gotten so close to him. Then she'd slept with him. Getting closer, both physically and emotionally, was making her overthink. She'd become open, even vulnerable, with Sawyer, and the sensation didn't come naturally. She detested feeling like, somehow, she might lose.

She'd lost her dad when he walked out, and she'd almost lost the inn. She didn't want to lose Sawyer.

Beth finally fell asleep dreaming of horses and storm clouds.

The next morning, she had a dozen calls to make and two meetings, but all she could think about was Sawyer.

This was exactly why she'd told herself to focus solely on the wedding. Business first, all else later, if ever at all. Because relationships were messy and took up time and energy. Dramatic distractions she didn't have time for. Sawyer might be warm and welcoming and wonderful, but now here she was. Unable to focus, worried more about his call than the call about a potential new wedding.

She fought not to scream in frustration.

Instead, she threw herself into the tedious tasks of her day. She went to the post office, the grocery store, and the drive-through pharmacy. She called her mom just to check in and say hey and give an update on Cece. She did everything on her list and some on Cece's, all to ignore the fact that Sawyer still hadn't called.

Chapter 17

Sawyer scrubbed both hands through his hair again and opened the photo on his phone for what was probably the tenth time.

Shelby, with her hair pulled back and a big, bright smile on her face as she walked a horse through a meadow of bluebonnets. The photo made life look like it was all a freaking Hallmark card.

Next to her, Clay Reynolds wore a smile to match. In the next photo, he touched her hand, taking a horse's reins from her.

They shared an obviously intimate smile.

"Dammit." Sawyer tossed down his phone.

He hadn't realized how much he'd wanted to be wrong about Garrett's fiancée until the very moment he saw that photo.

He should've been warm and content, holding Beth, basking in the aftermath of the best night of his life. He should've been spending quality time with the woman of his dreams.

Instead, he'd had to rush off for fear of getting sick at the sight of that photo.

How could Shelby do this? His brother was going to be devastated.

"I see it all the time," the PI had said when Sawyer had demanded to meet with him late last night.

"And you're sure they were *together* together?"

"They didn't make out or have sex in the field, if that's what you're asking. If they had, I'd have proof of that too. That's the job. But look at 'em. They ooze love-struck and all that crap. And you should've seen him help her down from that horse. I know a pair of people who have been messing around when I see them. Sad, really. People are hardly ever faithful. If they were, I wouldn't have a job."

A year ago, Sawyer would've agreed with him about people never being faithful.

Heck, a month ago Sawyer would've agreed. But Beth had changed all that.

She trusted Shelby, and he couldn't imagine her trusting anyone conniving enough to cheat on her fiancé.

She'd changed him and his view of people. Given him hope. She was as forthright and direct as anyone he'd ever known, and that meant something.

He hadn't been completely upfront with her regarding his suspicions about Shelby, or hiring an investigator, but he'd started hoping he was wrong. He'd almost come to accept he was off base about the whole thing, and why sabotage everything with Beth over a bad hunch? He wouldn't dare.

But his hunch had proven to be right.

He'd wanted to see what Beth and Garrett saw in Shelby, and believe that people could be sincere when it came to love. But they were as wrong and as blind as he'd been with Melissa.

He couldn't let himself think too long about an even worse truth: that perhaps Beth wasn't blind at all. That, somehow, she knew about Shelby and Clay all along, and lied too.

No.

There was no way that was possible. He wouldn't let his mind go there.

No matter how guilty Shelby was in her actions, he knew Beth would be more shocked than anyone to learn the truth.

A knock on his office door pulled him from the dark path of his thoughts.

"Are you going to eat breakfast?" Lina called through the door.

"No, ma'am. Thank you, though. I've got a lot to do this morning." And his appetite was long gone.

He dragged a rough hand through his hair again and threw on a hat.

Shelby would be awake by now. He'd confront her, once and for all, without Garrett or anyone else making excuses for her. He'd take care of this and save his brother from making the worst mistake of his life.

Sawyer barely registered the drive over to the Meyers estate. He drove up to their big brick house, with two-story white columns, on the hill. The house fit the family.

And to think his brother was going to marry into this family.

A severe-looking woman answered the door. Hair pulled back tight, black-framed glasses to match her pitch-black dress. "May I help you?"

"I'm here to see Shelby."

"And who, may I ask, is calling?"

"Sawyer Silva," he said, imagining the woman could probably place a curse on someone like him if she got it in her mind to do so.

"If you'll wait in the sitting room, I'll return with Miss Meyers."

"I'll wait out here," he said. Then added, "If that's okay."

She gave a quick nod and Sawyer moved away from the front door before she could change her mind.

He wasn't setting foot in a house that could have Evelyn Meyers lurking around any corner.

"Sawyer?" Shelby stepped outside and closed the door behind her. "Hey, there. I thought Beatrice had lost her mind when she said you were here to see me. But here you are."

"Here I am." He reached into his back pocket for his phone.

"I'm so glad too. Listen, I know we had an awkward start, but I had so much fun last night. I think we're going to make great—"

"Explain this." He thrust his phone, with the picture of her and Clay, in her face.

"Family," she finished, her brows knitting together as she took the phone. "What is this?"

"You tell me. Because it looks like you and Clay Reynolds are having a time of it in some field."

"A time of it?"

"Yeah. Cozied up, thick as thieves and everything else."

"Are you suggesting that me and Clay…that we—"

"Are seeing each other behind my brother's back? That's exactly what I'm saying."

"Sawyer!" She feigned shock with a hand over her

heart. "I am not dating Clay. I'm not doing anything in-appropriate. This is just a misunderstanding because Clay and I—"

"Then why did you lie?"

"What?"

"You lied and said you were trying on wedding dresses that day awhile back, but I saw the two of you, outside of Carson, in that diner, snuggled up beside each other, having lunch."

All of the color drained from her face.

"Then you told Garrett you went shopping with your momma in Austin, when I saw you at Northcliff Ranch, giggling and flirting with Clay. You lied about that too."

"This is not what you think, and I promise you I would never giggle while at a ranch."

"I am not going to let you do this to my brother."

"Do what? Sawyer, you've completely misunderstood this situation. I can explain."

"You've tried explaining before. I knew you were lying then and I should've stopped you, but I didn't. And you kept on lying, straight to my face. Straight to Garrett's face. I tried to tell him and he got mad at me for doing the right thing! He refused to believe me, but now there's proof. You can't lie your way out now."

"Lie my way out of what? Sawyer, this is just a picture of me—"

"Cheating on my brother."

"Clay is my trainer!" Shelby yelled and thrust the phone into his chest. "He's my horseback riding instructor. He's been teaching me to ride for weeks now. Or trying to, at least, but I'm failing miserably."

He could've sworn her eyes were welling up. Probably crocodile tears from getting caught.

"I fell when I was ten, broke both arms, and I've been terrified of getting on a horse ever since. I haven't been on one since then, so you can imagine how that makes me feel, living smack-dab in the middle of horse country. I swore I'd never touch a horse again, but Garrett loves to ride. I didn't even tell him I couldn't ride until recently, because I could tell all of my excuses about not going were wearing thin, and it's embarrassing! But Clay finally got me on one a couple of weeks ago, and I didn't die."

Sawyer stared at her flushed face, her hands finally settling by her side.

How could she not know how to ride at all? Even if awkwardly? Poorly at worst? But to not ride at all made no sense. Riding was just something people did.

At least, it was what his people did.

"You've told me you were trying on dresses, then you were in Austin," he said. "And now you expect me to believe you, after I know you lied about where you were?"

"You know what, Sawyer?" She threw her hands up again, color rushing up her neck. "I don't care what you believe."

"What?"

"You heard me. You've got this all wrong, but you don't even care. You got it in your mind from the very beginning that I was no good, so it doesn't matter what I say. You didn't want me marrying Garrett from day one, and all you've done for weeks is try to ruin our relationship and wedding."

"That is not true. I tried to like—"

"Beth keeps trying to tell me how great you are, but she's wrong."

He felt his neck go hot too. "Leave her out of this."

"You know there's no way I can. You saw to that the moment you started trying to ruin everything."

"I have proof that you're running around on Garrett and that's all that matters." Sawyer turned and left before he could say something he'd regret.

His boots fell heavy across the front porch and yard, and he barely remembered getting into his truck and speeding away.

Of course Shelby would deny cheating till the cows come home. She'd lie straight to anyone's face, that much was proven. He'd get nowhere trying to have her confess. No admission of guilt, no shame. No apology and no sorrow.

He'd have to tell Garrett himself. Show him the pictures and break his brother's heart.

Garrett was at his house, sitting on the front porch as he worked on his laptop, Dodger wedged in beside him. Dodger jumped down as soon as he saw Sawyer's truck.

The last time he'd seen the dog was when they were both mad at him, storming out of the stables.

He hoped today didn't end worse.

"Hey, man." He lifted his coffee mug from a small table. "Figured I'd be seeing you this morning."

"Yeah." Sawyer settled into the chair next to him. "I came by to talk."

Garrett cocked an eyebrow. "Talk, huh?"

"Yeah."

"Now, why don't I like the sound of that?"

"I don't..." Sawyer didn't finish the sentence as he sat down. "I just want to say, first of all, I actually had a good time yesterday. Last night, I mean. With you and Shelby."

"I did too. It was nice."

"Yeah." It'd been months, maybe more than a year, since he and his brother had just hung out and laughed.

He hadn't realized how much he missed it until they were laughing together, trying to outdo one another in mini-golf.

He loved his brother, and it pained him to have to do this.

"I...I just want you to know, I wanted to like her. I really did. But..." He gave up on saying the words and passed Garrett his phone instead.

Garrett studied it in silence.

"I'm sorry," Sawyer managed to say.

"For what? What am I supposed to be looking at?"

"That's Shelby."

"Yeah, I know that's Shelby, but why are you showing this to me?"

"She's with Clay Reynolds."

"Okay."

"Okay?"

"Yeah. I mean, come on, Sawyer. You know she called me as soon as you left her house, right? And I couldn't make heads or tails of everything she said, but she told me about her riding lessons and Clay. I vaguely remember the name from high school, but I don't know the guy. What I do know is I'm flat-out shocked she's within ten feet of that horse. She's scared to death of them, but other than that, I don't see why you're showing me this."

"Garrett, she's *with* him. She's been with him. Since you announced your engagement. That's who I saw her with in Carson, and again at Northcliff Ranch. She's running around with Clay Reynolds."

"Sawyer, we've been through this."

"Then why won't you believe it? You said yourself she's scared of horses, so why else would she be around Clay except to be around *him*."

"She's around him to learn to ride. Are you trying to piss me off again?" Garrett slid his hand across Sawyer's screen once, twice, and then stopped. "Why do you have multiple pictures of my fiancée?"

Sawyer ground his back teeth together, trying to keep cool.

"Did you have her followed? You did, didn't you?"

"I had to."

"Dammit, Sawyer." He threw Sawyer's phone back to him.

"I had to know what was going on. I tried to get to the truth at breakfast that morning, but she lied. She just kept lying. This was the only way to know for sure."

"What did you do?"

"I tried to protect you. I don't want you to get hurt."

"What did you do?"

"I hired a private investigator to prove she's cheating on you."

Garrett was on his feet in an instant, his laptop where he once sat. He moved so fast Sawyer barely saw it happen.

Sawyer stood up as well. "I hired an investigator. Look," he said, before his brother could open his mouth and get even madder. "I didn't want to. I put it off for a long time, but I kept seeing her with this guy. I saw them in restaurants together, then at Northcliff Ranch. And when I'd ask her about it, she'd lie. I had no choice."

"You could've chosen to mind your own business."

"I didn't—"

"You could have chosen to trust Shelby, and me, to manage our own relationship."

"I don't want you to go through what I went through."

"But that's exactly what you're doing. You're trying to put me through the same thing that happened to you."

Sawyer froze. That simply wasn't true. He'd never put his brother through the pain he dealt with. He managed to shake his head, but no words would come.

"Can't you see what you're doing? If what you're saying about Shelby was true—which I don't, for one second, believe it is—then you aren't going to save me from anything. You're digging around to find out the worst, dredging it all up. You're telling me I'm in the exact same situation you were in. My heart wouldn't be any less broken because it's you telling me that Shelby is with some other guy. In fact, I'd rather find out myself or from her, if it were even true."

Sawyer shook his head again. "I'm not . . . I don't want you to get hurt."

"Too late." Garrett pointed at Sawyer's phone. "*This* hurts me. You doing that, spying on her, hurts me. And if it were true, I'd be even more hurt by finding out this way. I don't know how to make you understand that."

He didn't know what to think, what to say. He'd told himself he was only trying to save his brother from the kind of hurt he knew too well, but was that really the whole truth?

Was it even possible to save someone from that? Or was he really just trying to catch Shelby wronging his brother? Because he wasn't able to catch Melissa until it was too late.

Pain creased his brother's brow, his eyes hard and cold.

Sawyer knew betrayal, and all he'd wanted this whole time was to spare Garrett.

But this time, Sawyer was the betrayer. He'd hurt his brother two-fold in his mission for the truth.

"You had no right to spy on my fiancée. You've hurt me and you're hurting the woman I love."

"I—"

"Just stop this." Garrett slammed his laptop shut. "You've got to let this go, if you want to be a part of our lives. Drop it and apologize to Shelby, or you can forget being a part of this wedding or anything else."

Garrett scooped up his computer and coffee cup, and went inside, Dodger right behind him. He locked the door behind him, leaving Sawyer standing there. Alone.

How had this whole thing gone so wrong?

Sawyer dragged a hand through his hair.

He'd been trying to do the right thing. Look out for his brother. But all he'd done was hurt him, and now Garrett was talking about him not even being in his life?

His mind raced back over everything he'd done, from the time he saw Shelby in that diner to sitting at breakfast with everyone the next day. Or did it go back even further than that?

When did he decide his brother shouldn't be with Shelby Meyers?

Chapter 18

She was with Cece, knee deep in tulle, when Shelby showed up, banging on the back door. She waved frantically through one of the door's little windows.

"What in the world?" Cece asked.

"I don't know." But she could see Evelyn popping her head up behind Shelby.

Aurora stepped over the fabric, preparing herself. Evelyn popping up places was never a good sign, but she opened the door.

"Shelby, hey! Evelyn." Beth's stomach tightened at the look on Evelyn's face.

"We need to talk." Evelyn barged right in.

"Mother." Shelby used a tone that Beth had never heard come out of her friend's mouth.

"Well, we do. It's her man causing all the problems."

"Mother."

"What's going on?"

"Sawyer Silva," Evelyn answered. "That is what's going on."

"Please let me speak," Shelby snapped.

"Then speak!"

Cece looked away, clearly uncomfortable.

Shelby turned to Aurora, stress and anxiety etching little lines in her pretty face. "Sawyer came to see me today."

"For...a visit?" Beth asked hopefully.

"To confront me."

The tightening in Beth's stomach turned to a knot of lead.

"He had a picture of me taking riding lessons and accused me of cheating on Garrett with my instructor."

Heat rushed up Beth's neck, surely blotching her skin like a rash. Not this crap again.

"I've been taking horseback riding lessons for weeks now, and I haven't told anyone, not even you. But Sawyer has been suspicious of me ever since we got engaged, and apparently that's why? I guess. He thinks I've been having an affair this whole time."

"Is that why he—"

"Yes! He basically accused me of running around on Garrett a few weeks ago while we were at breakfast with his family. I didn't know it at the time, but he'd seen me with my instructor after practice. We were having lunch together, but that was it. I swear that's it. I'm not cheating on Garrett and—"

"Shelby." Beth grabbed her friend's flailing hands and held them tight in her own. "I know you aren't cheating on Garrett. You don't have to defend yourself to me. I've known you since before you started dating. You aren't like that. Sawyer is just..." The tightness from her stomach clenched her chest. "I don't know what is going on with him."

"He's a troublemaker," Evelyn snapped. "That's what's going on with him."

Shelby glared at her mother and Evelyn clammed up again.

Beth had never seen her friend actually stare her mother down or stand up to her.

Shelby refocused on Beth and squeezed her hands in return. "He's been spying on me. I know that much. Garrett found out he hired a private investigator to see what I was up to."

Beth's stomach curled. "He did not."

Shelby nodded, and Beth knew it was true. Even as her heart raged against it, her mind knew a fact when it heard one. "Oh my gosh."

"Garrett is furious."

"Rightfully so."

"I think they got into a big argument. I don't really know. All I know is I'm at the center of why." Shelby's eyes began to well up with tears.

"Don't. Don't you do that." Beth hugged her close. "It's not your fault they had a falling-out over this. It's Sawyer's. I'll...I'll deal with him. I don't want you to worry about this. I'll handle it." Though she didn't know how.

"Why does he hate me so much?" Shelby sniffed.

Beth wasn't convinced he did. She couldn't explain his actions, but she'd seen nothing in Sawyer that made her believe he hated anyone. "I don't think that he does. I...I don't think it's you who he hates at all. But I'm going to find out. You can count on that."

Shelby swiped at her eyes. "Don't feel like you have to do that. You don't have to say anything to him. It's not your job to fix this and it's a bad spot for you to be in."

"I'm going to say something to him, all right." Beth

insisted. Not only because of how much he'd hurt Shelby, but because he'd betrayed Beth's trust.

How could he still be on a tirade about Shelby when Beth had told him she was a good person? Didn't he trust her? "I knew he had some trust issues, but I didn't know they were this bad. I didn't think it was like...this." Beth shook her head. "I can't believe he did this."

She wanted answers.

She deserved answers.

Was this why he'd left her bedroom last night? Lying about something with the horses when all along he was out to punish her best friend?

And hiring someone to spy on Shelby!

How was he capable of doing such a thing? The man she knew, and had fallen for, wasn't someone who'd sneak around and hire investigators and be bent on destroying his brother's future marriage.

None of this made sense.

And yet, here they were. The truth was, Sawyer had been spying on Shelby through an investigator. He'd been a giant monkey wrench in the wedding plans practically the entire time.

Her mind went right back to their confrontation in the sitting room at Orchard Inn, to them arguing about his overinvolvement in the whole affair.

Even then, he'd been threatening to sink the wedding. He'd been ready to pull his emotional and financial support way back then.

Had he lied about changing his mind when they called a truce at Frank's?

Had he been spying on Shelby and intending to destroy her happiness this whole time?

"Are you okay?" Shelby reached for Beth's arm.

"I'm fine." Beth jerked away, her gaze flying to Cece's.

Her sister's eyes widened. She would know, instantly, that Beth was far from fine.

"Why don't you..." Cece managed to get around the tulle without the aid of her crutches. "We will take care of the Sawyer situation. You two don't need to worry about a thing." She took Shelby's arm and began moving toward the door.

If it were only Shelby here, Beth would've broken down right then and there. But she refused to lose it in front of Evelyn.

That would never happen.

"Beth can call you later, okay?" Cece gave Shelby a look loaded with meaning.

"Oh. Yes." Luckily, Shelby seemed to get it. "That would be good. We can go and let you guys handle this."

"Handle it how?" Evelyn asked. "I want to know what's going to be done about this instigator who's been stalking my daughter. Or I will deal with it myself."

"It will be taken care of, Mother." Shelby took her mother's arm. "We're leaving."

Beth wanted to be proud of her friend for finally going toe-to-toe with her mother, but she was too wrapped up in everything else falling apart.

Shelby eventually got her mother out the door, and Cece closed and locked it behind them.

She made her way back to Beth's side. "Are you okay?"

"You shouldn't be walking around without your crutches."

"Forget my darn ankle for two seconds. This is about you."

Beth turned and started winding up the tulle to put it away. "I will be fine."

But right now, she didn't know what to feel.

Waffling among shock, fury, and hurt, she couldn't seem to land on any single emotion.

Beside her, Cece sighed and rubbed her arm.

How could Sawyer even be capable of this? Didn't she know him at all?

At first, sure, she'd let herself get closer to him so she could keep an eye on him. She'd feared he might try to torpedo the wedding and keeping a potential enemy close was the best course of action.

But that motivation had quickly changed.

Every second of every moment she was around him, she'd grown to like him more. With a love of family and valuing honest, hard work, he was supposed to be a kindred spirit. Putting those he loved and his responsibilities above himself as much as Beth did, he understood her.

She'd thought they were in sync, that their relationship was going somewhere.

But all along, he'd been working against her, her friend, her business, and her family?

Her chest ached at the realization.

Beth stared down at the tulle in her hands, the fine weave of the fabric blurring into a watery abstract.

"Oh, Beth." Her sister's voice came from a distance, someplace far, far away.

Her mind raced and her heart hurt.

She fell for Sawyer long before she fell into bed with him, but the truth was, she didn't know him at all.

He'd been bent on ruining everything from the very beginning, and she'd been sleeping with the enemy.

*　　*　　*

Sawyer texted her right before he came over. We need to talk was all the text said.

He had to know that she knew. He had to realize that, after Garrett, Shelby would've come straight to Beth with what had happened.

With the truth.

"I know you've probably already talked to Shelby," he said as she opened the back door. "But just hear me out."

She didn't want to hear him out.

She wanted to scream and cry. How could he? How could he ruin something so great with his suspicions and insecurity?

And she didn't mean the wedding.

But she let him in.

"You can come in," she said with ice in her voice. "But keep your voice down. We have guests at the inn and you've done enough damage. I don't need you causing a scene and upsetting guests."

"I have good reasons for what I did with Shelby," he said, his voice low and even.

She hated that he still had that kind of control over himself. "I don't care about your reasons and I don't want to hear them."

"What?" He sounded generally confused that she didn't care what he had to say.

Beth pointed her finger. "You heard me. Nothing justifies spying on your brother's fiancée and my dearest friend."

"I saw her out with Clay Reynolds long before I ever thought to have her looked into."

"So?"

"So, I didn't hire someone to check up on her because I'm some paranoid jerk. I had every reason to be suspicious. Eating out at restaurants together, cavorting around a ranch together. What was I supposed to think?"

"That the woman your brother loves is innocent until proven guilty. You're not supposed to think the worst of her."

"I tried," he insisted. "I asked her about it, and she lied, making up stories I know weren't true, about shopping with her mom. I was well within my right mind to find it suspicious."

"You weren't within your rights to have her stalked. The girl was taking riding lessons, for crying out loud. As a gift for your brother."

"Then why didn't she tell me the truth when I asked her weeks ago?"

"Because it was supposed to be a surprise. And it's not like she's not going to run around advertising she can't ride to you, the king of horses." Beth bit off the last few words with more than a little attitude.

Sawyer flinched and blinked at the venom in her tone.

"She fell when she was a kid and she's been terrified of horses ever since. Then she goes and falls in love with a guy who grew up on a horse ranch and loves to ride. She's always been embarrassed about her fear and inability. So why would she ever confide in you?" Her voice was getting louder, but she didn't care. "You've done nothing but push her away since you found out they were engaged. What reason would she have to trust you with a secret?"

Her anger and indignation boiled up and spilled over,

and she let it spill. "And here's something that might be new to you: It's none of your business. Shelby doesn't answer to you. She doesn't owe you anything. She's not the one who cheated on you."

"That is not fair."

"It's the truth, whether you want to hear it or not. You can't punish her or any other woman who comes into your life for the actions of someone else."

"I don't trust her."

"It's not just that, Sawyer. You didn't trust me. I told you she was a good person and there'd be no way she'd cheat on your brother. You should've believed me, trusted in me and my judgment and my word, even if you can't trust anyone else."

A deep line creased Sawyer's brow as he frowned. "I don't understand why you're being like this. I tried to do the right thing. Why are you so mad at me?"

"Because you hurt me," she snapped, her voice wobbling at the end. "You didn't just hurt my friend, you hurt me too."

"I..." Panic filled his brown eyes. "I didn't mean to. That's the last thing I'd ever want to do."

"But you did."

"I...I'm sorry."

"Sorry doesn't make it all go away." She shook her head so hard her hair whipped against her face. "You saw what you wanted to see, because you refuse to trust anyone, including me. And if you can't trust me, then you don't need to be with me."

"Beth, please." He stepped toward her, but she moved away.

"There's nothing else to say. I think you should go."

She crossed her arms and swallowed the knot in her throat, fighting against the tears.

"I don't want to—"

"Go, Sawyer." She ground out the words. "I don't want you here."

Chapter 19

The next day, Sawyer attempted to get back to work and focus on business, but every effort failed.

Garrett had told Uncle Joe and Lina about what he'd done. They'd all avoided him yesterday and had given him the silent treatment all day today.

He threw himself into manual labor to cope. After he checked on Amber, he started shoveling straw in the stables. It was work normally left for the hired help, but he needed something to do.

His mind was a wreck, and the only way to make it stop chewing on his fight with Beth was to exhaust himself physically.

He backed his truck up to the stable and lowered the gate. The back was stacked high with bales wrapped in twine. He took off his outer shirt and put on his oldest boots, which stayed in the truck.

One by one, he tossed bales off the back of the truck. A huge pile took up the entrance of the stable when he was done.

It wasn't the most efficient way to work, but he didn't even care. If he worked himself to death today, all the better. He deserved to ache in every bone and muscle the way he ached inside.

"If you can't trust me, then you don't need to be with me."

Beth's words echoed in his mind and around the stable.

"I don't want you here."

He picked up two bales and walked them all the way down to the farthest stall, dropping them outside the stall gate.

"Hey, Winston." He patted the old fella who peeked out at the noise. "Just me out here working." He stroked the horse and Winston nuzzled toward his face. "Me and my guilt, I guess. But you still like me, don't you, Winston?"

Horses were a lot easier than people.

Feed them, give them water, treat them right and consistently so, and always operate under the same expectations and consequences, and there were no problems.

People, on the other hand? Expectations differed wildly, and changed on any given day, as did the consequences.

He went back for more bales, walking them two by two down the corridor.

Like the consequences of a well-meaning, well-intended inquiry into a future sister-in-law.

He would've understood if Garrett and Shelby, and Joe, were a bit upset, and even gave him a tongue-lashing for butting in. It would've stood to reason if Uncle Joe had a come-to-Jesus meeting with the two brothers and sorted things out.

But this?

Iced out of his family, his brother not wanting him in his life at all right now, and Beth... Well, she was gone.

He'd lost her.

Over this!

Sawyer cursed under his breath and went back for more bales. Sure, he could've gotten a wheelbarrow, or any number of tools to make the task easier, but he didn't need easier.

Right now, he needed grueling, punishing work.

He needed something to hurt physically the way he hurt mentally because he didn't understand.

How had he ended up the bad guy in all of this? How had he pushed his brother so far, and driven Beth away?

He kept moving the hay to each stall until his shoulders ached. Once done, he took off his gloves and got a swig of water from his thermos. With his forearm, he swiped the sweat from his brow, then arched his back in a long stretch, letting out a disgruntled groan.

Winston popped his head out again, and this time Dolly, one of the mares, did the same.

"Sorry, guys. Just me. Being mad at the world. It's okay."

After he downed about half the thermos, he searched for one of the large forks to start pitching the hay.

The best one was leaned up against the wall by Winston, so he started at that end, cutting the twine with the Swiss Army knife from his back pocket and opening the stall to get Winston to back up in the stall.

"Easy does it, buddy. Just some fresh bedding hay to keep things comfy around here."

Looked like Winston had taken care of some business as well, so Sawyer cleaned that up first, before forking in the fresh hay.

He chuckled at the work, thinking he'd have to do this

in every single stall today, and he didn't mind. Typically, this was done for him, with him only occasionally doing grunt work.

He wasn't above it, but it simply wasn't in his usual rotation anymore. He'd served his time throughout childhood and his teen years, up until his early twenties. After that, he'd moved on to managing the broader operations of the ranch, being molded and shaped to take over someday.

Getting back to the basics, the day-to-day, wasn't a bad thing at all.

In life, sometimes you needed to shovel a little stink to remember who you were.

And he was Sawyer Silva, a stand-up, genuine guy, who said what he meant and meant what he said.

He stuck the pitchfork into the ground and put his hand on top of the handle.

So why in the world hadn't he just been honest with Beth about seeing Shelby out with Clay? Why hadn't he just taken his brother to lunch and told him why he was worried?

Why hadn't he pulled Shelby aside and talked to her about seeing her in that diner outside of Carson, or at the ranch that day?

He imagined talking to the girl in confidence.

"Hey, I saw you with Clay Reynolds. It's just the two of us talking here, so what's going on? It looks suspicious as all get-out, and I want to understand, because I'm trusting you've got a good reason to fib about it in front of my brother."

How differently would things have gone? Would she have told him then about her childhood fall? That she was terrified of horses? Would she have then asked Sawyer for help?

If Shelby wanted to learn to ride, he could've taught her. He was a heck of a lot better than Clay.

So why hadn't she come to him?

Sawyer pitched the other bale around Winston's stall and talked to him before leaving. "I guess I'm not always the most approachable guy in the world. I'll give her that. But Clay?"

He shook his head.

He felt bad for Shelby, for her fear of his favorite creature. He wouldn't wish a bad fall on anyone, but he hadn't known.

Had he known, he would've helped.

Instead, he'd been against her.

He moved on to Dolly's stall next, cutting the twine and digging into the hay with the pitchfork.

"Heh." And didn't that kind of symbolism just smack you upside the head?

Him out here, with a pitchfork, like the dang devil.

That's how his family saw him now. All of them. Even though he'd been trying to do the right thing.

Beth saw him as something even worse.

But anyone who'd seen what he saw at that diner in Carson would've thought and done the same.

Wouldn't they?

Beth said he saw what he wanted to see. Because he refused to trust.

He didn't *want* to see Garrett's fiancée hurt him! That was ludicrous. But Beth insisted he could see nothing but the worst in people.

Beth.

He hadn't thought this would cost him the one thing he was beginning to trust. Something he could believe in.

He didn't realize she'd see his actions as a betrayal. But could he blame her?

Sawyer swallowed his emotions down hard and moved on to the next stall.

It was Amber's stall.

His chest tightened, and inside, his heart twisted.

He'd never meant to hurt Beth with any of this. The reality that he would hadn't even occurred to him. If he'd known, he would've... he would've what?

Stopped everything.

He cared for her so much. He hadn't considered he might lose her over this. If he'd known then what he knew now, he would've handled everything differently.

And everything coming out about Shelby learning to ride? How was he supposed to know?

Who, in the whole Hill Country of Texas, didn't ride horses before they could even drive a car?

Everyone was furious with him.

"I'm surprised you're even talking to me." Amber came to him as soon as he opened her stall. He stroked her short mane and checked the growth and development of her hindquarters.

She came from prime stock and would make someone an amazing horse one day. If she kept growing as he predicted, he may even be able to sell her for top asking price to race. It was in her blood, as her dad was a derby winner.

"Remember the lady from the night you were born?" Sawyer grabbed a brush and began grooming Amber, even though she didn't really need it. "Pretty, auburn hair, kind of like yours. She cried when you were born. Yeah, you remember." He sweet-talked the horse as he tended to her.

"I don't know but…I think I messed up with her. Big time." And he couldn't shake the feeling that nothing would fix what he'd done wrong. "See, I—you don't really know this about me yet, but I can be stubborn. And I got it in my head that something was true, so I was bound and determined to prove it. I'm like a horse with blinders, except worse." He finished brushing Amber's tail and ran his hand back up her side until it rested at her shoulder. "I pushed Beth away because I was so dead set on proving I was right."

He moved around her to finish up her hay, and she stared at him with huge brown eyes.

"Somehow, I have to fix this mess I created."

Amber whinnied and tossed her head, checking out her fresh hay.

"Any ideas how? No. You'll get back to me if you think of something, right?"

He left her stall feeling only slightly better than when he'd started. He shoveled hay for hours, until all but the last bit of it was spread across each stable. He was drenched in sweat, with hay stuck to his jeans and bare arms, and still his mind jumped from thought to thought, replaying every word he'd said, everything he'd done. Analyzing and re-analyzing each thought. Second-guessing each and every action and reaction.

And he *never* second-guessed himself.

But this was Garrett and Beth and everyone he cared about.

Was it possible he was that wrong? About everything?

He'd never misjudged anything that completely. It couldn't be.

But maybe there was a first time for everything. If he was wrong about the situation with Shelby, then what else had he been wrong about?

"Are you gonna stay out here all night or come in and face the music?"

Sawyer turned to find Uncle Joe standing in the open stable door, backlit by the disappearing sun.

He'd spent all day out here with the horses and his thoughts.

"You're speaking to me now?"

"Don't get smart with me, boy. I'm offering you an opportunity here."

Sawyer jabbed the pitchfork into the last of the hay.

Boy.

He was a grown man and he'd handle this like one. "I'll be in after a while, when I'm finished. But I'm not going to be your punching bag over this. I'll listen and talk, but—"

"You're just so doggone stubborn you can't even admit it when you know you screwed up."

"What?"

Joe walked over to him, checking in some stalls as he passed. He stopped in front of Sawyer, resignation and a little sadness in his gaze.

"I think you get it from your dad," he said. "And our whole side of the family, truth be told. Silva men didn't say they were sorry. Are you kidding? Your dad would've never spoken again before admitting he was wrong. I think we both grew up and never once apologized to one another. About anything. Though Lord knows we should've."

Sawyer glanced down at his boots.

He wished he could say he knew his dad well enough to understand, but all he could do was imagine.

"What I'm saying is, you didn't grow up hearing a lot about people messing up and being sorry for their actions. Eating crow and making amends and all that. Though I know you've got it in you, because I've heard you say sorry before. I know you took Beth out after y'all had a dustup at her inn, because you told me. So I know you're capable."

Sawyer opened his mouth to object, but Joe wouldn't let him get a word in.

"What I don't get is why you can't see how wrong you are now and apologize. After the stunt you pulled, you ought to be seeking forgiveness and taking your licks. And just be glad they aren't any worse than they are."

"Joe?" Lina's voice reached them before she appeared at the end of the stable.

"Aren't any worse than they are?" Sawyer barely registered her presence as his voice went up a notch. "You-all haven't said a word to me in almost two days. Garrett doesn't want anything to do with me and told me to stay away from his wedding and him, and Beth wants me out of her life. I'm out here and everyone I care about hates me. How, exactly, could this be any worse?"

"You could be dead," his uncle deadpanned.

With a roll of his eyes, Sawyer put up the pitchfork, preparing to walk out.

"No, I'm serious. You ain't dead, son. And you aren't beyond forgiveness. Which means you've got a chance to realize your mistakes, fix them, and make it right."

"There's no way Beth or Garrett will forgive me. Definitely not Shelby."

"Do you want to be forgiven?" Lina asked softly, drawing his attention. "Because if you do, then it means, on some level, you recognize you did something wrong."

"And first, you've got to admit it." Joe followed. "You can't stick to this stubborn Silva mantra of being a man above making mistakes. It ain't healthy."

Sawyer studied the hay at his feet.

"Daggum it, Sawyer!"

"How am I supposed to know?" Sawyer shouted. "How do I know if I was wrong? Not about hiring the private investigator. I know I should've handled that differently. I screwed up big time there. But how do I know Shelby is telling the truth? How does Garrett know for sure? How do you?"

Uncle Joe's voice was calm and steady. "How does anyone know? People lie all the time for all kinds of reasons."

"Exactly!"

"But the people who love you don't lie. They are true. Their love is true. And that's the love Shelby has for Garrett. She's telling the truth because there's no way she'd be deceitful or hurt him. Anyone can see that's true. It's obvious, unless you've been so blinded by hurt that you can't see it."

Sawyer's gaze went to Amber's stall, and, deep inside, he knew it was true.

He could barely believe in Beth's feelings for him,

and he was a part of that relationship. She was the first person he'd trusted in ages, and still he struggled to have faith.

How could he believe in someone like Shelby, whom he barely knew?

"But it's not all your fault," Joe said, his hand settling on Sawyer's shoulder. "Having to look out for me and your brother, growing up so fast. And after the way that girl did you, it stands to reason you'd be suspicious of folks. But at some point, you have to get past that and move on. You can't go punishing the people who try to get close to you, all because you're too stubborn to let go of being wronged. Are you going to push Beth away? Punish her for what Melissa did?"

The mention of Beth's name brought a bristling chill to Sawyer's skin, even in the heat. He moved away from his uncle. "Don't bring her into this."

"She's in it, son. Whether you like it or not. And if you don't figure this out and recognize where you went wrong, you'll lose her for good."

"I've already lost her."

"No, you haven't."

"How would you know? What do you know about women?"

"More than you think," Lina answered.

Sawyer's gaze fell on Lina, to where she'd moved to Uncle Joe's side, and taken his hand.

His mind flew back to something Garrett had said about Joe and Lina hanging out more.

So many things clicked together at once.

Joe and Lina's shared laughter and glances, their knowing looks. The little touches and casual flirting.

Joe and Lina were together. They were a couple.

Sawyer motioned between them. "So this is…how long has this been going on?"

"You mean us being in love?" Joe asked.

Sawyer almost fell over. "In love?"

"Long enough," Joe said.

"Several months now," Lina clarified.

Several *months*?

Sawyer looked around out of habit, wanting to find Garrett to help carry this news. Their uncle was in a romantic relationship?

Joe had finally put himself out there, and found the courage to care about someone other than him and Garrett.

A partner.

He'd opened up, let Lina in, and become someone's boyfriend.

And Sawyer'd had no idea.

"Son, she's been staying at the house full time the last few weeks. What'd you think was going on?"

"He's been busy." Lina elbowed him. "With his wedding planner. I mean planning."

Joe gave her a toothy grin. "Oh, that's right."

"Does Garrett know?"

"No," Lina said.

"I think Garrett knows there's something going on between us," Joe added. "More clued in than you, obviously, but he doesn't know for sure."

Lina pulled his hand to her and placed a quick kiss on his knuckles.

Sawyer never thought he'd see the day. And when the day had come, he'd been so wrapped up in his own anger and resentment he hadn't seen what was happening right in front of him.

He was so blind.

Winston chose that moment to pop his head out of his stall and stare him down, as if to say, *Duh*.

If he was too blind to see a love that'd grown right under his own roof, every day, with him right there beside them, what else had he missed? Had he missed Shelby's love for Garrett too?

And what about Beth?

Beth, who'd made her way into his cynical heart, with her honesty and blunt manner. Beth, who trusted him enough to tell him about her childhood, her past, and her pain. She'd shared her worries about the future and how Garrett's wedding was the foundation of so much hope.

She'd trusted him, and, what's more, she'd believed in him. That he was the kind of man who said what he meant and meant what he said.

They'd been falling in love, whether he wanted to believe in and trust in it, or not.

And he'd betrayed them.

Sawyer groaned as he buried a hand in his hair.

He'd done so much worse than mess things up with a stupid investigator. He'd been wrong. On every level.

Chapter 20

Do you think twelve dozen white roses would be too much?" the voice on the phone asked.

Beth stared out the window of her office, to the peach trees beyond.

She'd done nothing but work eighteen-hour days for several days now, stare out this window, and sleep.

"Hello? What do you think about the roses?"

Beth snapped to and blinked hard. "Sorry. I'm so sorry. A dozen roses would be lovely."

"I said twelve. Twelve dozen, filling the foyer. Too much?"

She tried to imagine the foyer of Orchard Inn crammed unnecessarily with roses. "That might be . . ." The tackiest use of flowers, ever. "A little overwhelming. I think you could do two arrangements and put that money toward flowers in the ceremony or reception."

"You're probably right." The bride-to-be let out a long sigh. "Okay, that's all the questions I had for today, thanks."

But she'd have more tomorrow, and more the day after that. Beth had spoken with this bride every day for the past week. Didn't matter, though; it was another booked wedding, not like she had anything else to do but work, and it kept her mind off of—

"My pleasure," Beth said, chopping off the end of that thought.

"Bye," the bride chirped.

"Goodbye," she managed after the line died.

The wedding-planning business was flourishing, Orchard Inn was more vibrant than ever, but the joy and motivation Beth typically felt were muted. Dull.

The wedding was moving forward, Orchard Inn was on the upward climb, but the success lacked the sparkle it would've had just a few days ago.

Without Sawyer, without the person who knew what it meant to succeed for more than just yourself, without the person she'd thought understood her, she felt hollow.

Still, she was working harder than she ever had. If she worked long and hard enough, she wouldn't have to think about him.

Or how much she'd been hurt.

She especially wouldn't have to think about how she'd asked for it. No one to blame but herself, seeing as how she was stupid enough to break her own rules.

Family first, work a close second. She was young and had plenty of time for romance and focusing on herself. For now, her priority was securing the future of Orchard Inn and the livelihood of her sisters.

But she'd gotten off course with Sawyer. Shirked her responsibilities and spent her time doing silly things like long walks and horseback rides, kissing in parks and opening up her heart.

How ridiculous to think she could have it all: juggle work, a big wedding, and have time for a relationship.

Something always suffered when you mixed in feelings. And this time, it was her.

She'd gotten too close, developed feelings for him, and
even started falling in—

No.

She wasn't going to let her mind go there.

"Knock, knock," Aurora said after she'd already
popped her head into Beth's office. "How are you doing?
You okay?" She had a look on her face that said she knew
Beth wasn't okay.

Both of her sisters were aware she hadn't been okay
in days.

"Would you move so I can get in the door?" Cece
asked from the hallway.

"Fine." Aurora stepped in and then both sisters crowded
her desk.

"Are you hungry at all? You need to eat."

"No. My appetite is completely gone."

"But it's after dinner. You haven't had anything since
breakfast and that was just a banana. You need to eat
something."

Beth shook her head.

"I made fresh peach pie."

Beth's salivary glands perked up at the mere mention
of pie.

"It smells incredible too." Cece lured her further with
a big smile and a nod.

"I changed up my recipe a little, adjusted the filling
and tried a whole new thing with the crust. The peaches
are insanely fresh."

"First harvest of the season. C'mon, Beth, you have to
try some. Please?"

"Okay, okay." Beth caved.

She forced herself up out of her desk chair and followed her sisters to their private living room area.

There, on the center ottoman, sat a serving platter with a round dish covered by a crisp blue gingham towel, a suspicious-looking carafe of dark liquid sitting next to it. But the scent filling their entire living room distracted her from wondering about the liquid.

Warm peaches, vanilla, a sweet sugary aroma, and a hint of cinnamon.

"Wow, that smells divine."

Aurora kneeled down beside the ottoman and picked up the pie knife. "This pie better taste divine or I'm going to be mad. I've tinkered with the recipe for a while now. I know perfection is a slippery slope, but I'm hoping."

Cece eased herself onto the sofa. "I'm sure it's amazing. You slice, I'll pour." She reached for one of the three glass tumblers filled with ice, poured in the dark liquid, and splashed cream on top of it before passing it to Beth.

"What is this?"

"Umm, iced coffee?"

Beth sniffed her glass. "That seems unlikely. Try again."

"Cece wanted to try her hand at mixology."

"Uh-huh. Then what am I about to drink?"

"It's a White Russian. Kahlúa, vodka, and a splash of cream."

"I can't have this. I've barely eaten all day. I'll be sloshed."

"No, you won't. Just sip on it and you'll be fine. You deserve a drink." Cece clinked Beth's glass with hers and they all took a sip.

Aurora then placed a slice of pie in front of her. "Plus, you're about to eat right now."

Cece put down her glass and squeezed Beth's hand. "You need this. Trust us."

Naturally her sisters were worried about her, but she didn't want them to be. She'd be fine. And they needed to concentrate on the inn and keeping the momentum going with the upcoming weddings.

Beth looked around. "Cece. Where are your crutches?"

"I don't need them anymore. I can walk with the boot on, no problem." Cece pulled her pie plate closer.

"Did the doctor say that was okay?"

"I say it's okay because I'm getting around great and I feel just fine. We aren't worrying about me right now, remember? We're worrying about you."

"Let's eat up before it gets cold." Aurora passed out the forks, effectively ending the discussion.

Beth took her first bite of pie, and her eyes rolled back inside her head. "Oh my gosh."

The tart sweetness of peach exploded on her tongue. Not syrupy sweet or mushy like canned peaches, the freshness came through strong. The fruit was firm, full of flavor, accentuated by vanilla and cinnamon sugar, but not overpowered. The crust was light, crispy, and somehow soft, with just enough of a buttery smoothness and a hint of salt to complement the peaches.

"This is seriously the best peach pie I've ever had," Cece said with her mouth full.

Aurora took another bite, clicking her tongue a few moments later, sniffing her dessert like a sommelier sniffing wine. "Y'know what?" She prepared another bite on her fork. "This is a darn good pie."

Cece laughed and nodded. "Yeah it is!"

They all finished their slices in record time, and then stared at each other silently for a moment.

Cece was the first to crack. "Y'know, I think I might have just a little bit more."

"Me too," Beth said immediately.

"Just, like, a half slice."

"Exactly. A half slice. Just another taste."

"Yep." Cece kept nodding as she cut them both a piece that was the exact same size as their first.

They ate and chatted about their days, the new guests in the inn, the upcoming weddings. Basically anything except Sawyer.

She'd told her sisters about him coming over, their argument, and their breakup. They'd both been at the inn when he'd visited, but they'd had the good graces to stay in their rooms and pretend they hadn't heard a word.

They knew exactly what he'd done, and how much he'd hurt Beth, but they wouldn't touch on the topic of Sawyer unless she did.

Sisters knew better.

Beth set down her plate and picked up her White Russian. "That was amazing, Aurora. I don't know how, but we should get that on the menu for a wedding. Completely nontraditional, but still. People need to have that pie."

Aurora beamed, and her happiness and pride warmed Beth's heart. The warmth was a welcome change from the frost she'd felt for days.

"It's funny you say that, because I've come up with an idea for Shelby's wedding cake."

"Yeah?" Beth sat up a little straighter.

"Cece helped me test out a small one and it turned out great. I'm going to do a peaches-and-cream wedding cake."

"And it is so good it'll knock everyone's socks off." Cece clapped at the announcement.

"I love that idea," Beth exclaimed.

"I got the idea from the raspberry crème cake from the wedding tasting."

"But this is so much better," Cece interjected.

"It will be a vanilla cake with peaches-and-cream filling, made with fresh peaches from our orchard, of course. And the frosting will be buttercream. Fondant holds up better, but the taste is meh."

"And the rosettes. Tell her about the rosettes," Cece said.

"I'm going to make little rosettes out of fresh peaches, to decorate the cake. I thought it'd look perfect since her floral arrangements include apricot-colored roses."

Beth gazed at her sister, amazed.

The cake sounded perfect for Shelby and Garrett, as well as delicious. "I love that idea. I'll run it by Shelby tomorrow."

Aurora finished her drink, shaking her head. "You don't have to. I've already talked to her about it. She's thrilled."

"She came by the other day and tried some of the sample," Cece added. "She loved it."

Beth wasn't even aware Shelby had been by the inn. Then again, she'd been holed up in her office for days now, and her sisters wouldn't disturb her.

"Wonderful. We can check that off the list. I'll contact the florist. Make sure nothing clashes with peach."

"Already taken care of." Cece sipped her drink. "I

talked to the florist yesterday. The flowers are cream, shades of peach, and varying shades of greenery. We're all good with coordination."

Beth sat back in awe. Her sisters had taken care of everything. They'd stepped up and had the little details under control. They didn't need her there leading the charge or managing outcomes.

They were flourishing without her oversight.

She should be thrilled, or at least relieved. Instead, the hollowness inside grew larger. She wanted her sisters to do well, be successful, operate the inn and the wedding business to its fullest potential.

But these triumphs were bittersweet.

"We just want you to know that Shelby's wedding is going to be the best wedding this town has ever seen," Cece assured her. "Since there was a little dustup with Evelyn coming by the other day, I went by to see her and Shelby yesterday. Just to reassure them and update them on where things stand. I figured it's something you would've done."

Beth nodded. Something she would've done if she weren't holed up in her office, trying to mend a broken heart.

"Ugh!" The sound was out of her mouth before she could stop it. "Sorry." But she was just so . . . so . . . annoyed! With herself, with Sawyer, but mainly with herself.

She'd let a man break her heart and then take her away from what made her happy. Working with her family. Who was she anymore?

"I'm just— I'm so mad!" Beth exclaimed.

Aurora moved closer, bringing the carafe with her to refill Beth's glass. "Of course you are. You have every reason to be."

"But I'm mad at myself too." She held out her glass. "I got all sidetracked because of Sawyer. I lost sight of my purpose, because of a man. I was supposed to be focusing on Orchard Inn and our wedding-planning business, but instead I was out with Sawyer, going on dates, bebopping all over town, wrapped up in him."

"You're allowed to have fun." Cece moved closer too. "Don't beat yourself up for having a life."

"But having a life meant letting him in. I'm lucky he didn't ruin the wedding and everything else with it."

"He wasn't going to ruin everything," Cece assured her. "We'd never let that happen."

"And so what if he had?" Aurora shrugged and took a long sip.

Beth and Cece both stared at her, slack-jawed.

"Um, we could've lost the orchard and the inn," Beth pointed out. "Your investments, our future. It could all be gone if we don't have a good season."

"I know that." Aurora pulled in her legs and crossed them. "But what I'm saying is, that's all material stuff we'd lose. Don't get me wrong: that would suck, but we'd recover."

Beth couldn't fathom her sister's meaning. "How? This place is more than just a structure and our money, though. It's our connection. To our childhood, to each other."

"Yeah, but even if this place crumbled to the ground tomorrow, we'd still have each other. We would still be here. That's what I'm saying."

Cece seemed to take that in. "Yeah, and this place isn't our main connection. We're sisters. We're family. We are what makes us, Us. Not this place."

"Anyway, I'm just saying, I thought I had it all figured

out when I went to LA, right? Thought I knew exactly what I wanted and where I was going. But the truth is, life changes, stuff happens. And it turns out I'm way more resilient than what I thought. One guy, even a guy like Sawyer, isn't capable of ruining everything. Trust me on this. He might screw up big time, but he can't ruin you, or us, or Orchard Inn."

Beth understood what her sister meant, and where she was coming from, but it was hard to describe how Sawyer had hurt her. "I thought he understood how important this wedding was to me, and I thought he believed me when I told him Shelby would never cheat on Garrett. And"— she took a steadying breath—"turns out he didn't trust or understand me at all."

The realization hurt more than she wanted to admit.

But she admitted it anyway.

"And I'd started thinking he might even be the one?" she confessed, her voice shaking with the admission.

Immediately, her sisters consoled her. Cece rubbing her arm, Aurora's hand on her back.

"It's silly, I know. I've only been around him a few weeks so how could I possibly think—"

"It's not silly," Cece insisted. "I've always heard the heart knows."

"No, it is silly. I let myself get caught up, even though I swore I wouldn't get derailed by relationships. Now is for ensuring Orchard Inn is solid, and focusing on my goals. I always planned on dating and guys and relationships and love coming into life later. On down the road, at some other time."

With a soft laugh, Aurora patted her back. "Honey, I don't think you get to plan for love or when people come into your life. In my experience, life never works like that. Or like anything you plan."

"I'm with Aurora." Cece reached for the carafe to pour all that remained into their glasses. "What if, for love, yours isn't on down the road? What if love is here now?"

"What?"

"I know you're hurting now, but I don't know that it means you should turn your back on life and fall back into work being all you do."

"I'm not—"

"You haven't left your office in days. All you've done is sit in here, working on prospects or staring out the window."

"You're hiding," Cece agreed. "You're hiding from your personal life, and you can't. You know he'll be at the wedding. He'll make up with his brother and you'll have to see him again."

"I don't know if they'll make up."

"Of course they will. Sawyer will realize what a jerk move he pulled, and they'll make up. The three of us always do."

"And you'll have to face him." Cece reached for her hand. "But even if you didn't, you've still got to get out and live your life. You can't have a life in your office. You're always thinking about us, and the inn, and the business, but right now you need to be thinking about yourself."

Her sisters weren't wrong, but the truth was, running a business was easier than dealing with a romantic relationship. Relationships were messy. Just look at the mess she was in right now!

"I get what y'all are saying, and I promise, once these next few weddings are over, I'll work a little less and have a little more fun."

Aurora set down her empty glass. "No. Not after the next few weddings. Now. There are three of us running this inn now. It's not all on you. Don't get so caught up in work, thinking you can have fun in the future, that you forget to live your life right now."

What would that even look like?

All she'd ever known was managing everyone and everything, except for her time with Sawyer.

She tended to guests and vendors and family over herself, but the one who really needed her attention right now was herself. She needed to live now.

And right now, that meant dealing with her feelings for Sawyer.

Her eyes filled with tears. "I think I loved him."

"Come here." Her sisters wrapped their arms around her.

"I do. I really do. I let him in. I let my guard down. I wanted to spend time with him. I skipped work to hang out with him!"

Cece brushed her hair back. "And that's saying a lot."

"He made me feel good. Happy. I thought he understood. I thought he got me."

Aurora nodded and passed Beth her drink to sip.

"But the whole time he was just spying on Shelby."

"I don't think he was *just* spying on Shelby. From what I saw that night of Cece's accident, it was pretty obvious he was falling for you too."

"Then why wouldn't he listen to me? Why didn't he believe me when I told him Shelby was a good person and faithful? Why didn't he listen?"

"Because he's a man." Aurora laughed.

Beth rolled her eyes.

"No, I'm serious. I've dated a lot of guys. A lot more than both of you, and they don't always hear you. They may listen, but that doesn't mean they hear you. Not very well, at least. And usually not the first time you make a point. A guy like Sawyer? Who does he ever have to listen to? People listen to him, not the other way around."

"That is true." Cece nodded and sipped. "It's probably a new experience for him. An amonaly. Anemone. Anomaly!" She giggled.

Aurora took her glass away. "That's enough White Russian for you, but the point is a good one. I don't think Sawyer meant to hurt you. Or anyone, actually. He was only thinking about protecting Garrett. Like a horse with blinders on."

"Yes!" Cece flapped one hand and pointed at her. "And he just charged forward."

"Yep, and hurting you wasn't intentional. You were collateral damage."

She didn't want to be any kind of damage. She wanted him to realize what he'd done and do a complete turnaround about his brother's marriage. She wanted an apology, and she wanted him back. "What am I supposed to do?"

"Tell him how you feel."

"Yep." Cece nodded in quick repetition. "And tell him that he screwed up. Big time."

She should. She was always outspoken, and this situation certainly shouldn't be any different. "I'm going to do it!" she declared. "I'm going to tell him he should've listened to me. And that I'm hurt and angry because I care about him."

"Yes!" Cece pointed at her.

"I'm going to tell him exactly how I feel."

Aurora took Beth's glass away too. "But maybe not right now."

"Nooo," Cece drew out the word. "Definitely not tonight."

"Agreed." Aurora laughed. "I think nothing tonight but sleep."

Beth imagined calling Sawyer now. Not a good idea. She wanted to be clear and concise when making her point. Regardless, she'd be emotional, but right now sleeping was a good idea.

First sleep. Tomorrow, she'd deal with Sawyer.

Chapter 21

Sawyer had been up for hours when Uncle Joe ambled into the kitchen the next morning.

In fact, he'd barely slept a wink. The winks could wait. He had fences to mend.

"What's all this?" Joe asked, staring at the spread of food on the counter.

"What's it look like? I made breakfast."

Uncle Joe humphed as he surveyed the food.

"I made a breakfast casserole, some cinnamon rolls that just came out of the oven. Ready-to-bake ones, but still good. Coffee is brewed and I put out some fruit and spreads."

"What's the occasion?"

Sawyer put the plate full of hot cinnamon rolls on the counter and faced his uncle. "An apology, and a congratulations. With breakfast."

Lina chose that moment to walk into the kitchen. "Look at this! You cooked! Something smells delicious!"

Her enthusiasm helped. "Thanks. I'm sorry for yesterday. For everything. You two became a couple and I was too wrapped up in my own stuff to even realize. I'm sorry for my attitude, what I said, but mostly for what I did with Shelby and Garrett."

Both of them studied him, and Joe picked up one of the cinnamon rolls.

"I'm really happy for both of you. This is...this is great news. And I'm going to apologize to Garrett and Shelby after this. I was out of line. Regardless of what I intended, my actions were wrong. And hurtful."

Joe stepped forward, already chomping on his roll. "I'm impressed—with the apology, the congrats, the food, and you. Look at you, growing the heck up."

"Thanks?"

"You're welcome." Joe eyeballed another roll.

"How about some fruit instead?" Lina suggested before turning to Sawyer. "Apology accepted. From Joe too. He'd say it himself except his mouth is full of cinnamon roll."

"Hey," Joe said while chewing.

"I'm sure you'll work things out with your brother too. And with Beth."

Beth.

That was a big one. And he had no idea where to start. He didn't have a lot of experience with screwing up and then trying to make it right. Instead, he tried just not to screw up at all.

One thing he did know was that first he had to make things right with Shelby.

As protective as Beth was over family and friends, going to her first, without making amends with her best friend, would be a dead end.

"How are you going to apologize to Shelby and your brother?" Lina asked, reading his mind.

"I don't know." He needed to make it up to them somehow. He'd tried to interfere at every turn and been totally unsupportive.

So...maybe he should do the opposite?

But how was he supposed to be boldly supportive of their wedding and marriage? Hire a sky writer? Big bag of cash?

No, those were tacky, even if people tended to love big bags of cash.

"I need to show them both that I'm sorry and that I've got their backs. I don't think a plain ole 'I'm sorry' will do. They deserve more than that from me."

Lina sipped her coffee, deep in thought. "I think it just needs to be from the heart. You're sincere, and they'll know you mean it."

Sure, all of that was true, but he wanted to do more. He had to go big. Texas big.

The idea struck like lightning. "I know what I should do!"

"What is it?"

Sawyer shook his head. "You may try to talk me out of it, but it's the perfect way to say I'm sorry."

"Sawyer." His uncle's voice held a tone like he already knew Sawyer's plan.

Didn't matter. His mind was made up. There was only one way to show Shelby, and Garrett, that Sawyer wanted her to be part of this family.

A couple of hours later, he was back on Shelby Meyers's front porch, his hat in his hand—literally and figuratively.

This time, Shelby came to the door, a look on her face that could strip leather. "Sawyer Silva, don't you make me forget my manners. I think it's best that you don't come around here anymore."

"I'm sorry," he blurted before he could come up with any prettier words or she could run him off.

"What?"

"I'm sorry, for what I said, what I did, everything. I was wrong and stubborn and, well, I was mean to do you that way. And I am so sorry."

She blinked at him with huge brown eyes. Then those eyes turned to puddles. Her lip quivered and Sawyer panicked.

"No, no. Don't—don't cry. I know I hurt you, and I wish I could take it back. I could kick my own tail for doing you that way. You've only ever been nice and—"

Shelby let out a shaky breath and then tears rolled down her cheeks.

"Uh-oh. Um. Please don't do that. Don't be upset. Garrett is going to kill me. I know you love him. And I want us to be family."

Both hands flew to her face as a small cry escaped her lips.

He was about two seconds from a stress-induced heart attack when she lunged forward and threw both arms around him. She squeezed him tight and cried into his shirt.

Sawyer stood frozen for a moment, then his brain kicked in to what was happening.

Shelby was accepting the first half of his apology.

"There, there now." He patted her back because he didn't know what else to do. "It's okay. I know I was a jerk. I'm sorry I hurt you."

Eventually, she managed a sniffle and swiped at her eyes.

"All I ever wanted from you was your acceptance," she managed.

"I know."

"And your approval."

"I know." He shook his head. "I know that now. And turns out, I'm a more ornery cuss than I realized. I have a hard time letting people in and trusting them, and I took it out on you. But you have my acceptance now. And my approval."

"I do?"

"Yeah, one hundred percent. And as a gesture of just how much I support y'all's union, I have something for you. An, um, an apology gift, I guess."

"What is—?"

"Come on, I'll show you."

Shelby swiped at her eyes again, pulling herself together as she followed him.

But she started sniffling again when they turned the corner and she saw the horse trailer. "Sawyer, what is—?"

"I want you to meet someone." He unlatched the door and led little Amber out onto the driveway. "This is Amber. Amber, this is Shelby. Your new owner."

Shelby's gaze flew to his. "Her wha— You ... What?"

"I know you're only learning, and you may still be nervous a lot, but bonding with a horse this young, especially if you come and groom her every day and talk to her, she'll be your best chance at a horse you can trust, and one who knows you as well as you know her."

"Sawyer..." Shelby's eyes filled again.

"I want you to have her. She's from the best line I've got, and you deserve her. I don't want you to be afraid of riding any more than I want you to be afraid of me. We're going to be family, and I want you to be happy and comfortable at the ranch. And with the extended family." He stroked Amber's mane.

"I don't know what to say?" Shelby's voice shook.

"Say hey to your new friend here."

Shelby approached slowly, palm out. Amber sniffed her and nuzzled her, and let Shelby stroke her head, all the way up to her ears.

"She's beautiful," Shelby said.

"I know. Prettiest foal we've seen in years."

"Are you sure about this?"

Sawyer took in Shelby's smile, her ease with Amber, and the way she was no longer crying but breathing easily and calmly. "Never been surer about a new owner."

Shelby rubbed the back of her knuckle above Amber's nose. "Have you, um, talked to Beth yet?"

Just the thought of it made his stomach clench with nerves. What if she wouldn't forgive him? What if he'd lost her forever?

"Not yet. I wanted to see you first. Make things right with you before I went to her."

Shelby nodded. "Good call." She turned to him. "You're a wise man, Sawyer Silva. If you really want to make things right, in your life and everyone else's, go see her right now. Set things straight and then snap her up and give her the life you both want. The life y'all deserve."

Chapter 22

A bright beam of sunlight chased her under the duvet, stalking her.

Beth's head throbbed, her eyes burned, dry and raw. Her phone pinged with a text, but she couldn't bring herself to come out from under her protective shield.

What had Cece put in those White Russians? Besides vodka and Kahlúa?

No, wait, that was probably enough.

She groaned aloud at the second ping, but eventually her phone was quiet and she drifted back to sleep.

Then a soft, repetitive knock came on her bedroom door. "Beth?" Aurora called. "Beth?"

"Go away."

"No."

"Y'all tried to poison me."

Aurora came into her room unapproved. "No one poisoned you. You had two and a half drinks, you silly lightweight."

"My head hurts."

"Hydrate." Aurora tapped her shoulder with a glass of water. "I brought you some Tylenol too."

Beth crawled out of her cocoon and folded the edge of

her covers over her lap. She took a long swallow of water, two Tylenols, and more water. "Thank you. I love you."

"I know."

"Even though you poisoned me."

Aurora laughed. "We're never going to hear the end of you drinking those, are we?"

"No."

"Yay. Well, keep drinking your water, drink water all day, and eat a burger and fries for lunch. You'll be just fine."

"Why aren't you hungover?" Beth stared up at her sister, who appeared bright-eyed and bushy-tailed.

"Because I am not an amateur. I ate actual food yesterday, not just pie, and drank twenty-four ounces of water before bed. You live, you learn." Aurora patted her head gently.

"I take back what I said. I hate you."

"I know you do. Oh, and Sawyer is here to see you."

Beth coughed up her sip of water. "What?"

"Sawyer. He's on the back porch."

A vise squeezed her chest. Why was Sawyer here? She was supposed to call him up today. Tell him how she felt and give him another earful of what he'd done wrong.

"Why is he here?"

Aurora plopped down on her bed. "Not sure how I'd know the answer to that question, but I'm going to hazard a guess that he's here to win you back? Maybe? He looks pretty repentant. I mean, as much as a six-foot-tall brick-house cowboy can."

Beth nudged her sister with her foot. "I can't see him like this. I probably look awful."

"Oh, you totally do."

Beth pulled the covers back up with a groan.

"But I don't think he cares." Aurora tugged the covers down until she and her sister made eye contact. "Why don't you go wash your face and brush your teeth, and then go talk to him? I'll stall him."

She lurched forward and hugged her sister. "Thank you."

"Ugh, get off me. You've got five minutes." Aurora left and Beth rushed to the bathroom to clean up.

Even if Sawyer wasn't here to make up, she didn't want him seeing her like this. Exactly five minutes later, she was clean-faced and fresh-breathed, walking out onto the back porch in shorts and a T-shirt she'd thrown on.

"Hey," she managed, clearing her throat when she saw him.

He looked the same as he always did. Tall and unyielding, but his smile made her melt. "Hey," he said, his voice quieter than normal.

"Sorry you had to wait."

"No, it's fine. I don't mind." He glanced around. "Can we sit?" He motioned to the rocking chairs.

"Sure." She took her usual chair, and he sat beside her, pulling his a little closer and angling it to face her a little more.

"I went by to see Shelby this morning," he said.

Her heart galloped in her chest. "You did?"

"To tell her how sorry I am, for what I did, and the things I believed."

Somehow, her heart managed to pick up speed. "And did...did she accept your apology."

"Well, first she cried. A lot."

Beth smiled despite herself. "Sounds about right."

"She did that for a little while. Then she said all she'd wanted was my acceptance."

She nodded. "That sounds right too."

Sawyer reached for her and took her hand. "Beth, I've been awful about this whole wedding. I was suspicious and shut off from ever even giving Shelby a chance, and I should've told you what I was worried about, what I was thinking. I didn't realize it until the other night, but I'd made my mind up as soon as I heard Garrett was engaged. I was so caught up in seeing him going through what I went through that I couldn't see anything else. I hurt you in the process, and I am so sorry. I should've listened to you and trusted your judgment."

Beth bit her lip to keep it from trembling.

"I didn't expect to get close to you. But I did. Because you're smart and caring and beautiful and strong. And protective like me. I screwed it up. I know what I did was awful, but I promise I will only ever be completely open with you from now on and, I hope, maybe in time, you can forgive me?"

With a great deal of effort, she kept the tears at bay, and nodded. She had some things she wanted to say, but she was afraid she'd cry if she started talking.

"Will you say something?" he asked.

Well. She could try.

"I...I was just hurt by what you did."

"I know."

"No, I don't think you do. See...you hurt my friend because you thought the worst of her. But you hurt me because...because I was falling for you."

Sawyer's breath caught.

"And I don't want to be with a man who doesn't trust me or believe me."

He was immediately beside her. "You won't be. I promise. If you'll give me another chance, I'll prove to you how much I believe you, and believe in you. I'll make up for the awful things I did."

Beth reached for him, touching his hair, cupping his cheek. "Not all the things you did were awful, and I'm not perfect myself. We all deserve a second chance."

Sawyer leaned forward and pressed his lips against hers.

He kissed her until the worry and doubt began to melt away. Sawyer was human. Sometimes he seemed so much larger than life that she forgot he was as fallible as anyone else.

Beth leaned back enough to meet his gaze. "So, did Shelby forgive you?"

"She did. And I may have made amends with a little gesture."

"What kind of gesture?"

A smile crept across his lips. "You know Amber? We were there for her birth? She now belongs to Shelby."

Her jaw dropped. "You didn't. Sawyer, that is a very nice gift." And very thoughtful, considering the circumstances. "I bet she bawled."

"There was a little bawling, yeah." He chuckled. "And she hugged me, and accepted me and my apology so wholeheartedly I felt like an even bigger heel."

Beth smiled. "That sounds exactly like Shelby. I'm glad you're getting to know the real her, and that she forgave you."

He caught her chin, his brown eyes bottomless. "But do you forgive me? It's all pointless without you."

Sawyer would always be there for her, supportive and strong. He'd ensure she remembered to live her life instead of only managing other people's.

With him, she wanted to do so much more than work. She wanted to experience each day, even without planning. From the ordinary to the amazing, she chose to spend it with Sawyer.

"I forgive you," she said, and pulled him down for another kiss.

He kissed her like she was the air he breathed. Like he would never get enough.

"I thought I'd lost you," he said, his voice gravelly with need. "I never would've forgiven myself for ruining this."

She pressed her lips to his, silencing his doubt. "You don't have to worry about that now."

He slid his hand down to the small of her back, arching her into him. "I'm going to make it up to you, though. You'll see."

Her smile felt wicked. "Do you want to start now?" She raised an eyebrow.

Sawyer had her on her feet, leading her to her room, before she could blink.

As he eased her onto her bed, he smiled. "I was wrong earlier. I'm not just falling for you, Beth Shipley. I love you."

Nothing could stop the smile that took over her face, her soul. "I love you too."

Chapter 23

Beth smoothed down her cream-colored maid of honor dress and hurried over to Garrett.

"Are you sure Dodger is going to walk down the aisle obediently and not take off after some squirrel mid-march?"

Garrett patted the pocket of his tux. "Dog treats. My magic wand. He'll be glued to my side."

Beth took in the dog's bright eyes and bow tie. "You better behave," she told him. "Okay, then y'all can get in position as soon as—" Her breath caught.

Sawyer.

He joined them, and he was the best-looking thing she'd ever seen in her life.

Didn't he know this was the bride's day?

"Hey." He kissed her on the cheek.

"Hey yourself."

"You look beautiful, baby," he said.

Her face felt like she'd landed on the sun. "Not so bad yourself."

Garrett cleared his throat. "Can I get married now?"

"Right." Beth shook the Sawyer-induced fog from her head. "Sorry. Y'all take your places. Go."

The two of them, along with Dodger keeping lock-step like a good boy, took their places at the altar. Beth hurried around to the side of the house, where Shelby waited, looking like a woodland fairy princess in her ivory A-line gown and small white flowers attached at the crown of her veil. Her bouquet was a bundle of white roses, white peonies, and the greenery of eucalyptus and dusty miller.

"You look like a princess."

Shelby pinched her quivering lips together. "I feel like a princess. Like the luckiest girl in the world."

Beth opened her eyes wider and fanned her face. "Stop that or you'll ruin your makeup and I'll ruin mine."

"I'll try."

"How about we get you married?"

Shelby nodded, sniffing back her emotions.

Beth left her as Shelby looped her arm into her father's and headed toward the aisle. The string quartet played softly and she stood a little taller, doing her best to glide down the aisle without trembling.

The day was finally here.

She'd planned this wedding in the shortest time frame yet, but so much had happened it seemed ages had passed.

When she said yes to this wedding, she didn't even know Sawyer Silva. Now look at them. Look at him.

He beamed as she came to a stop on the other side of the altar, a knot forming in her throat.

She was not going to think about the two of them and how much she loved him and weddings and— Stop it.

The quartet transitioned seamlessly into Pachelbel's Canon in D.

Shelby rounded the corner and floated down the aisle like a dream. Beth glanced at Garrett, to find his eyes misted over. Next to him, Dodger looked up at him expectantly, then to Shelby.

His tail beat against Garrett's pants leg like he was equally as smitten with the newest member of their family.

The sting of joyful tears threatened, and Beth willed them back down. Not now, not yet. She could get through this and bawl after all the pictures were done.

Garrett and Shelby shared their vows, but Beth barely heard them. Sawyer kept smiling at her, and it was all she could do to keep her feet on the ground.

"You may kiss your bride," she heard the minister say, and everyone began clapping.

Her gaze drifted to her sisters, sitting in the front row, as beautiful as ever. Next to them sat Joe and Lina, holding hands, glowing. Joe swiped a tear away with his free hand, the big softie.

They both looked ten years younger than the day she'd met them.

The new Mr. and Mrs. Silva led the recessional up the aisle and Sawyer held out his arm for Beth.

"You ready?" he asked.

For whatever life had in store, she thought. Beth took his arm and held him tight.

A few hours later, she sipped her champagne, finally able to breathe for a moment and simply enjoy the evening.

The outdoor wedding and reception venue was perfect for the relaxed yet classy vibe Shelby was after, and there were enough high-end accoutrements to keep Evelyn and the Fredericksburg society snobs happy.

Her friend glowed with joy as she danced with her husband. They'd all been through a lot of pain and growth with the planning of this wedding, and each of them deserved this moment to bask in the beauty and success, but none more so than Shelby.

"You're over here alone, staring and smiling, so I'm going to take that as a good sign." Cece joined her, walking slowly with the boot, but in good spirits. She lifted up her margarita in an air toast. "You did it. You pulled off the wedding of the season and managed to just about completely book out the inn for weddings through the spring and summer."

Beth clinked her glass against her sister's. "*We* did it."

Cece quirked her lips. "Yeah, I suppose. But mainly it was you."

Beth fought the blush rising in her cheeks. "Have you seen Sawyer lately?"

"Earlier I did. I think he was rehearsing his best-man's toast on the back steps and asking me where I got this prickly-pear margarita. I think he's nervous about talking in front of all these people."

"I'm sure he is. He hates being the center of attention. How's the margarita?"

"Best I've ever had. Seriously. Try this." Cece passed her glass and let Beth have a sip.

Sweet with a wisp of tanginess and a bite of tequila. "That is tasty."

"Aurora let me help her work up the final recipe. We came up with a zesty version, too, that has a punch of heat, but figured the nonheat version would appeal to a larger crowd."

"You guys did a great job. Where is Aurora?"

"She hasn't left a ten-foot radius of the wedding cake. She's keeping a hawk eye on it, though I'm not sure why. I think she's just nervous about what people will think, or that it might—I don't know—spontaneously implode."

They both laughed at the visual.

"It's not going to implode, and it will taste divine. It's by far the most beautiful cake I've ever seen."

Beth searched the crowd until she found Aurora only a few feet away from the cake, watching it like a mother watches her newborn.

"Hey, beautiful!" Sawyer approached, tucking his toast note cards into his jacket.

"Whatcha got there?" She slipped a finger into his lapel.

"What? Nothing."

Beth tilted her head, more than a little surprised. "Are you really that nervous?"

"Huh?"

"About the toast."

"Oh. Yeah. But it's my job. Just have to get it over with. You want a drink or anything?"

Okay, he was officially acting weird. "I have a drink." She held up her champagne glass as proof. "Are you okay?"

"Yeah, no. I'm great. Let's dance." He took her hand and pulled her to the dance floor without waiting for an answer.

Beth found room on one of the high-top tables to set her drink, and let herself be hurried to the parquet floor they'd put down this morning. Above it, a white tent, strung with lanterns and tiny lights, lit the dance floor and the band.

Shelby's parents were dancing, and Evelyn looked

happy—finally. Joe and Lina laughed as he twirled her, and Beth caught how happy that made Sawyer.

"I love them together," she told him.

"Right?" His smile grew bigger. "Never would've predicted it, but they're so great together."

Beth took his hand and let him lead.

Sawyer was a surprisingly good dancer. Or maybe not so surprisingly anymore.

She remembered being shocked at his more cultured side early on. Her cowboy loved more than just horses and his ranch. He knew about art and wine, and dancing, apparently.

The band began to play a slower song and Sawyer pulled her close. "Now what are you grinning about?"

"You."

"What did I do?"

"Nothing. Just being you."

His smile stole her breath. "You should be smiling about yourself. I've heard people oohing and aahing about the wedding and this reception while I was walking around. The lanterns look great, all the white flowers and greenery. It's like a garden. And oh, man, that cake looks delicious."

"That was the goal. A sort of enchanted garden. With peaches and peach trees too."

"You and Orchard Inn are going to be the toast of the town."

She didn't bother to stop her huge grin.

"You're going to be a very busy lady from now on. My girl, in high demand."

Beth giggled, burying her face into his neck. "Oh, stop it. Not really. Keep going."

"Think we'll manage to find time for each other?" he asked.

She straightened, only to find him grinning. "You know we will."

"Yeah, I know we will." He spun her with the music. "Just keeping you on your toes."

And boy was he good at that.

They danced to almost every slow song and fast song alike. They took breaks for his toast, and hers, and to debate on whose brought more tears from the crowd. They ate cake.

Oh, heavens, the cake.

Beth had two slices, figuring she needed it with all the dancing. Cece, ever the best hype-woman in the world, couldn't stop raving about it.

Aurora's cake was nothing short of phenomenal. Moist and flavorful. Beth was pretty sure she saw Shelby tear up again when Garrett fed her a piece for the photographer.

And if supply and demand were any indication of success, the barely one-eighth of the bottom layer remaining on the table meant everyone would soon be wanting an Aurora specialty.

After cake, and more dancing, it was finally time for Garrett and Shelby to leave the venue and head to their honeymoon suite down the road. Tomorrow they'd leave for Hawaii.

"Come on, you're going to want a good spot to see this." Sawyer took Beth's hand and led her to the front steps of the inn.

In lieu of sparklers or confetti, the couple had opted for lighted tree branches, fitting the garden theme, and the guests lined the driveway, creating a kind of arch over the couple's path.

As everyone gathered, Shelby joined them, her dress bustled to reveal the ivory-colored cowboy boots on her feet.

The slow clomping of hooves got louder as Garrett came around the corner with two horses, one a black stallion, and the other a very light gray.

Beth's hands flew to her mouth, a knot in her throat, and stomach, as Garrett helped his new wife onto the docile quarter horse.

Shelby took the reins like a pro, having worked with her new instructor several days a week for the past few weeks.

Her huge smile told the tale, full of joy and pride.

"She did it." Beth clutched Sawyer's arm.

"Yeah, we practiced that about fifty times with her in an old prom dress. I thought Uncle Joe was going to bust a gut laughing."

Garrett mounted his horse and Shelby showed complete control as she maneuvered her horse to ride along beside him.

"She's doing great." Sawyer looked almost as proud as Shelby.

"She had a great instructor."

"Eh, she's just a good student." Sawyer beamed as his star pupil rode by.

Shelby and Garrett waved to the crowd as they rode down the center of their lit path, on their way to begin a life together.

The lump in her throat felt ready to choke her, and Beth's heart was so full she thought it might burst.

"I may need that drink now," she whispered to Sawyer.

"You big softie." He kissed her on the temple.

His eyes looked a little misty too.

"C'mon. Let's try a margarita, and I want to show you something."

There was no wait at the bar, as most of the guests had begun to depart when the bride and groom left. Only close family remained, picking over the cake and dancing to the last songs.

After their drinks, Sawyer led her away from the dance floor and onto the soft grass of the orchard.

"I'm going to ruin these shoes." Beth tippy-toed.

"Here." Sawyer scooped her up into his arms, making her squeak, and kept walking.

"What in the world? You're going to hurt yourself."

"Hardly. I've carried bags of feed your size."

Beth laughed, tossing her head back, marveling at the clear night sky and the stars above.

She couldn't believe her blessings. This wedding, this inn, this family. This man.

Just a few short months ago, they were either in jeopardy or nonexistent. Look at how much had changed.

"Here we are," Sawyer said, and set her on her feet next to a peach tree strung with tiny, battery-operated lights.

"How did you—?"

He patted a bench that'd been placed by the tree. On the bench was a large, flat, rectangular package.

"What's this?" she asked as she sat next to the package.

"Guess you better open it and see."

She quirked her lips as she eyed him. "What are you up to, Sawyer Silva?" Beth tore into the package, always loving a present and a surprise.

Inside lay a canvas full of color. Vibrant greens and blues, brown and touches of orange. It was the painting of the peach orchard they'd seen at the festival that day, in the art booth.

"You didn't!" She touched the corner of the canvas.

"I did. I could tell it spoke to you. I got myself one with the horses."

"Oh, Sawyer." She lifted the canvas from the package to hold it up in the light. "It's beautiful. I don't know what to say." She lowered the canvas back down to find Sawyer on one knee.

Her hands began to shake.

"You said it looked like home. Beth, you look like home to me. I'll never forget that day, getting to know you, realizing there was something there. I didn't know where things would go with us, but I knew I wanted to find out. And when I thought I'd lost you, I was miserable. I don't ever want to be without you. I want to be there for you, and with you. I know I was full of doubt when it came to believing love could happen so quickly, but I was wrong. You've made me a believer. I want us to have a life together, full of joy and family, and even work and stress. All of it. I want to do all of it, with you." He reached into his jacket's inner pocket and pulled out a diamond ring. "Beth Shipley, will you marry me?"

She gingerly laid down her new painting, and then all but tackled him as she flew into his arms.

"Yes!" She wrapped her arms around his neck. "Yes, yes, yes!"

She was somehow managing to laugh and cry as he kissed her, and her hands were still shaking when he slid the princess-cut solitaire onto her finger.

It was absolutely perfect.

"Whew!" he said, kissing her again as they got to their feet.

Beth laughed, burying herself in his hug. "What do you mean, 'Whew'? Like I wasn't going to say yes?"

He chuckled and kissed the top of her head. "Well, I was hoping and counting on you saying yes, but the 'Whew' was because I got through it without messing up." He patted his breast pocket. "I didn't even need my note cards either."

Beth pulled away with a laugh. "Is that what Cece saw you practicing? We thought it was your best-man speech."

"I know you did." Sawyer winked. "Told you I'll keep you on your toes."

And she couldn't wait.

Don't miss the next book
in the Orchard Inn series!
Coming Winter 2023

About the Author

Heather McGovern writes contemporary romance in swoony settings. While her love of travel and adventure takes her far, there is no place like home. She lives in South Carolina with her husband and son, and one Maltipoo to rule them all. When she isn't writing, she enjoys hiking, scuba diving, going to Disney World, reading, and streaming her latest favorite on television.

You can learn more at:

HeatherMcGovernNovels.com
Facebook.com/Heather.McGovern.Author

Please turn the page to read
A WEDDING ON
LAVENDER HILL
by Annie Rains!

Event planner Claire Donovan loves giving clients
the weddings of their dreams. But that gets tricky
when she has to work with the man who recently
broke her heart—Bo Matthews. As the son of the
groom and owner of the perfect venue in Sweetwater
Springs, Bo will be impossible to avoid. But can
Claire be this close to her sexy ex without falling for
his charms all over again?

FOREVER

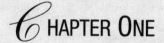CHAPTER ONE

*C*laire Donovan had a bit of a reputation in Sweetwater Springs. She loved to shop.

As an event planner, she was always looking for a special item to make the *big day* just a touch more special. Last week she'd found a clown costume for a purse-size Chihuahua to wear to its owner's eightieth birthday bash. It was a huge hit with the crowd; not so much with the little dog, who yapped, ran in circles, and tore at the shiny fabric.

The only shopping Claire would be doing this morning, however, was glancing in storefront windows on her way to meet with her newest client, Pearson Matthews. Claire's reputation extended beyond shopping. In Sweetwater Springs, she was also known for being professional and punctual, and for putting on the best parties in town.

She passed Sophie's Boutique and admired the window display, wishing she had more time to pop inside and say hello to the store owner—and try on one of those dresses that she absolutely didn't need. Then she opened the neighboring door to the Sweetwater Café and stepped inside to a cool blast of air on her face. She was instantly accosted by the heavy scent of coffee brewing. *Best aroma in the world!*

"Good morning," Emma St. James said from behind the counter. She had the smile of someone who'd been sniffing coffee and sugary treats since five a.m.

"Morning." Claire glanced around the room, looking for Pearson. The only people seated in the coffee shop though were two twentysomething-year-old women and a man with his back toward her. Judging by his build, he was in his twenties or thirties and liked to work out. He wore a ball cap that shielded his face. Not that Claire needed to get a good look at him. If his face matched his body, then he was yummier than Emma's honeybuns in the display case. Claire would do better to have one of those instead.

Pulling her gaze away from him, she walked up to the counter.

"Your usual?" Emma asked.

"You know me so well."

Emma turned and started preparing a tall caffe latte with heavy cream and two raw sugars. "Your mom was here the other day," she said a moment later as she slid the cup of coffee toward Claire.

Claire's good mood immediately took a dive. She loved her mom, but she didn't exactly *like* her. "Oh?" she said, her tone heavy with disinterest. "That's nice."

Emma tilted her head. "She asked about you."

"Well, I hope you told her that I'm fine as long as she stays far away."

"She said she's going to AA now," Emma told her as she rang up Claire's items at the register.

Drinking had always been Claire's father's problem though. Nancy Donovan had so many other, more pressing issues to deal with, none of which Claire wanted to concern herself right now.

She paid Emma in cash, took her coffee and bagged honeybun, then turned and looked around the shop once more.

"Are you meeting someone here?" Emma asked.

"Pearson Matthews. I guess he's running late," Claire said, turning back.

Emma shrugged. "Not sure, but his son is over there." She pointed at the man in the ball cap, and Claire nearly dropped her coffee.

What is Bo Matthews doing here? She didn't have anything against his father, but the youngest Matthews son ranked as one of her least favorite people in Sweetwater Springs. Or he would have if he hadn't left town last April.

Bo glanced over and offered a small wave.

"Maybe he knows where his father is," Emma suggested.

A new customer walked in so Claire had no choice but to step away from the counter. She could either walk back out of the Sweetwater Café and text Pearson on the sidewalk or she could ask his son.

You hate him, she reminded herself as attraction stormed in her belly. She forced her feet to walk forward until she was standing at his table.

Hate him, double-hate him, triple-hate him.

But *wow,* she loved those blue-gray eyes of his, the color of a faded pair of blue jeans. The kind you wanted to shimmy inside of and never take off.

"What are you doing back in town?" she asked, pleased with the controlled level of irritation lining her voice.

He looked up. "I live in Sweetwater Springs, in case you've forgotten."

"You left." And good riddance.

"I had a job to do in Wild Blossom Bluffs. But now I'm home."

Like two sides of a football stadium during a touchdown, half of her cheered while the other side booed and hissed. She was not on Team Bo anymore and never would be again. "Where is your father?"

"I'm afraid he couldn't make it. He asked me to meet with you instead."

Claire's gaze flitted to the exit. Pearson Matthews was her biggest client right now. He was a businessman with money and influence, and she'd promised to do a good job for him and his fiancée, Rebecca Long. Claire also had her reputation to maintain. She took her responsibilities seriously and prided herself on going above and beyond the call of duty. Every time for every client.

And right now, her duty was to sit down and make nice with Bo Matthews.

* * *

Bo reached for his cup of black coffee and took a long sip as he listened to Claire do her best to be civil. If he had to guess, the conversation she really wanted to be having with him right now was anything but.

"The wedding is two months away," she said, avoiding eye contact with him. "We're on a time crunch, yes, but your father could've called and rescheduled the initial planning session." Her gaze flicked to meet his. "It's not really something you can do."

Bo reached for his cup of coffee and took another sip, taking his time in responding. He could tell by the twitch of her cheek that it irritated her. She couldn't wait to get out of that chair and create as much distance between them as possible. Regret festered up inside him. He couldn't blame her for being upset. He'd handled things with her all wrong last year. "There's a problem with the wedding."

Claire's stiff facial features twisted. "What? Pearson and Rebecca called the wedding off?"

"No, unfortunately," he said, although that would've made him happy. Bo had been certain his dad would eventually come to his senses about marrying a woman half his age. Then, a few months ago, the lovebirds had announced they were pregnant.

"If the wedding is still a go, then what's the problem?" Claire lifted her cup of coffee and took a sip.

Naturally that brought his focus to her heart-shaped lips. He'd kissed those lips once—okay, more than once—and he wouldn't mind doing it again. Clearing his throat, he looked down at the table. "Rebecca is in preterm labor. The doctor put her on hospital bed rest over the weekend. She's not leaving there until the baby is born. Not for long at least."

From his peripheral vision, he saw Claire lift her hand to cover that pretty pink mouth. "That's awful."

He nodded and looked back up. "She wants to be married before little Junior arrives, which could be a couple days to a couple of weeks from now, if we're lucky."

Women weren't supposed to be beautiful when they frowned, but Claire wore it well. "So the wedding is postponed?" she asked. "Is that why Pearson sent you here to talk to me?"

"Not exactly. Dad and Rebecca want to speed things up a bit. Rebecca can get approval to leave the hospital, but only for a couple hours."

"Speed things up how much?"

Bo grimaced. This was a lot to ask, but his dad was used to getting things done his way. Pearson Matthews demanded excellence, which was one of the reasons Bo guessed he'd hired Claire in the first place. "They want the wedding to happen this weekend."

"What?" Claire nearly shouted.

"No expense spared. Dad's words, not mine."

She shook her head and started rattling off rapid-fire thoughts. "I don't even know what they like or what they want. I haven't met with Rebecca for planning yet. She's the bride, it's her wedding. Today is Thursday. That only gives me—"

"—three days," he said, cutting her off. "They want to marry on Saturday evening."

Claire's face was flushed against her strawberry locks. Her green eyes were wide like a woman going into complete panic mode. He'd seen her in this mode when she'd woken up beside him in bed last spring, and that had been his fault as well.

She pulled a small notebook and pen out of her purse and started writing. "I guess I could meet with Rebecca in her hospital room to discuss colors and themes."

Bo cleared his throat, signaling for Claire to look up. "About that. Dad doesn't want Rebecca involved. No stress, per doctor's orders. Dad wants you and me to plan it."

Claire's mouth pinched shut.

Yeah, he wasn't exactly thrilled with the idea either. He had other things to do than plan a shotgun wedding that he didn't even want to happen. For one, he had architectural plans to finish by Friday for a potential client. Having just returned to town, it was important to reestablish his place as the preferred architect in Sweetwater Springs.

"You and me?" She folded her arms across her chest. "I don't think so."

He shrugged. "Dad said he'd double your fee for the trouble."

That pretty, heart-shaped mouth fell open. After a moment, she narrowed her eyes. "What's in it for you? Aren't you busy?"

"Very. But despite his poor sense in the love arena, Dad has always been there for me. He even bailed me out of jail once."

Her gaze flicked away for a moment. Claire had told him about her family history during their night together last spring. Not that he hadn't already heard the rumors. Her dad was a drunk, now serving time for a DWI. Claire's mom couldn't hold down a job and had a bad habit of sleeping with other women's husbands.

Most notably was her mom's affair with the previous mayor of Sweetwater Springs. That had ensured that the Donovan family's dirty laundry was aired for everyone to talk about.

Claire was cut from a different cloth though, and she did her best to make sure everyone saw that.

"Why am I not surprised that you would've spent the night in jail?" she asked with a shake of her head. The subtle movement made her red hair scrape along her bare shoulders.

"I guess because you have low expectations for me."

She pinned him with a look that spoke volumes. "How about *no* expectations?"

Maybe that was another reason Bo had agreed to help with this farce of a wedding. Claire might never forgive him, but maybe she'd stop being angry at him one day. For a reason he didn't want to explore too deeply, he hoped that was true.

* * *

Saying yes to this request would be insane.

Claire lifted her coffee to her mouth, wishing it had a splash of something stronger in it right now. "Okay, I'll do it." She'd never bailed on a job, and she wasn't about to start now.

Even if the wedding was in three days. And she had to plan it with Bo Matthews. And... "Oh no."

"What?" he asked.

"There aren't going to be any venues available. You can't book a place three days out. Everywhere in town will be taken. I wouldn't even be able to empty out a McDonald's for them to get married in with this short a notice."

Claire's hands were shaking. *The best and nothing less* was her personal motto. But she wasn't going to be able to deliver this time. There was no way. Her eyes stung with the realization.

"What about the Mayflower?" Bo asked.

That was a popular restaurant that she sometimes reserved for less formal events. "It'll be booked."

"The community center?"

Claire rolled her eyes. "Such a male thing to say. No woman dreams of getting married at the local community center." Claire dropped her head into her hands. *Think, think, think.*

She listened as Bo rattled off some more options, and shot them all down without even looking up.

"A wedding should be about the people, not the place," he said a moment later.

She looked up now. "I wouldn't have pegged you as a romantic."

He smiled, and it went straight through her chest like a poisonous barb. "It's true. If two people are in love, it shouldn't matter where they are. Saying vows under the stars should be enough."

She swooned against her will, immediately imagining herself in his arms under said stars. She'd danced with him at Liz and Mike's wedding reception last year. And he'd smelled of ever-greens and mint. She remembered that when he'd held her in his arms, she'd thought he was the perfect size for her. Men who were too large put her head level at their chests. Too small put them face-to-face, which was just awkward.

But in Bo's arms, her head was at the perfect height to rest on his shoulder. Close enough to where she had to tip her face back to look into those faded denim eyes behind the Clark Kent glasses.

Bo reached for his coffee. "I couldn't care less where they get married. They'll be divorced within the year if my dad maintains his track record."

Right. Rebecca would be the third Mrs. Matthews.

"Maybe Rebecca is *the one*," Claire said, feeling a wee bit of empathy for the man sitting across from her.

"Nah. But I am going to have a new brother. *That* I'm excited about."

"You'll lose your spot as the spoiled youngest," she pointed out.

"Trust me, I was never spoiled." He tipped his coffee cup against his lips and took a sip. "I started working at the family business as a teenager after school. Dad made me save every penny to put myself through college."

Claire already knew the history of Peak Designs Architectural Firm and how it had grown from a one-man show to employing all three of Pearson's sons. Bo was the architect of the group. The middle son, Mark, was in construction management with the company. Cade did landscape design. The project he'd done that Claire liked best was Bo's own yard on Lavender Hill. The landscape, covered with purple wildflowers, was open and elevated over the water, with Bo's home—one of his own designs—seeming to touch the sky. She'd often looked out on that home while canoeing downriver and thought to herself that it was one of the most romantic places on earth.

"I've got it." She bolted upright. "Your place on Lavender Hill is the perfect place for a wedding!"

"My place?"

"I'm assuming your yard isn't taken for the weekend."

"It is. It's taken by me. No."

His expression was stiff, but she wasn't going to be deterred.

"Yes," she countered, leaning forward at the table. As she did, she caught a whiff of his evergreen scent, and her heart kicked at the memories it brought with it. Him and her, kissing and laughing. "It's your dad, your stepmom."

He groaned at the mention of Rebecca.

"And you owe me."

His eyes narrowed behind his glasses.

Yes, she knew she'd gone into his hotel room on her own volition last year. But he'd never called the following day, and she'd hoped he would. Instead, he'd taken a job in Wild Blossom Bluffs and promptly left town. She'd pined for his call even after the rumors had started popping up about them. Some people, more accurately, had compared her to her wanderlust mother. In reality, only a handful of people had talked, but even one comparison to Nancy Donovan stung. Claire wasn't like her mom and never would be.

Bo stared at her for a long moment behind those sexy glasses of his and then cursed under his breath. "Fine," he muttered. "You can have the wedding at my place."

CHAPTER TWO

$\mathscr{B}$o was in over his head, and he'd barely waded into the water.

Helping Claire pick out colors or themes for his dad's wedding was harmless enough. Inviting her into his home on Lavender Hill, letting her rearrange things, and set up for a wedding was another.

And even though he was convincing himself of how awful this new turn of events was, there was some part of him that was excited to spend time with her. The night they'd shared last spring had been amazing. Being best man at the wedding of his childhood buddy and the woman who'd left Bo at the altar a year earlier had promised to be akin to having his appendix removed sans anesthesia. Instead, as the night was ending, Bo found himself kissing Claire, who'd tasted like some exotic, forbidden fruit. They'd both been too drunk to drive home and had gone up to the hotel room he'd booked. Best night of his life without question, even with hindsight and the events that followed tainting it.

In the morning when he'd woken, he'd watched Claire climb out of bed, looking sexy as anything he'd ever laid eyes on.

She'd had that sleepy, rumpled look he found so attractive. She'd smiled stiffly and had made some excuse about needing to go. Then he'd promised to call later, knowing good and well he wouldn't.

That was his main regret. What was he supposed to say though? *That was fun* or *Have a nice life*? Claire was the kind of woman who men fell in love with, and he wasn't a glutton for punishment. He'd gone that route once and had been publicly rejected by Liz. He didn't fancy doing it again.

He also hadn't looked forward to seeing Liz and Mike be newlyweds around town. So he'd taken a job opportunity outside of Sweetwater Springs to clear his head. Putting the lovely Claire out of his mind, however, hadn't proved as easy.

His cell phone buzzed in the center console of his car. He connected the call and put it on speakerphone. "Hello."

"Our new stepmom is in the hospital?" his older brother Cade asked.

"That's right. She's at Mount Pleasant Memorial on bed rest. And she's not our stepmom yet...not until Saturday," Bo corrected.

"So I hear. You're planning the wedding with the event planner? Isn't she the one you disappeared with after Liz and Mike's wedding?"

"Yes and yes," Bo said briskly. "I plan to give her free rein over all the details. Dad said money was no object, and I trust Claire's taste. I just hope she doesn't mess up my house in the process."

"Your house? That's where you're having it?"

"Outside." But guests had a way of finding themselves inside at events, either to use the bathroom or to lie down when they weren't feeling well. Bo wasn't naive enough to think that wouldn't happen. His cousins would likely want to put their small children to sleep in one of his guest rooms.

"Well, I'd say 'Let me know if I can help,' but…" Cade's voice trailed off.

"But you'd be lying."

"And I'm an honest guy," Cade said with a chuckle. "No, seriously. I'm designing some gardens behind the Sweetwater Bed and Breakfast right now. It's a big job, and Kaitlyn Russo wants it done before the Spring Festival and the influx of guests she has coming in for the event."

"It's okay. Claire will do most of the work. She's top-notch."

"You speaking from experience there, brother?" Cade teased.

Bo ground his back teeth. "I already told you what happened." And he took offense at people jumping to the worst conclusions about Claire just because of who her parents were. "Listen, I have to go," he said as he pulled into the driveway of his home. He'd taken years to design this house himself, working nights while creating the plan. He loved every curve and angle of the structure. He loved the rooms with their high ceilings. His bedroom even had a skylight that allowed him to stare up into the sky while lying in his bed at night. Set on a hill, the house overlooked the river and the mountains beyond. *This* was his idea of heaven. He'd missed it while he'd been licking his wounds in Wild Blossom Bluffs. But now that he was back, he didn't plan on leaving again.

He walked inside, went straight to the kitchen, and grabbed an apple. Taking it to his office, he started working on the proposal designs for Ken Martin. Landing this contract would be good for business.

An hour later, he let out a frustrated sigh. He couldn't concentrate. All he'd been able to think about was that night he'd shared with Claire last spring. And the next three days he'd get to spend with her.

* * *

Claire had briefly considered going to school to become a nurse. Then her grandmother had fallen sick during her senior year of high school, and Claire had spent quite a few months visiting her at Mount Pleasant Memorial. That experience had ended any nursing dreams. She didn't like hospitals. Didn't like the sounds, the smells, or the dull looks in the eyes of the people she passed.

Making her way down the second-floor hall, Claire avoided meeting anyone's gaze. She liked being an event planner because most of the time people were happy. They were excited and looking forward to the future.

Just like the patient she was here to see.

Stopping in front of the door to room 201, Claire adjusted the cheerful arrangement of daffodils she'd picked up at the Little Shop of Flowers on the way here and knocked.

"Come in," a woman's voice called.

Claire cracked the door and peered inside the dimly lit room. Rebecca was lying in bed wearing a diamond-print hospital gown. The TV was blasting a soap opera, and she had a magazine in her lap. "Hi. How are you feeling?" Claire asked, stepping inside.

"Like a beached whale," Rebecca said with a small smile. She was practically glowing with happiness.

"Well, you definitely don't look like one. Pregnancy looks great on you," Claire said. "I know you're not supposed to be doing work of any kind right now so I'm only here as a friend. I brought you flowers."

"Oh, they're so beautiful!... And that rule about no work of any kind is Pearson's," Rebecca added in a whisper, even though no one else was in the room. "He's so protective toward me. It's adorable, really."

Rebecca also had that look of love about her. Her brown eyes were lit up and dreamy. Bo might not think what his father and

302

Rebecca had was real, but Claire always got a good feeling for her clients. She could tell who was legit and who was getting married for all the wrong reasons. Maybe the baby was speeding things along, but Rebecca loved Pearson. It was as clear as her creamy white skin.

"I agree with Mr. Matthews. You should be taking it easy. We don't want that baby of yours coming any sooner than he needs to."

Rebecca sighed. "It's just, I've been dreaming about getting married since I was a little girl," she confided. "I wanted more time to plan this out and do it right."

"Relax. If you and Pearson are there, it will be perfect," Claire said, remembering how Bo had told her something similar this morning. "All you'll remember by the time it's over is the look in his eyes when he says I do. Assuming you can see through the blur of your own tears."

Rebecca's lips parted. "Wow. You're good."

"Thanks. And don't worry—your wedding day is going to be everything you ever dreamed."

"I hope so. The main thing I want now is to have it before the baby gets here."

"We'll make sure that happens," Claire promised. "Do you have any favorite colors?"

Rebecca drew her shoulders up to her ears excitedly. "I was thinking that soft purple and white would be pretty."

"That's a nice springtime combo." Claire pulled a little notebook out of her purse along with a pen and wrote down Rebecca's color preference. "I'll see if Halona at Little Shop of Flowers can do some arrangements in those colors. Maybe with a splash of yellows and pinks as well for the bouquets."

Rebecca's eyes sparkled under the bed's overhead light. "Perfect."

"What about food? Since it's such short notice, I was thinking we'd skip a full dinner and just have light hors d'oeuvres at the reception. And drinks too, of course, for everyone except you." Claire winked at the bride-to-be.

They sat and chatted for another ten minutes while Claire wrote down a few ideas. Then she stood up and shoved her little notebook back into her purse. "I promised I wouldn't stress you out so I better go. You need your rest. But I'm so glad we got a chance to talk. I'm clearing my schedule for the rest of the week to focus solely on your big day."

And not on Bo Matthews. Which would be easier said than done, since she would be spending the next several days at his house.

"Thank you so much," Rebecca said, bringing a hand to her swollen stomach.

"You're very welcome." With a final wave goodbye, Claire headed back down the hospital halls, keeping her gaze on the floor and not on passersby. She resisted a total body shudder as the smells and sounds accosted her. Once she was outside again, she sucked in a breath of fresh air. She walked to her car, got in, and then drove in the direction of Bo Matthews's home on Lavender Hill.

Butterflies fluttered up into her chest at the anticipation of seeing him again. But this was just business, nothing more, she reminded herself. And that was the way it needed to stay.

* * *

After a walk to clear his head, Bo settled back at his desk and worked steadily, making good progress on his proposal. Somehow, he put Claire out of his mind until the doorbell rang. Just when he'd gotten into the zone. With a groan, he headed to the door and opened it to find Claire staring back at him for the second time today.

She looked away shyly and then pulled the strap of her handbag higher on her shoulder as if she needed something to do with her hands. Did he make her nervous?

What would've happened had he called her the morning after they'd spent the night together? Would they be a couple right now? Would she be stepping into his arms to greet him instead of looking anxious and agitated? Would she be pressing her lips to his in a kiss that promised to turn into more later?

Bo cleared his throat and then gestured for her to come inside.

"I thought I'd go ahead and get started," she said. "I want to walk around the yard and get a good feel for the size and layout so I know where we can set up chairs and a gazebo."

"Okay." He was working hard to keep his eyes level with hers and not to admire the pretty floral dress she was wearing and the curves that filled it out so nicely. She had shiny sandals strapped to her feet that glinted in the light of the room.

"I stopped by to see Rebecca on the way here and brought her flowers." Claire held up her hand. "Don't worry. I didn't cause any stress. But she did give me her color preferences though."

"That's good," Bo said.

"I was thinking we should keep things simple. Even though your father said no expense spared, less is more depending on the venue. Your yard is the absolute perfect place for a wedding. The view is amazing, and as long as there's good music and food, it'll be as nice as some of the bigger events I plan in pricier spots."

Bo wasn't going to argue with her about saving money. Especially since his father was likely to have another wedding sometime in the next five years if history repeated itself.

"Feel free to walk around and do whatever you need to do," he said. As long as she kept her distance from him. He needed to work, and he had a feeling his brief streak of productivity was now broken for the rest of the afternoon. "There's a spare key on the kitchen counter for you to use over the weekend. You can come and go as you need." He gestured toward the back door. "That'll take you to the gardens. Let me know if you have any questions."

"Thanks." She turned and headed in the direction he pointed. His gaze unwillingly dropped as he watched her walk away. With a resigned sigh, he returned to his office to work.

This is going to be a very long three days.

An hour and a half later, he lifted his head to a soft knock on his open door. Then the door opened, and there was Claire, her cheeks rosy from her walk outside. The wind off the river was sometimes cool this time of year, and the humidity had left her hair with a slight wave to it. "Sorry to disturb you."

She'd been polite and civil toward him since their new arrangement. Whatever resentment she harbored toward him, she'd locked it away for the time being. The same way he was doing his best to keep his attraction toward her under wraps. "What do you think?" he asked. "Will Lavender Hill work?"

She nodded. "You have quite a few acres of land. We'll need to set up a few Porta Potties somewhere out of sight so that guests don't come in and out of your house all night. I think three will be enough, and I know a company that can arrange that on short notice. I'll also be having wooden fold-out chairs delivered. We rent them, and the company typically picks them back up on the day after the ceremony. The ground is nice and firm, and I checked the weather for Saturday. Sweetwater Springs isn't expecting rain again until later next week."

"Sounds like everything is falling into place."

"There's still more to do, of course. There are so many things to consider when you're planning an event for nearly a hundred people. But first I was thinking about having some food delivered. I'm starving, and I can't think when my stomach is growling. Are there any pizza places around here that deliver?"

He thought for a moment. "Jessie's Pizza delivers. It's my favorite." Just thinking about it made his mouth water. "The number is on my fridge."

She gave him a strange look as if she was debating whether to say something else. With a soft eye roll that he suspected was at herself rather than him, she folded her arms across her chest and met his gaze. "Are you hungry? I certainly can't eat a whole pie."

This was where he should practice self-control and say no. "I haven't eaten all day, actually. But if we're sharing, I'm buying. It's the least I can do considering the pinch my dad has put you in."

"Great. What do you like on your pizza?"

"I like it all," he said, not intending for the sexual tone in his voice.

Claire's skin flushed. "Okay, well, um...I'll let you work until it gets here," she called over her shoulder as she headed back out of his office.

Work. Yeah, right. With the anticipation of eating his favorite pizza with Claire, his brain had no intention of focusing on architectural plans right now. The only curves he was envisioning were those underneath that floral sundress she was wearing.

CHAPTER THREE

*W*hile Claire waited for the pizza to arrive, she sat at Bo's kitchen counter and made a to-do list. Priority number one was lining up all the services for Saturday's wedding. Years of planning events meant she had close contacts for everything. Most would drop whatever they were doing and work extended hours to meet her needs. She'd already spoken to Halona about the floral arrangements, and that was a go. *Thank goodness.* She jotted down several people she planned to call after lunch, and then she found her mind wandering while she drew little hearts on the side of her paper and thought about Bo.

Whoa! She wasn't going down that path again. It'd been a long hike back the last time. Being seen coming out of Bo's hotel room had been mortifying enough. Even worse, she'd left that morning so smitten with him that she couldn't see straight. He was charming and funny, and undeniably gorgeous. She'd always thought so. He had this Clark Kent sexy nerd look about him that just *did it* for her.

Bo also had muscles plastered in all the right places. Not too bulky. No, his were long and lean. They'd run their hands all over each other's bodies last spring. That night had been hotter than anything she'd ever experienced, even though their clothes had stayed on—mostly. She was drunk, and he'd said he didn't want to take advantage of her. So they'd spent the night driving each other crazy with their roaming hands. They'd also spent it talking and laughing. Then, after Claire had left the next morning, it was out of sight, out of mind for Bo. But not for her.

The doorbell rang. As she walked down the hall, she turned at the sound of heavy footsteps behind her.

"I told you I'd pay." Bo caught up to her and reached to open the door ahead of her.

A young, lanky, twentysomething guy held a box in his hand. "Someone ordered an extra-large pizza and chicken wings?"

Bo glanced over his shoulder. "Wings, huh?"

Her cheeks burned. "I'm going to be here a while tonight so I thought it'd be a good idea to have plenty of fuel on hand." And pizza and wings were her biggest weaknesses, right after the clearance racks at Sophie's Boutique. And Bo, once upon a time.

Bo chuckled as he pulled out his wallet and paid the guy at the door. Taking the food, he closed the door with his foot and walked past her into the kitchen. "I'll get the plates. There's sweet tea and soda in the fridge. Help yourself."

She opened the fridge and peered inside. A man's fridge said a lot about him. If there was more alcohol than food, that might be a problem. Bo appeared to have only one bottle of brew, and a healthy selection of fresh fruit and vegetables were visible in the drawers. She reached for the pitcher of tea and brought it back to the counter, where Bo had put out two plates. The open box of pizza was at the center of the kitchen counter.

He placed a slice of pizza on each plate and carried them to the table. "I have two glasses over here," he said. "You can bring the pitcher over."

Apparently, they were eating together. She'd just assumed that he would take his food back to his office and work.

He glanced at her for a moment. "Everything okay?"

She softly bit the inside of her cheek. She'd already had breakfast with the man. Lunch too? Her stomach growled. "Yep. Just fine." She moved to the table and took a seat, where the delicious smell of Italian sauce and spices wafted under her nose. "Mmm. If that tastes as good as it smells, I'm going to be having seconds."

Bo laughed. It was a deep rumble that echoed through her. "It tastes even better than it smells," he promised. "Jessie's is the best."

Her eyes slid over as he brought the slice to his mouth and took a bite. A thin string of cheese connected his mouth to the pizza for a moment, reminding her of all the pizza commercials on TV. Bo could be the guy in those commercials. Watching him bite into a slice of pizza would have her craving it every time. Craving *him* every time.

She lifted a slice herself and took a bite, closing her eyes as her taste buds exploded with pleasure. "You're not kidding," she moaned. When she looked over, he was watching her.

She swallowed. "It's very good."

For the rest of the meal, she kept her eyes and moans to herself as she filled Bo in on Rebecca's thoughts for the wedding. "She's really excited. She has the bride-to-be and the mother-to-be glows combined."

Bo grunted.

"I've known Rebecca ever since she moved to town two years ago. I don't think she's the type to marry someone for anything other than love."

Bo finished off his third slice and reached for his glass of tea. "It's just hard to fathom that a twenty-eight-year-old woman would want to marry a fifty-year-old man."

Claire laughed. "Love is crazy that way. It doesn't let you choose who you fall for."

"True enough. Maybe if you did, it would turn out a whole lot better."

She knew the whole ugly story about his ex-fiancée, who'd fallen in love with his best friend. Even after their betrayal, Bo had stood in as best man for the wedding that had led to him and Claire spending the night together.

"Have you ever been in love?" he asked, surprising her. They'd talked about a lot that night last spring, but that topic hadn't come up.

She nearly choked on her bite of pizza.

"Sorry. You know my history. It's only fair."

She reached for her glass of tea and washed down her bite. "I've been in what I thought was love in college. It was really just infatuation though."

"How do you know the difference?"

"Well," she said, chewing on her thoughts, "infatuation fades. Love survives even after you know about all the other person's faults. Sometimes knowing the faults makes you like them more... This is not personal experience talking, of course. I'm talking as an event planner who has worked with countless couples in love. I've seen couples crumble under the pressure of big events, and I've seen others come out stronger."

He wore an unreadable expression on his face. "I guess I could say I've seen the same in my line of work. Making plans for the house you want to grow old in can be as stressful as it is exciting. Couples have torn into each other in the process, right in front of me. At those times, I'm almost glad that my ex walked away from me." He sat back in his chair. "That just meant I got to plan the home of my dreams all by myself. No drama involved."

Claire shook her head. "Well, you did a great job. This could very well be my dream house," she said. "I haven't seen the upstairs, but I'm sure it's just as perfect as the downstairs."

"I'll have to give you a tour at some point."

She shifted restlessly. Was his bedroom upstairs? She didn't think stepping inside alone with him would be wise. Probably asking him the question that sat right at the tip of her tongue wasn't wise either. She asked anyway. "Why didn't you call?"

Bo shifted his body and his gaze uncomfortably. She needed to know though. Yes, he'd left town, but he hadn't gone far and not for good. "I needed some space from everything. It had nothing to do with you. It wasn't personal."

But it was to her. She hadn't felt so connected to anyone in a long time. They'd had such a great time, and he'd promised to call. Only he never did. He must have been hurt watching his ex marry his best friend, and he'd used her as a crutch to get through the night. That was all.

"I see," she said briskly. Then she started cleaning up her lunch, even though she could stomach another slice of pizza or a chicken wing. What she couldn't stomach was continuing to sit with Bo right now.

"I had a good time that night," Bo said, as if backtracking from his response. "A *very* good time."

"So good that you never spoke to me again."

"We didn't sleep together, Claire. Why are you so mad at me?"

She slammed her paper plate and napkin in the trash and then whipped around to look at him. "Is that what defines whether a guy calls the next morning? Sex? You know, forget I asked the question. Forget everything. I have work to do and so do you."

* * *

312

It was well after eight p.m. when Claire arrived home. Her slice of pizza and sweet tea had worn off midafternoon, and she'd been running on adrenaline and fury since then.

It wasn't personal.

Those three little words had burrowed under her skin and had been festering for the last several hours. How dare he? She'd shared intimate details of her life with him that night. Hopes and dreams. She'd told him about her dysfunctional childhood that she never spoke of with anyone. It was *very* personal to her.

Stepping into her bedroom, she shed her clothes and traded them for something comfy. Then she turned off the lights, climbed into bed, and reached for the book on her nightstand. She kept rereading the same line because her brain was still trained on Bo. It'd only been one night, but that night could've filled several years' worth for some couples. She always left a wedding feeling romantic and hopeful for her own happily ever after. Like a fool, she'd felt there was a potential for that with Bo.

A few days later, she swung by his house on Lavender Hill. Instead of finding Bo, she'd run into his brother Cade, who'd informed her that Bo had taken a job out of town. He didn't know when Bo was coming back, but it wasn't anytime soon. With him, Bo had taken a little bit of her pride and a big piece of her foolish heart.

Well, not this time. In fact, she wasn't even going to waste any more energy being mad at him. Bo was right. This wasn't personal; it was work.

* * *

Bo startled at the sound of his front door opening and closing early the next morning. He jolted upright, realizing he'd fallen asleep at his desk, which wasn't uncommon. His muscles cried out as he moved. Even though he was only thirty years old, he was too old to be grabbing shut-eye in an upright office chair.

"Bo?" Claire's voice called out from the front entrance hall.

How had she even gotten in? Oh, right. He'd given her a key.

"Bo?"

He stood and met her in the hallway. Unlike him, she appeared to be well rested. Her hair was soft and shiny—perfect for running his fingers through. Today she was wearing pink cropped pants along with a short-sleeved top featuring a neckline that gave him ample view of her breastbone—the sexiest nonprivate part of a woman, if you asked him. Claire's was delicate with a splash of freckles over her fair skin. He'd spent time sprinkling kisses there once.

And if he didn't stop thinking about it, he was going to have a problem springing up real soon.

"I brought you a cappuccino and a cream cheese bagel." She lifted a cup holder tray and a bag from the Sweetwater Café. "And you look like you could use it." She laughed softly. She'd been royally ticked off the last time he'd seen her. What had changed since then?

"I fell asleep working on my latest design," he told her.

"And you have the facial creases to prove it." She smiled and breezed past him, leaving a delicious floral scent in her wake. He followed her into the kitchen and lifted the coffee from its tray.

"To what do I owe this act of mercy?" he asked suspiciously.

Claire lifted her own cup of coffee. "I'm calling a truce. What happened last spring is done and over. We won't think or talk about it ever again."

He sipped the bittersweet brew. The only problem with that suggestion was that he'd been thinking about that night for the past twelve months.

"I can put it behind me. It wasn't personal for you so I'm assuming you can as well." She notched up her chin, projecting confidence and strength even though something wavered in her eyes as she waited for him to reply.

"I can do the same," he lied.

"Great." She smiled stiffly. "Then I need your assistance this morning. If you're available."

"I got a lot done workwise last night so I guess I have some time. What do you need?"

"I brought some fairy lights to hang outside. You have some great gardens. Your brother Cade is so talented." She shifted her gaze, almost as if looking at him directly made her uncomfortable. "Since the ceremony will be at night," she continued, her voice becoming brisk, "I thought fairy lights in your garden beyond the arbor will add to the romantic feel. Do you have a ladder?"

"Of course."

"Great. I'm just going to take a walk around out there while you finish your cappuccino and bagel. I usually walk in the mornings down my street, but when I woke this morning, I just couldn't wait to go for a stroll behind your house. If that's okay?"

"Sure. I need to shower. I'll meet you out there with a ladder in about twenty minutes." Showers and coffee were his usual morning ritual. Perhaps he should start adding in a morning walk as well. Especially if it included a gorgeous redhead with dazzling green eyes.

He grabbed his cappuccino and went upstairs to prepare for the day ahead. It was Friday. Last night, he'd made a lot of progress on the Martin proposal. Tonight, he was meeting the couple over dinner to discuss his plans. He hated the social aspect of his job. Going to the Tipsy Tavern downtown with his buddies was fine, but having a nice dinner and wooing potential clients made his skin itch. It was a necessary evil though. He'd just have to suffer through it and hopefully come out of the night with a contract.

* * *

The gardens were a feast for Claire's eyes, but watching Bo string those fairy lights over the last hour was even yummier. His arms flexed and stretched while he hammered nails into the wooden posts that weaved in and around his garden. And the tool belt he'd looped around his waist was a visual aphrodisiac.

"You okay back there?" Bo asked, glancing over his shoulder.

She jolted as if she'd been caught with her hand in the proverbial cookie jar. Nope, she'd just been checking out the way he filled out the backside of those jeans. Her gaze flicked to his eyes, which were now twinkling with humor. *Yeah*, he knew exactly what she'd been doing. "Fine."

"Fine, huh? A woman who says she's fine never is. Am I hanging these things to your satisfaction?"

"You are. I might have to contract you for all my jobs."

"As much as I'd love to be at your beck and call, I'm afraid I already have a job that keeps me pretty busy." He climbed down the ladder and folded it, then carried it out of the garden and toward the arbor that had been delivered yesterday evening. He set the ladder back up and climbed to the top.

Claire handed him another string of fairy lights. "I'm meeting with the caterer in an hour and then swinging by the Little Shop of Flowers after that. Since your father asked you to help, I thought you might be interested in coming along."

Bo looped the lights around the arbor with an eye for spacing them out perfectly. "I'm not sure I'm the best person to ask for opinions on catering or flowers. Can't you get one of the women in that ladies group you go to?"

The group in question was a dozen or so Sweetwater Springs residents who regularly made a habit of having a Ladies' Day (or Night) Out. They went to movies, had dinner, volunteered for community functions, anything and everything. It was girl power at its finest.

"I spoke to Rebecca, but you know your dad's tastes. I always like to represent the groom as much as the bride. Going to a wedding or anniversary function that is one-sided is a pet peeve of mine."

She watched him shove his hammer into the loop on his tool belt. Part of her physical attraction to Bo was his intellectual look, complete with glasses and a ready ballpoint pen always in his pocket. He had those thoughtful eyes too, always seeming to be thinking about something.

But this handyman look was really appealing as well. She'd created an online dating profile on one of those popular websites a couple of months back with the ladies group, but she hadn't activated it. She was a bit chicken, and the spring and summer were her busy months for planning events. Maybe she'd make it active in the fall and expand her search for bookish professionals to include muscle-clad guys who did hard labor. Bo was a perfect blend of both, except he wasn't available. After the way his ex betrayed him with his best friend, he might never be again.

He climbed back down the ladder and faced her. "I've got a proposition for you. I'll go with you to meet the caterer and look at flowers if you have dinner with me tonight."

She blinked him into focus. "You mean a date?"

"No."

She swallowed and looked up at the work he'd done with the lights, pretending to assess the job. Why had her mind immediately jumped to the conclusion that he was asking her on a date? If he was going to do that, he would have last spring. "Why do you want me to have dinner with you?"

"I'm meeting a potential client and his wife. It's social as much as it is business, and I hate doing these things alone. So yes, I guess they'd see you as my date, but—"

"It isn't personal," she said with a nod. "Fair enough." She jutted out her hand.

As his hand slid against hers, her body betrayed her iron-clad decision not to want him. Those hands were magic, she recalled. The stuff that her fantasies would forever be made of.

She quickly yanked her hand away. "Deal."

* * *

Two hours later, Claire was standing beside Bo and sampling finger foods and hors d'oeuvres at Taste of Heaven Catering. Claire usually came to her friend Brenna Myer's business with the prospective brides and grooms. It was usually them sampling the cheese, crackers, and little finger sandwiches.

"This is divine," Claire said with a sigh. She turned to Bo. "What do you think?"

"It's good," he said with a nod.

Claire punched him softly. "It's better than good. Are you kidding me?"

He chuckled softly. "Okay, it's the best thing I've put into my mouth in a long time."

Those words sliced right through her like a knife on that soft cheese spread in front of them. *Get it together, Claire.*

Brenna was watching them the way she usually did with the clients that Claire brought in. Claire guessed that her friend, who was also a member of the Ladies' Day Out group, was scrutinizing every facial reaction and weighing whether her potential clients were satisfied.

Speaking of clients... "Do you think Pearson would like it?" Claire asked Bo.

"My dad is a carnivore. Put any meat in front of him, and he's a happy man."

"Especially with Rebecca at his side," Claire said, throwing in two cents for her currently bedridden client. If Rebecca made Pearson happy, then Bo should be happy too.

"Great. We'll definitely have a spread of various meats then," Brenna said, pulling a pen from behind her ear and writing something down on her clipboard.

"And the cheese," Claire said. "What pregnant woman doesn't love cheese?"

"I don't know any," Brenna said on a laugh. "You'll probably want something sweet as well."

"That's what I'm looking forward to sampling." Bo rubbed his hands together as a sexy smile curved his mouth.

"You have a sweet tooth, huh?" Claire asked.

"I do."

"Me too," she confessed. "Brenna's cheesecake squares are my favorite. I swear that's what she named this business after. They are the epitome of what heaven would taste like if it was food."

Brenna laugh-snorted.

Bo was also grinning. "Then we need to add them to the menu," he said, turning to Brenna.

"Oh no. This event is not about me and what I like," Claire protested. "It's about your dad and future stepmom."

The word *stepmom* drew a grunt from him. "We're the ones planning this wedding, and if cheesecake squares are your favorite, then cheesecake squares it will be."

Claire melted just a little bit at his insistence. "Let's add some chocolate maroons and white chocolate-dipped strawberries as well," Claire said, with a decisive nod in Brenna's direction. Those were also one of her favorites, but Rebecca had also mentioned how much she enjoyed those.

By the time they left Taste of Heaven, their bellies were full, and there was no need for lunch.

"That was actually a lot of fun." Bo walked on the traffic side of the sidewalk as they strolled down Main Street to their cars. They'd driven there separately so that she could go home and prepare for tonight.

"It was. Thanks for coming."

"Well, as you pointed out, it's my dad and his soon-to-be wife. Coming along with you is the least I can do. Plus, now I get you tonight." He raised his brows as he looked at her.

It wasn't a date. He'd said so himself. But her heart hadn't received that message, because it stopped for a brief second every time he looked at her.

He opened her driver's side door and then stared at her for a long, breathless second.

There went her heart skipping like a rock over Silver Lake. He leaned forward, and she forgot to breathe as his face lowered to hers and kissed the side of her cheek. Part of her had thought maybe he was targeting her mouth. Would she have turned away? Probably not.

"See you tonight." He straightened, holding her captive with his gaze.

Maybe she should've held on to her anger at him. At least that would have buffered this bone-deep attraction that she couldn't seem to kick.

"Yes. Tonight." She offered a wave, got into her car, and watched him head to his own vehicle. She could still feel the weight of his kiss on her cheek. His skin on hers. She touched the area softly and closed her eyes for a moment. When she opened her eyes again, she saw a familiar face crossing the parking lot.

Everything inside her contracted in an attempt to hide. Luckily, her mom didn't seem to notice her as she walked to her minivan and got in. Seeing Nancy Donovan was just a reminder of everything Claire wanted and didn't want.

She wanted respect, success, and a man who wanted her as much as she wanted him.

She didn't want to lose her heart or her pride to an unavailable man. No, Bo wasn't married, which was the kind of guy her mom preferred. But he was no less on the market. Being with him tonight would have to be more like window shopping. Claire could look, but there was no way she was taking him home.

$\mathscr{C}$HAPTER FOUR

$\mathscr{B}$o wasn't sure if he was more nervous about meeting with the Martins tonight or about spending the evening with Claire.

He pulled up to her house, parked, and headed up the steps. As he rang the doorbell, he felt empty-handed somehow. Maybe he should've stopped and gotten flowers. That would've been stupid though. This wasn't a real date. But the tight, hard-to-breathe feeling in his chest begged to differ. It was a blend of anticipation and nerves with a healthy dose of desire for this woman.

The door opened, and Claire smiled back at him. She had on just a touch of makeup that brought out the green of her eyes. She'd swiped some blush across her cheeks as well, or maybe she really was flushed. With her strawberry tones and fair skin, she seemed to do that a lot.

There was something between them. There always had been. Their chemistry was off the charts, but it was more than that. Claire was funny and smart, and he admired the heck out of her. She would've had a right to view the world with bitterness and skepticism as much as anyone. Instead, she seemed to have unlimited optimism, and she romanticized everything. Bo could learn a lot from this woman, if he chose to spend more than three days with her.

"You're staring at me," Claire said. She looked at what she was wearing and back up at him with a frown. "Do I look okay? I wasn't sure what to wear for a business dinner, and there was no time to go shopping for something new. I can go back upstairs and change if you think this isn't good enough."

"It's perfect. You look beautiful." And heaven help him, it was all he could do not to move closer and taste those sweet lips of hers.

"Great," she said. "Let me just grab my purse. You can come on in."

Bo stepped inside her living room and looked around. It had been her granddad's place before he'd moved south to Florida and left it to her. Bo had never renovated a historic home before, but his mind was already swimming with ideas on how to modernize it just a touch by adding more windows for natural lighting.

As he waited for her to return, he walked over to the mantel and looked at the pictures encased in a variety of frames. There was a photo of Claire with her grandparents, who'd done a good bit of raising her while her parents shirked their duties. He thought he remembered that her grandmother had died several years back. There was one of Claire and her brother, Peter, whom Bo hadn't seen in quite some time. He wasn't even sure what Peter had been up to in the last decade since high school graduation.

Claire breezed back into the room. "Okay, got my purse, and I'm ready to go."

Bo turned to face her, and his breath caught. He wasn't dreading tonight's dinner like he had been this morning before inviting her along. On the contrary, now he was starting to look forward to it.

When they got to the restaurant, Ken and Evelyn Martin were already seated and waiting for them.

"Oh, you brought a date," Evelyn said, looking between them with a delighted smile. "This is such a nice surprise."

Bo wondered if he should clarify that Claire was just a friend. Evelyn didn't give him time to say anything, though, before launching into friendly chitchat.

"I'm Evelyn, and this is my husband, Ken," she said, reaching for Claire's hand.

Bo pulled out a chair for Claire and sat down while they all made their acquaintances. Then he made the mistake of looking around the restaurant. On the other side of the room, his vision snagged on Liz and Mike. They were expecting their first child if the rumors were true, which in Sweetwater Springs was fifty-fifty. A mix of emotions passed through him.

"I'm so glad you could meet us tonight," Ken said, pulling Bo back to his own dinner party.

Bo nodded. "Me too."

Liz had never been *the one* for him. He had come to terms with that during his time in Wild Blossom Bluffs. Perhaps he should walk over and thank them for that invitation to their wedding last year, because it'd led to an amazing night with the woman beside him. The *only* woman he had eyes for in the room tonight.

* * *

Claire had thought since this was a business dinner, that it would be tense or maybe a little stuffy. The Martins were probably twenty years older than her, but even so, Claire was having the best time. The older couple picked on each other in the most endearing way. And since Bo was paying, Claire helped herself to a steak with two sides of vegetables and a glass of wine. She didn't feel bad about it either. This was payback for last spring.

They might have called a truce this morning, but she hadn't forgotten.

"It must be so rewarding to plan so many life events for others," Evelyn said, stabbing at a piece of shrimp on her plate and looking up at Claire.

"Oh, it is. I couldn't imagine myself doing anything else."

"I was a schoolteacher for thirty-one years," Evelyn said proudly, "and I loved every moment. If you love what you do and who you're with, life is always a party."

Claire was midway through lifting her glass of wine to her lips, but she paused to process that statement. "I love that philosophy."

"Well, it's true. I fell in love with Ken thirty-three years ago, and we haven't stopped partying since."

Ken Martin reached for her hand.

After that, the conversation turned to Bo's architectural proposal. The Martins loved all his ideas, and they seemed to love him too. Why wouldn't they? She hadn't been lying when she'd told him earlier that he was talented. He was. He was the architect behind the designs for so many of Sweetwater Springs' big businesses and houses. He was amazing.

By the time they left the restaurant, Bo and the Martins seemed like old friends. And Claire was totally and completely smitten with her date. Exactly like she'd promised herself she wouldn't be. But being with him was so easy.

He walked her out to the parking lot and, like a good gentleman, opened the passenger door for her.

"Thank you," he said, once he was behind the wheel. He pulled out of the parking lot and started to drive her home.

"It was no problem. I had a good time, and I had to eat anyway, right? Thanks for buying me dinner. Usually, the night before a wedding, we'd be doing a dress rehearsal. But nothing is the norm about tomorrow's ceremony." She was chattering away for some reason.

"Looks like we make a good team."

There was a smolder in his blue eyes when he looked over. Was she imagining that?

"Yes, I guess so."

"Maybe you could call me for all your catering and flower needs, and I could ask you to be my date for all my client meetings."

She knew he was only teasing. "I daresay, you'd grow tired of sampling food and picking out flowers." She cleared her throat. "I saw Liz and Mike. You were fixated over there for a moment at dinner."

She saw the muscles along his jaw tighten. "They didn't stay long, thankfully."

"Is it hard to see them together?"

"A little," he admitted. "Not because I still love her. Just knowing that they did things behind my back. Trust isn't an easy thing to repair." He sucked in a deep breath. "All for the greater good, I guess. They have a baby on the way, from what I hear."

Claire had heard the same. She reached a hand across the car and touched his shoulder, wanting to offer comfort. The touch zinged through her body. She hadn't touched this man since last spring. She'd made a point not to. Now she felt his hard muscles at her fingertips, and her body answered.

She yanked her hand away and turned to look out the window. "Not every woman would do that to you, you know."

"I never thought Liz would do that to me. Or Mike. So no, I don't know." There was an edge to his voice, making her sorry she'd even brought it up. He was obviously bitter about relationships now. No doubt that spilled over into his view on his dad and Rebecca's nuptials tomorrow.

They rode in silence for a few minutes, and then Bo turned on the radio.

Claire looked at him with interest. "Jazz? I would've pegged you for classical."

To her relief, the hardness of his face softened.

326

"I've always thought classical was boring. I played the saxophone in high school band."

"I remember. Do you still play?"

"I have the sax, but all the neighborhood dogs start howling when I put my lips to the mouthpiece."

Claire laughed. "I play piano. I had six years of lessons."

"Really? I thought we spilled all our secrets the night we spent together." His gaze slid over. There was a definite smolder there, contained only by thick-rimmed glasses.

He pulled into her driveway and cut off the engine. "I'll walk you to your door."

"How about a nightcap? I have wine. Or beer if you'd rather." What was she doing? She'd resolved earlier this afternoon not to take him home with her.

"I'm not sure you can trust me not to kiss you if you invite me in," he admitted.

Gulp.

Without thinking, she ran her tongue along her bottom lip, wetting it. Which was just silly because she absolutely was not going to kiss this man. While her mind was starting to make a rational argument for saying good night, her body was warming up for first base, maybe second.

Bo leaned just slightly and tucked a strand of her hair behind her ear. Then his fingers slid across her skin as he took his time with the simple gesture. Her heart pattered excitedly. Then she leaned as well, almost against her will. One kiss wouldn't hurt anything, right? One tiny, little…

His mouth covered hers in an instant, pulling the plug on her mind. Her thoughts disappeared along with everything else, except Bo. It was just him and her and this scorching-hot kiss. His hand curled behind her neck, holding her captive. Not that she wanted to pull away. Nope. She was close to climbing across the seat and straddling him at this moment.

He tasted like white wine from the restaurant. Smelled like a walk through Evergreen Park. Kissed like a man who wanted her every bit as much as she wanted him.

She heard herself moan as their tongues tangled with one another. She remembered this. How good he kissed. It was like a starter match lighting a fire that burned in her belly. He broke away and started trailing soft kisses down her cheek and then her neck. There was a slight scruff of a five o'clock shadow on his jawline. It felt sinfully delicious.

She tilted her head to one side, giving him access. Eventually, his mouth traveled to her ear and nibbled softly. That fire in her belly raged to a full-on hungry blaze.

"That nightcap sounds good," he whispered, tickling the sensitive skin there. "And I don't want to think about Liz and Mike anymore tonight."

Claire's brain buzzed back to life. That was exactly why he'd invited her back to his hotel room last spring. She was a distraction, nothing more.

She opened her eyes and pulled away just enough to look at him. This was a mistake. There was no denying that she had it bad for this guy, but he wasn't emotionally available and she wasn't going to be used.

"Actually, I'm really tired." She averted her gaze because looking in his eyes, heavy lidded with lust, might sway her sudden resolve. "I'll see you in the morning. There are a few last-minute touches to do before the wedding. Thanks for dinner. Good night." She pushed her car door open, slammed it shut, and hurried up the porch steps as if running for her life.

But she was really running for her heart.

* * *

What happened tonight?

Bo sat out on his back deck and looked out to the garden. He'd turned on the fairy lights they'd strung earlier, giving the yard an ambient glow. Claire was right. It was a romantic touch.

He still couldn't decide if he was glad or disappointed that she'd slammed on the brakes to their make-out session. Going inside with her would have almost definitely led to her bed, and he didn't think Claire was the kind to have sex casually.

He'd been in a different place in his life last year. Liz and Mike's affair had plunged a knife through his heart, and he wasn't sure he'd ever be able to pull it out. It'd been hard to breathe for a long time after that. He'd dated casually, hooked up a few times, but he had no interest in anyone.

Until Claire. She'd sparked something deep inside him that was terrifying to him back then. The thought of allowing himself to have actual feelings for a woman felt like marching himself right up to Skye Point and preparing to jump off without a parachute. It was nuts.

But now...

He liked her. She evoked feelings he'd never experienced before. Not even with Liz, whom he'd planned to spend his life with.

Damn. He wasn't sure what exactly had happened tonight; all he knew was he needed to fix it. After tomorrow's wedding, there'd be no need to see Claire anymore. Not unless he climbed that proverbial mountain and forced himself to look off the ledge and jump. Getting into another relationship was a risk. Claire could hurt him even more than Liz had. But would she?

An hour later, he dragged himself to bed and flopped around restlessly until he drifted off. After what seemed like just a few minutes, he awoke with the chirping of springtime birds nesting by his window. A slant of sunlight hit his face, prompting him to sit up and shuffle down the hall. He made coffee, enough for two, and then showered.

Claire still hadn't arrived by the time he'd dressed and started preparing breakfast—also enough for two. A little worry elbowed its way to the forefront of his mind. Had he scared her off last night? He knew that she'd be here to finish the job no matter what. He trusted that she wouldn't let his dad and Rebecca down.

He trusted *her*.

That one thought stopped him momentarily in his tracks. His heart was more easily won than his trust, but it appeared that Claire had captured them both.

He continued walking to his office and opened his computer to scan his email. There was already a message waiting for him from Ken Martin:

> Loved having dinner with you and Claire last night. Evelyn and I both love your plans for the mother-in-law suite we want to add on. We were unanimous in our agreement that you are the right man for the job. We'd love to work with you. We'd also love to have you and Claire over for dinner at our place again sometime soon. She's a keeper. A wise man wouldn't let her slip away.
>
> Ken

Bo pumped a fist into the air. The deal was done. Success! He reread those last two lines.

It was good advice, and he planned on taking it.

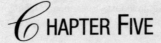

CHAPTER FIVE

$\mathcal{C}$laire was taking her time getting ready to go to Lavender Hill this morning. When she'd agreed to this business arrangement, she'd resolved not to let herself fall for Bo again. And who fell for a guy after only a few days anyway?

Apparently, she did. She wasn't in love with him, no. But she was long past lust.

Claire gave herself one last glance in the mirror. She hadn't put on the beautiful dress she'd purchased at Sophie's Boutique a few weeks back just yet. She still had work to do at Bo's house. Speaking of which, she guessed it was time to go.

She headed to her car, got in, and then, continuing to procrastinate, veered off toward the Sweetwater Café for a strong cup of coffee.

A few minutes later, Emma smiled up from the counter as a little jingle bell rang over Claire's head.

"Good morning, Claire," Emma said with all the warmth of one of her delicious hot cocoas. "You have a big event this evening."

"I do." Claire gave a nod. On the morning of a special event, she was usually buzzing with so much energy that she didn't even need to stop by the Sweetwater Café, even though she always did anyway. "Are you going to be there?" Claire asked.

"I wouldn't miss it. Rebecca is one of my favorite customers. I'm so happy for her."

"So you're not against the marriage because of the age gap?"

"No way. Not if she's happy, and I wholeheartedly believe she is." Emma was already preparing a cup of coffee for Claire per her usual specifications.

Claire fished her debit card out of her purse as she waited.

Turning back to her, Emma narrowed her eyes. "And you've been holed up for the last couple of days with Bo Matthews, I hear."

"Because the wedding is at his house," Claire clarified, handing her card over. "Not for any other reason."

Emma swiped the card and handed it back. "I wouldn't blame you if there was. He's hotter than that cup of brew you're holding. Don't tell him I said so though. He's not really my type."

Claire grabbed her cup of coffee and took a sip. Bo was *her* type. "No? What is your type?"

Emma shrugged. "I dunno. Chris Hemsworth, maybe."

"You do realize that he's a world-famous movie star, and that it's very unlikely he'll walk into your coffee shop, right?"

"Yeah, yeah. Just a technicality. It could happen," Emma said with a soft giggle.

Yeah, and Bo could realize he was falling for Claire too. Which would never happen.

Claire started to turn and leave, but Emma grabbed her forearm.

"I have to warn you," she said, biting down on her lower lip. "Your mom is here."

"What?" Claire looked over her shoulder, and sure enough,

there was Nancy Donovan. How had she missed seeing her when she'd walked in? And why hadn't Emma warned her sooner? Not that it would've helped. There was only one way out and it was past her mom.

Claire turned back to her friend. "Thanks for the heads-up. I'll see you tonight." She took her cup of coffee and turned to leave. As she headed toward the exit, her mom's gaze flicked up and stayed on her. Her mouth curved just slightly in a sheepish smile. Then she lifted her hand and waved.

Crap. If Claire kept walking, she'd be the bad guy here, and that wasn't fair. Claire was always the one trying to help her parents growing up. She was the one victimized by their lack of attention and their shaming of her family's name.

Forcing her feet forward, Claire walked over to her mom's table and slid into the booth across from her. "I can only stay a few minutes," she prefaced.

Her mom nodded. Soft lines formed at the corners of her eyes and mouth as her smile wobbled. "I'm just happy to get to talk to you. How are you?"

Claire swallowed, wondering if she should answer that question truthfully. And if so, what was the honest answer? Work was great, but her personal life was all screwed up because she'd once more allowed herself to have feelings for Bo. "Swell. And you?"

"Better these days." Her mom molded her hands around her own cup. "I'm working on things I wish I'd worked on a long time ago."

"Hindsight and everything," Claire said, hating how sarcastic she sounded. She blew out a breath as she looked around the shop and shook her head. Then she turned back to her mom. "Look, I'm sorry. I don't mean to be so rude."

"It's okay," her mother said. "I deserve it. I was hoping that we could work toward having some sort of relationship again though. Even if it's only five minutes every now and then over coffee."

Claire stared at the woman in front of her. Time hadn't been kind, mostly because of the way Nancy had chosen to live her life. "How's Dad?"

"Jail has helped him sober up. He's going to stay dry once he gets out next month," she told Claire with a hopeful lilt to her voice. "We're going to get a second chance to do right by each other. That's what we both want."

Claire sucked in a deep breath and let it go. It was hypocritical of her to expect Bo to believe his dad could change and settle down with Rebecca when she couldn't do the same with her own parents. It was easier said than done though. "I hope that happens, Mom."

They spoke for a few minutes more, and then Claire pushed back from the table and stood. "I really do have to go...But maybe we can do this again."

Her mom's brows lifted. "Really?"

"I'm usually here on Saturday mornings"—Claire shrugged a shoulder—"so maybe I'll see you next weekend."

"Yes. Maybe you will." Her mom reached for Claire's hand and gave it a quick squeeze, the closest to a hug that either of them were ready to give. "Thank you."

As Claire walked out of the coffee shop, she felt lighter. Maybe her mom would let her down again. But there was also the possibility that she wouldn't this time. Claire had always been an optimist. She never wanted to lose hope that things could change for the better.

There was no hope for Bo changing his mind about love and romance though. No matter how much her heart protested that maybe, just maybe, there was.

* * *

Claire had drained her cup of coffee by the time she pulled into Bo's driveway. She was surprised to find him outside setting up the chairs.

"Wow. You've been busy," she said, walking toward him. She kept her shoulders squared. Kissing him last night didn't change anything. She wasn't going to let it affect the task at hand.

Straightening, he looked at her. He was all hot and sweaty, with the same ball cap on that he'd been wearing at the coffee shop a few days before. "I promised to help, so I am. Ken Martin emailed this morning and offered me the contract, by the way."

Claire's smile was now sincere. "That's great, Bo. I thought he would. Last night went really well." Except for that last part.

Judging by the look in his eyes, he was thinking about that too.

"I'm, um, just going to call Halona and Brenna and make sure everything's on track. I'll use your kitchen for that, if you don't mind."

"I don't. There's coffee, eggs, and bacon in there too. I made plenty this morning."

It was official. Emma could have Chris Hemsworth, because he had nothing on Bo Matthews.

* * *

Claire was obviously ignoring him. Bo wasn't sure how to make things right, but he knew he wanted to. He wanted a lot more than that, and he was ready. Seeing Liz and Mike together last night at the restaurant had barely stung. In fact, he almost felt happy for the two of them. Yeah, they'd hurt him, but he knew they hadn't meant to.

Love didn't let you choose. He understood what Claire had meant by that now, because he was falling hard and fast for the sweet, smart, gorgeous event planner. *How the hell am I going to fix things with her?*

335

A delivery truck pulled into his driveway with SOUTHERN PORTA-JOHN written in large black letters on the side. Bo guided the guys toward the back of his house, where the porta-johns would be available to guests but not readily seen during the ceremony. After that, Halona Locklear showed up in a navy SUV with all the flower arrangements in the back. Claire came out of the back door to help her set things up.

It wasn't a good time to talk to her right now. Not when she had so many things to get done before tonight's wedding.

The next few hours were a blur of activity going on in and around his house. Brenna showed up with trays full of food. He helped her set up tables to display it all. A DJ showed up and set up a place to play music for the reception. The entire Ladies' Day Out group showed up after that and helped Claire with a host of other things that he never would've considered. They set out tablecloths and large baskets full of party mementos for the guests. Pearson's and Rebecca's names and the date were written on little paper hearts attached to each favor.

"Aren't these the cutest?" Lula Locklear asked as she walked up to peek inside one of the baskets. "The ladies and I were up all night making these." Lula was Halona's mom. She was often involved in the community, increasing awareness about her Cherokee Indian culture.

"They are," Bo agreed, unable to resist lifting his head and looking around to see where Claire was. He spotted her laughing with Kaitlyn Russo, the owner of the Sweetwater B&B. The sight of Claire happy and enjoying herself made his heart skip a beat. He longed to be the kind of guy who put that smile on her face.

"You are a man with the look of love," Lula said with a knowing nod. She followed his gaze to where Claire was standing. "She's such a nice girl. She needs someone who will treat her well." She gave him an assessing look as if trying to decipher if he was capable of being that kind of guy. *Was he?* "Maybe there'll be more weddings on Lavender Hill in the future," she said.

* * *

As the sun started to creep toward the mountains, the sky darkened, and guests started to arrive. Claire slipped on the beautiful satin dress she'd purchased from Sophie's Boutique and then headed outside to turn on the lights. The aroma of the food wafted in the air along with laughter and casual conversation.

Pearson and Rebecca would be on their way at any moment. Rebecca's obstetrician had okayed her to leave for two hours. That was enough time to greet guests, walk down the aisle, say their vows, and maybe even have a dance under the stars.

Claire sighed dreamily, imagining Rebecca getting the wedding of her dreams tonight.

Bo stepped up beside her, scrambling those happy thoughts and feelings. "I need to talk to you. There's a problem."

She whipped her head around to face him. "What kind of problem?"

"Rebecca is in labor. The wedding has been called off."

"What?" Claire's lungs contracted as if the wind had been knocked out of her. "But she wants to be married by the time the baby comes. She needs to get here."

Bo frowned. "I just spoke to Dad. Rebecca's water broke when she was putting on her wedding dress." He grimaced. "It's not going to happen tonight. They can do it after the baby is born. She can buy a new dress and have it anywhere or any way she wants."

Claire shook her head. "The only thing she really wanted was to exchange vows before she gave birth." Claire looked around at all the guests, seated in wooden fold-out chairs. The scenery was perfect. There were even hundreds of stars speckling the clear night's sky.

Her shoulders slumped as she blew out a resigned breath. This was out of her control, and she knew it. "I guess we'll tell the guests the news and send them all home." She hesitated before looking at Bo. Disappointment stung her eyes. She didn't want him to know that all she really felt like doing was sitting in one of those chairs and having a good cry on Rebecca's behalf.

"You stay here. I'll take care of the guests," he said.

"You don't have to. That's my job."

"You did your job already."

"Not really. The wedding is off. I've never let a client down before. Ever." And now she wanted to cry on her own behalf.

There was something gentle in his eyes when she looked up at him. "Stay here," he said again.

She watched him walk off toward the crowd, then she turned to face the garden. She wasn't sure exactly how long she stood there collecting herself before Bo came up behind her. When she turned, he was standing there with Pastor Phillips.

Claire started to apologize to the older man, but Bo patted the pastor's back and narrowed his gaze at her.

"Pastor Phillips is ready to go to the hospital."

Claire scrunched her brows. "What? Why?"

"Because there's a wedding to be had, and we don't have much time. If Rebecca wants to be married before my baby brother gets here, then that's what we'll make sure happens. Assuming we beat the clock."

Pastor Phillips chuckled. "My wife was in labor for twelve hours after her water broke with our first child. I think we'll be okay."

Bo reached for Claire's hand. "You've never let a client down, right? Why start now?"

"You don't even believe your father and Rebecca should be together. Why are you doing this?"

"Maybe I see things differently now. Because of you."

CHAPTER SIX

Claire grabbed the wedding bouquet before climbing into Bo's car. It was an assortment of purple irises and white lilies—exactly what Rebecca had requested. In fact, aside from wanting to marry before her baby was born, the flower preferences were the only other thing Rebecca had asked for.

After a short drive, Bo parked in front of the labor and delivery wing, and they hurried inside. Claire clutched the arrangement tightly as she walked beside him toward the elevator. Pastor Phillips had driven separately. Hopefully he wasn't far behind.

"What's wrong?" Bo asked. "You were talking as fast as I could drive on the way here."

Claire shook her head. "A hospital isn't exactly my favorite place. I watched my grandmother die here." And ever since, Mount Pleasant Memorial had carried nothing but bad memories for her.

They stepped inside the elevator, and Bo reached for her hand. He didn't let go once the door opened on the second floor. The feel of his skin against hers distracted her from the repetitive beeping sounds and the smells of disinfectant as they walked.

"Let's make a few happy memories here today, shall we?" he asked, giving her a wink that short-circuited all the negativity in her mind.

"There's nothing more joyful than a wedding. I've always thought so."

His smile wobbled just a little as they walked.

"I'm sorry. I guess weddings hold as many bad memories for you as hospitals do for me."

"I used to think I never wanted to go to another wedding again. But there's nowhere I'd rather be tonight than at this one with you."

Her heart fluttered. "Same. Even if it is at a hospital."

They stopped behind Rebecca's door, and Claire knocked softly.

A moment later, it cracked open, and Pearson Matthews peeked out at her. Claire had seen him many times over the years. His presence was always confident and commanding. Now he looked like a man juggling half a dozen emotions: excitement, fear, anxiety, exhaustion, confusion, joy.

"How is Rebecca feeling?" Claire asked.

In response, they heard Rebecca groan in the background.

"The baby is coming fast," Pearson said. "What are you two doing here?"

"You couldn't come to the wedding so we brought the wedding to you," Bo answered. "Do you think Rebecca is up for it?"

Pearson smiled at his son, a dozen new emotions popping up on his face. "I think that will probably make her really happy...Thank you, son."

Claire's eyes stung just a little as she watched the brief father-son interaction. "Great. Can we come in?"

Pearson swung the door open wider. "Becky, look who's here?"

Rebecca looked between Claire and Bo and then to Pastor Phillips who stepped up behind them.

"Do you still want to get married before the baby arrives?" Claire asked.

"Yes." Rebecca shifted and tried to sit up in bed. She was wearing a hospital gown instead of a wedding gown. Her hair was a little disheveled, and the makeup she'd put on for tonight's ceremony needed a touch-up. Even so, she was as beautiful as any bride Claire had ever seen.

Rebecca flinched and squeezed her eyes shut, moving her hands to her lower belly. "But we better do this fast," she gritted out.

Pearson went to the head of Rebecca's bed as Pastor Phillips opened his Bible to read a short passage. Afterward, he looked up at the bride and groom and read off vows that they repeated.

Bo never let go of Claire's hand as they stood witness to the happy union. It was quick, but no less perfect. A tear slid off Claire's cheek as Rebecca said "I do." Then Pearson dipped to press his lips to Rebecca's—their first kiss as man and wife.

Claire would've wiped her eyes, but one hand still carried the bouquet and the other was held by Bo. He squeezed it softly as he glanced over. There was something warm in his gaze that melted any leftover resolve to resist this man.

Rebecca pulled away from her husband and turned to her guests, which had expanded to include two nurses. "My bouquet, please."

Claire finally broke contact with Bo and handed the arrangement over.

"Okay, ladies. Arms up," Rebecca said. "Bouquet tossing time!"

"Oh, no. I'm already married," one of the nurses said with a laugh.

Bo stepped off to the side, leaving Claire and the second nurse in the line of fire. Claire usually removed herself from this moment at weddings too. Fighting with a bunch of single ladies over a superstition had always seemed so silly, albeit fun to watch. As the bouquet went sailing across the room though, Claire lifted her hands reflexively and snatched it from the air, much to the second nurse's disappointment.

"You're next!" Rebecca said with a laugh. Then she flinched again as another contraction hit her.

"Okay, that's it," the married nurse said. "I think your baby wants to join this party."

Rebecca opened her eyes. "Okay." She looked at Claire. "Thank you. For everything. This was absolutely perfect."

"You're welcome. But I couldn't have done this without Bo."

Rebecca looked at him with tears in her eyes. "Thank you too."

"That's what family is for, right? Welcome to the Matthews clan."

Pearson stepped over and reached out his hand for Bo to shake. He shook Claire's hand as well.

"We're going to give you two some privacy now," Bo told him.

"Don't go too far," Rebecca called from across the room. "Your baby brother will be excited to meet you."

Bo seemed a little stunned by the invitation to stay. He looked at Claire.

"I'm in no hurry to go home," she said. Nor was she in a hurry to leave Bo's side right now.

* * *

"That was amazing!" Claire said, leaning back against the headrest of Bo's car as he drove her to his home three hours later. "And your baby brother is adorable. I can't believe I got to hold a newborn who's only been on this earth for an hour. That was such a rush. And the wedding was perfect, even though we were the only ones in attendance."

He glanced over, feeling a sense of pride and accomplishment at helping to put that contented look on her face. "You pulled it off."

"*We* pulled it off."

From his peripheral vision, he saw her turn and look at him.

"You said it yesterday, and it's true. We make a pretty good couple." Her relaxed posture stiffened. "Team. We make a good team," she corrected.

"I liked it better the first way." He'd been waiting to talk to her all day. The hospital hadn't seemed like the right place, but now he couldn't wait any longer. He pulled into his driveway, parked his car, and then looked across the seat at her.

Her contented, dreamy look was gone, replaced by a look of confusion. It was just last night that they'd kissed in this very car, but it felt like a lifetime ago.

"I like you, Claire Donovan. I liked you last spring, but I was a coward. I'll admit that."

"Sounds about right," she agreed.

"I'd just watched my best friend marry the woman I thought I wanted. But I was wrong. I was so wrong. You're the woman I want, Claire. And I want you like I've never wanted anything in my entire life." His heart was thundering in his ears as he made his confession.

Her eyes became shiny for the hundredth time that night.

"The last few days have breathed new life inside me. I don't want to think about waking up tomorrow and not knowing if I'll see you." He ran a hand through his hair to keep from reaching out and touching her. "Claire, I want another chance with you. If you say yes, I promise I won't mess things up this time."

She was so still that he wondered if she was okay.

"Say something," he finally said.

"I'm hungry." After a long moment, her lips curved ever so slightly.

He cleared his throat and turned to look out at his yard. "Well, there's probably still some food left over from the reception. The guests each took some, but it'd be a shame for the rest to go to waste. I even think I saw Janice Murphy spike the punch on her way out," he said.

Claire gave a small laugh and nodded when he looked at her. "There's also a place to dance under the stars."

"The evening is set for romance," he agreed.

"So let's enjoy it and see where the night takes us. On one condition." Her expression contorted to something stern with just a touch of playfulness lighting up her eyes. "If it ends up leading somewhere nice, you have to promise you'll call me tomorrow."

He chuckled. "I promise that it will lead somewhere nice, and when it does, you might never get rid of me."

She looked up into his eyes and smiled. "I might never want to."

$\mathcal{E}$PILOGUE

$\mathcal{I}$n the blink of an eye, everything could change. Or in Claire's case, one month's time. That was how long it'd been since she'd planned Rebecca and Pearson's wedding. It had all happened so fast, but everything had fallen into place perfectly.

Claire stepped out of the dressing room at Sophie's Boutique and did a twirl in front of the body-length mirror. The cotton dress was a deep rose color with tiny blue pin dots in the fabric. The hem brushed along her knees as she shifted in front of the mirror.

"That's the one," the shop owner said, stepping up beside her.

"I feel a little foolish. It's just our one-month anniversary, but Bo told me to wear something nice."

"One month together is definitely worth celebrating. Where is he taking you?" Sophie asked. "Any idea?"

Claire shook her head. "No." It didn't really matter though. It was the gesture that melted her heart like a marshmallow against an open flame. He was always doing little things for her to show her how much he cared. "Okay," she said, looking down. "This is the one. I'll take it off and let you ring it up for me."

"Do you have the right shoes?"

Claire laughed. She loved to shop as much as the next person, but she couldn't wait to get home and ready for whatever Bo had planned for them. "I do. But thanks."

An hour and a half later, Bo picked her up at her place and started driving.

"You're still not going to tell me where we're going?" she asked.

He was dressed in nice jeans with a polo top and a sport coat. She was almost disappointed to have to go out tonight because she would have rather been alone with him. They'd spent a lot of alone time together over the last month, and she wasn't sure she'd ever get enough.

"That would ruin the surprise."

She huffed playfully. "Fine. How's baby Noah?" she asked. He'd told her he was stopping by the hospital this afternoon. It had been all she could do not to invite herself along, but visitors were limited to family right now. She was just the girlfriend.

"A genius," Bo answered. "He takes after me."

This made Claire laugh out loud.

"And he'll be leaving the NICU tomorrow. The doctor says he's ready."

"That's wonderful news. I'm sure Pearson and Rebecca are so happy."

He nodded. "They are."

Claire blinked as she looked out the window, recognizing the route. Surely, she hadn't gotten all dressed up just to go back to his place.

He turned the car onto Lavender Road and drove all the way to the end. After pulling into his driveway and parking, he turned to her. She blinked and kept her gaze forward. The fairy lights were turned on—they'd never taken them down—and a table was set up at the peak of the hill behind his house.

Bo stepped out of the car and walked around to open her door for her. Then they approached what he'd put together. There was a small vase of fresh flowers at the table's center, sandwiched between two candles, not yet lit. Another table was set up to the right with what appeared to be catered food from Taste of Heaven.

"A candlelit dinner under the stars." She turned and stepped into him, wrapping her arms around his neck and staring into his eyes. "All this just to celebrate one month of being together?"

He leaned in and kissed her lips, soft and slow. Nothing in her life had ever felt so right as being with him.

"No. All this is to tell you that I love you, Claire Donovan. I love you so much."

She blinked him into focus. A man had never uttered those words to her before, but they were music to her ears. She wanted to hear them again and again. "I love you too, Bo Matthews."

She laughed as he pulled her in for another kiss under the starry night sky. Then they had dinner and shared a dance before retreating to his room, where he repeated those three little words again and again.

About the Author

Annie Rains is a *USA Today* bestselling contemporary romance author who writes small-town love stories set in fictional places in her home state of North Carolina. When Annie isn't writing, she's living out her own happily ever after with her husband and three children.

Learn more at:

> AnnieRains.com
> Twitter: @AnnieRainsBooks
> Facebook.com/AnnieRainsBooks
> Instagram: @AnnieRainsBooks

For more from Annie Rains,
check out the rest of the
Sweetwater Springs series!

Fall in love with these small-town romances full of tight-knit communities and heartwarming charm!

THE BEACHSIDE BED AND BREAKFAST
by Hope Ramsay

Ashley Howland Scott has no time for romance while grieving for her husband, caring for her son, and running Magnolia Harbor's only bed and breakfast. But slowly, Rev. Micah St. Pierre has become a friend...and maybe something more. Micah cannot date a member of his congregation, so there's no point in sharing his feelings with Ashley, no matter how much he yearns to. But the more time they spend together, the more Micah wonders whether Ashley is his match made in heaven.

THE SUMMER SISTERS
by Sara Richardson

The Buchanan sisters share everything—even ownership of their beloved Juniper Inn. As children, they spent every holiday there, until a feud between their mother, Lillian, and Aunt Sassy kept them away. When the grand reopening of the inn coincides with Sassy's seventieth birthday, Rose, the youngest sister, decides it's time for a family reunion. Only she'll need help from a certain handsome hardware-store owner to pull off the celebration...

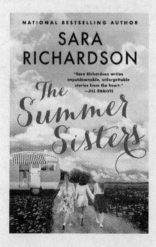

SOMETHING BLUE
by Heather McGovern

Wedding planner Beth Shipley has seen it all: bridezillas, monster-in-laws, and last-minute jitters at the altar. But this wedding is different—and the stakes are much, *much* higher. Not only is her best friend the bride, but bookings at her family's inn have been in free fall. Beth knows she can save her family's business—as long as she doesn't let best man Sawyer Silva's good looks and overprotective, overbearing, older-brother act distract her. Includes a bonus story by Annie Rains!

HOW SWEET IT IS
by Dylan Newton

Event planner Kate Sweet is famous for creating happily-ever-after moments for dream weddings. So how is it that her best friend has roped her into planning a best-selling horror writer's book launch extravaganza in a small town? The second Kate meets the drop-dead-hot Knight of Nightmares, Drake Matthews, her well-ordered life quickly transforms into an absolute nightmare. But neither are prepared for the sweet sting of attraction they feel for each other. Will the queen of romance fall for the king of horror?

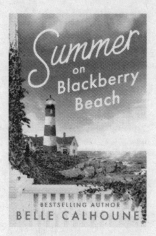
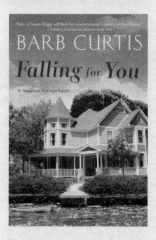

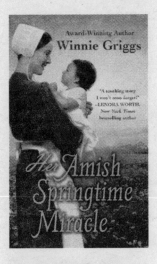

HER AMISH SPRINGTIME MIRACLE
by Winnie Griggs

Amish baker Hannah Eicher has always wanted a *familye* of her own, so finding sweet baby Grace in her barn seems like an answer to her prayers. Until *Englischer* paramedic Mike Colder shows up in Hope's Haven, hoping to find his late sister's baby. As Hannah and Mike contemplate what's best for Grace, they spend more and more time together while enjoying the warm community and simple life. Despite their wildly different worlds, will Mike and Hannah find the true meaning of "family"?

THE AMISH FARMER'S PROPOSAL
by Barbara Cameron

When Amish dairy farmer Abe Stoltzfus tumbles from his roof, he's lucky his longtime friend Lavinia Fisher is there to help. He secretly hoped to propose to her, but now, with his injuries, his dairy farm in danger, and his harvest at stake, Abe worries he'll only be a burden. Yet, as he heals with Lavinia's gentle support and unflagging optimism, the two grow even closer. But will she be able to convince him that real love doesn't need perfect timing?

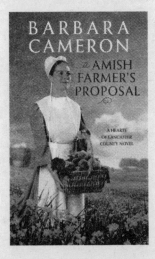